Undeniable Temptation

RECKLESS BEAT BOOK FIVE

EDEN SUMMERS

Dedication

To the readers, friends, and family who have joined me along this Reckless journey—thank you.

Prologue

L EAH STARED AT THE GLOSSY PAINT OF THE DOOR, THE HEAVY WOOD HOLDING back her dreams and protecting her from stupidity.

"Ryan, let me in." Fantasies and idiocy be damned, she needed to be in there with him. "Talk to me."

The response was an eruption of noise—a harsh shout, a smash, a thump. He was going postal, entirely destroyed from the news of his impending divorce.

"*Ryan.*" She banged her fist against the wood. "Open the fucking door."

Whispers skittered toward her, the flutter of curiosity coming from other hotel guests who cautiously stepped into the hall to snoop.

If she didn't smother this outburst it would become gossip column news. All those tabloid bastards needed was a sniff of drama and they'd pounce. There'd be photos, old or new, it didn't matter, and a provoking headline that lacked an ounce of truth. Then she'd have to deal with more chaos. More than the monumental amount she already predicted with his inevitable divorce.

"Ryan... *Please.*"

The heavy thud of approaching footsteps made her inch back. Then the door flew open, and before her stood the man she adored, his pain and anger transforming his usual at-peace appeal into something toxic.

"Ryan—"

"What do you want?" he sneered.

His gorgeous ocean eyes tried to belittle her, and the heavy rise and fall of his chest aimed to intimidate. His ferocity would've worked if she hadn't anticipated it. She had already prepared herself for the worst, because this moment was exactly that for him.

It was his time to break, and she had to be the one to pick up the pieces. Not because she hoped it would save their rocky friendship. Not because it was her job to do so. And definitely not because her feelings for him were far from platonic.

Nope. His appeal to her needy senses had nothing to do with this. None whatsoever.

She wanted to fix this because he deserved to be the one who was coddled for once. Every other member of Reckless Beat had stolen the dramatic limelight more than a handful of times over the years. Mason, Sean, Blake, and Mitch had all driven her crazy with moments of melodrama, while Ryan had been the peace and civility. The charmer. The goodness that kept her smiling.

"Get out of my face, Leah."

OK, so maybe he wasn't the peace and civility right now. But it was only a matter of time before the restoration of the man she admired.

She raised her chin, meeting his defiance with a dose of her own. "Let me in."

"Why?" He scowled. "Why do you care?"

Ouch. That hurt. "Don't take your anger out on me." She strode forward and squeezed past him into the suite. "We'll talk this out. It'll ease the shock."

She could smell alcohol. Scotch. It was potent, the mere scent like a tranquilizer to her senses. Obviously, she'd made the wrong decision to wait in the lobby for ten minutes so he could pull himself together. The only thing he'd been amassing was a more delirious arsenal for the impending explosion.

He wasn't himself. She couldn't see the gentle friend under his wavy shoulder-length hair and the close cropped beard. His fierce scowl washed away his easy charm, making her the tiniest bit fearful for his mental state.

"Yeah, we'll just talk this shit out and all my troubles will disappear." His tone dripped with sarcasm. "Then we can hug and laugh and braid each other's hair. Right?"

"Just get in here and take a seat." She entered the main room and winced at the opened bottle of Johnny Walker on the coffee table, half the contents already consumed. She hoped, for his sake, that he'd cracked the cap before today, otherwise he'd soon face plant into the carpeted floor.

"Come on, Ryan." She strolled into the kitchen, retrieved two glasses from the cupboard beside the fridge, and started to fill them with tap water. "Talk to me."

"About what?" He came into view at the end of the hallway. "You know as much as I do."

That was a lie. They hadn't been close for a long time. Not since Australia when she'd made the mistake of keeping the gossip about his wife's questioned fidelity to herself. Now she was banished from the insider knowledge of his private life. He didn't confide in her at all.

"I gather you weren't expecting the process server to show up today?" She turned off the tap and kept her gaze downcast, measuring her dosage to his pain.

The divorce papers had been handed over in a hotel ballroom across the city, while the band had been watching Sean and his dance partner rehearse an upcoming music clip. Ryan's enraged reaction to his induction into single status had been witnessed by the film crew, along with the security and dance team. All of them possible gossip leaks to the always starving paparazzi vultures.

"No, Leah," he grated. "I didn't know."

"Is there anything I can do? Do you want me to contact your lawyer? Or arrange for a flight back home?" She walked toward him and held out the filled glass.

"No. And I don't want your damn water." He shooed her with an abrupt wave of his hand. "You should go."

"I'm not leaving you alone."

"Then get Sean. Or Mitch. Or Blake. Or Mason." He made the distance to the scotch bottle in three steps, then swung it high to take a long pull. "Hell, get the concierge, for all I care. Anyone else would be better than you."

Bam. His cruelty made a direct hit to her chest, blood and sinew splattering everywhere.

"That's harsh." She kept her tone light, casual, hoping to smoothly transition him into a new headspace. "What have I done to deserve your anger?"

He shrugged. "I expect you knew she was going to blindside me. It wouldn't be the first time you've held back information."

"Don't be an ass." She didn't care how much alcohol was flowing through his veins, nothing excused such a low blow. Being his support was one thing. Becoming his punching bag was entirely another. "If I made an issue out of every article that claimed one of our group was cheating, or doing drugs, or on the verge of bankruptcy, I'd get no work done. And in the end, those claims about Julie were unfounded, so you need to get over the way I dealt with it."

He scoffed and took another gulp.

Jesus, he was seconds away from requiring a stomach pump. "Put the bottle down."

He stretched his arms wide, holding out the scotch, an entirely morphed Ryan standing before her. "Why don't you come and get it?"

Why? She schooled her expression and came up with a mental list of reasons. First and foremost—being close to Ryan wasn't a stellar idea. Two—the responding tippy-tap of her heart was a bad sign.

A very bad sign.

But he kept holding out the bottle, taunting her with the opportunity to help.

"Fine." She maneuvered around the coffee table. "Give it here."

He grinned, the curve of lips spiteful as he handed over her prize. "I should be happy, right? Now I get to do all those things I missed out on since vowing my life away."

"Sure." She searched for the bottle cap, the visual sweep of the floor, table, and couches coming up with nothing. "You're free to be yourself again."

"I'm also free to be a player." His words held the hint of a slur. "All those groupies will be at my disposal. And with the other band members now off the market, I'll be eating snatch for breakfast, lunch, and dinner."

She swallowed the bile rising in her throat. It was the alcohol talking. No question. Only the thought of him being a sleaze sat like a chunk of marble in her belly. "Getting a divorce doesn't mean you're exempt from morality. Separating from Julie isn't going to change who you are."

"And who am I?" He stepped toward her, encroaching on her personal space. "Who the fuck knows anymore?"

"*I* know." She stood tall, even though his proximity made her nervous. His uncharacteristic cursing, too. "You're not that guy. You were always faithful to your wife. You never wanted to mess around—"

"Yeah, and look how that paid off."

She placed the bottle down on the table and looked him in the eye. "Would you prefer if the divorce was your fault?"

"Oh, I know it's not my fault." He smiled, a fake, brutal curve of lips. "It's yours." There was no humor in his tone, no hint of amusement.

"What are you talking about?"

"Julie hates you. She hated how close we used to be and how every conversation revolved around my infallible band manager. Our friendship was the straw that broke that bitch's back."

A frozen knife sliced through her chest, slow and agonizing. "You're blaming me?"

"Maybe." He waved the seriousness away with a lazy hand. "It doesn't matter. It's over now."

"It fucking matters." She couldn't tell if this was truthful catharsis or alcohol-fueled lies. Either way, the news was butchering her. She'd done everything within her power to keep her feelings to herself. She'd refused to make her adoration known and become the other woman. All those years of restraint and she was still getting the blame? "Tell me the truth."

He shook his head and stepped closer. Too close.

Suddenly, answers weren't dire. The way the world shrank down to the two of them was apocalyptic. Nobody else existed in that panicked moment. It was only Ryan. Only love smothered in pain and coated in undeniable temptation.

"Do you miss the way we used to be?" He scrutinized her face, from the hair around her ears, to her cheeks, her eyes, and finally her lips. "Do you wish we could return to the way things were?"

"Of course I do." She swallowed, hard, and shuffled backward. He was crawling under her skin, sinking beneath her ribs, clutching at her heart. "You should already know that."

He took another step, and another, overshadowing her with his frame, stealing her confidence. The tips of his shoes brushed hers and the universe held its breath until she had the smarts to backtrack a little more.

"Ryan." His name was a warning. A plea. She was falling. Suffocating. She couldn't think past his proximity, or the accompanying daydreams. "What are you doing?"

"I can do whatever I want now, remember?" He took another step, forcing her to stumble into the wall. "What if I wanted to kiss you?"

Oh, god, yes.

Oh, hell, no.

She'd fantasized about his kiss for years, had yearned for it, pained for it. But there were infinite reasons why it could never happen. It wasn't just about his wife. The need for restraint came from Leah's job, their careers, the possible loss of her best friend even though he'd pretended not to hold the role since the band toured in Australia. If she lost the battle with her heart and slid down the slippery slope of seduction, she'd be in breach of contract. And a tight non-compete clause meant a similar role within the industry was impossible.

"Don't." That one, meek, vulnerable word was supposed to slay the threat of his lips and make him retreat. Only she couldn't summon a stronger complaint. She was speechless at the possibility of receiving her wildest dreams and scared beyond belief at the same time.

Her heart hammered. Her senses became acute. Every inch of her skin tingled with a blanket of goosebumps while her nipples tightened in anticipation. He took the final step, the one that brought them thigh to thigh, hip to hip, and pressed her ass against the wall. The clean cut of his beard was there. Right there. Within her grasp. She wanted to run her hand over it, to cup his cheek and tangle her fingers in his loose hair.

Everything slowed to frozen frames in time, one movement gradually morphing into the next. She had a decade to stop him. A lifetime passed under his advance, and still she did nothing as he encroached, his mouth descending inch by inch until finally those lips were brushing hers in the sweetest glide of dream fulfilment.

The contact was explosive. Her cheeks burned. Her lungs, too. Between her thighs a dull throb formed, spurring her to kiss him back and seize what she'd always wanted. Soft swipes of his mouth transformed into a lick of his tongue, the delicate intrusion parting her lips on a moan. Her hands moved of their own volition, gliding behind his neck, pulling him close, demanding more.

Nothing could break the perfection. Nothing but the taste of scotch on her tongue. The infusion to her palate was a wakeup call that announced he was under the influence of alcohol, while she was merely under the influence of lust.

Fuck. What the hell was she doing?

This was wrong. So horribly, horrifically wrong.

She snatched her hands from around his neck and pushed him away, her chest rising and falling as the intimacy became a mere memory.

He considered her with a frown, his lips kiss darkened, his eyes glassy with intoxication. "Don't deny you wanted that," he rasped. "You've wordlessly begged for it since we met."

Air left her lungs in a mass evacuation. He'd hit her right where it hurt, and without thinking she responded with one of her own. A physical one, where her hand slapped across his cheek with enough force to make both of them gasp.

He stiffened at the impact. She was traumatized herself. She'd never raised a hand to anyone before. Never even thought of it... Well, that was a lie. Anyone who knew Mason Lynch would attest to envisaging bodily harm against the egotistical lead singer. But this was different. This was Ryan.

Ryan possessed by liquor.

His cheek turned a dark shade of pink, the evidence of her carelessness seeping under his beard. Seconds passed in the measure of panted breaths. They stood staring at one another. Both of them in shock. Both of them blinking in slow succession.

She'd anticipated that a kiss between them would be devastating. Yet, none of her fantasies were this unforgiving. None of them tore her apart and left her to wither and die under his stare. Her imagination had always included the man who used to bathe her in compliments. Not this person who inflicted suffering on others in the hopes of lessening his own.

"Listen to me," she whispered. "You crossed a line. A phenomenally inappropriate line. Don't ever do it again. Do you hear me?"

He winced and for a second she glimpsed the real Ryan. The man who was kind and charming and sweet. "I'm sorry."

"So am I." She slid along the wall, not daring to make physical contact as she fled for the hallway.

"Leah, wait."

Hell, no.

She headed for the door, her steps clipped, her chin standing at a height that spoke of determination even though she was dying inside. Coming here was a mistake. Cataclysmic. And it wasn't because of her job, or his, or the impending divorce. Her monumental stupidity came from the incessant beat in her chest and the rolling tumbles of her belly that cemented the knowledge that one kiss had changed her forever.

One kiss had destroyed her.

And one was all she could ever allow herself to have.

MONTHS LATER
Orlando, Florida

RYAN FLIPPED HIS GUITAR PICK BACK AND FORTH BETWEEN HIS FINGERS AS HE followed the bee-line down the backstage hall toward the Reckless dressing room. He was dripping with sweat, from his face to his crack. Every limb was wet and thrumming with adrenaline, just the way he liked it.

Nothing compared to the high of a live crowd, especially when he'd been living his life in the gutter lately. The fans kept him going. They pushed him to forget about the single lifestyle he wasn't accustomed to and the estranged wife who was still trying to bleed more money out of him with the divorce settlement.

Julie was destroying him, one instigated lawyer interaction at a time.

"Great show, guys." Leah's voice came from the dressing room door and nudged at places in his chest that shouldn't be accessible.

Her sapphire eyes were bright, her flawless lipstick clinging to sultry lips while she grinned at their approach. He wasn't sure how she did it. The days were long, her tasks arduous, but she never appeared anything less than unstoppable. Even now, after a twelve-hour day, her short-sleeved dress was wrinkle-free and clinging perfectly to every inch of her body, all the way to her calves.

He'd rarely seen her in a state of anything less than excellence. It was how she worked, how she liked to be perceived. Strong. Sure. Capable. That was why his admiration for her had never wavered, even though she still found it hard to look him in the eye.

Not even his drunken kiss had unsettled her. Yes, initially she'd flipped out and skipped town, but her return had been uneventful. The only thing that changed was the cold shoulder she always had pointed in his direction.

"What are you doing here?" Mason asked from the front of the group. "You're usually hiding in your hotel suite by now, sleeping like a baby."

"I am not." She scowled. "I just refused to meet up with you after a concert because your ego resembles a needy five-year-old."

"I don't have a needy ego. I merely like to hear the details from a viewer's perspective. It's performance appraisal." Mason stopped at the door, holding the rest of the band from entering the dressing room. "I did look good on stage, though, didn't I?"

Leah rolled her eyes. "Thanks for proving my point."

Ryan withheld a smile. He missed her playfulness. That sarcastic edge and mischievous spark. One day soon he'd get it back. He just had to keep telling himself—right time, right place. The right time wasn't the middle of a tour when they were tired and lacking patience from all the sterile hotel rooms and cramped nights on the sleeper bus. And the right place wasn't a packed dressing room where there'd be an audience to his groveling.

But soon. He'd get them back to where they once were. Soon.

"Hurry up and get inside." She jerked her head toward the room. "We've got an impromptu meeting to get through before you can call it a night."

"With?" Sean shoved Mason inside and followed after.

Leah's expression tightened. "The label."

Someone from Grander was here? On tour? In the middle of the night?

Ryan stepped past her and into the dressing room, Mitch and Blake at his back. The sight of Scott on the sofa at the side of the room made his muscles tense. The guy sat like he was made of gold and sprinkled in silver. His suit was immaculate, his arms outstretched along the head rest, his leg crossed over the other knee.

"Where's my warm welcome?"

"Welcome, Scott." Leah pulled the door closed behind her. "Now can you tell me what was so important that you had to fly across the country instead of calling?"

Ryan spared her a quick glance to find her standing tall with a fake curve to her lips. She was nervous, or angry. He could never tell the difference with that expression.

"Things have been quiet on the publicity front lately." Scott gave them a sinister smile. "I thought I'd drop by and have a quick catch up to determine the problem."

"Problem?" Mason shook his head. "There's no problem. We've settled down and learned not to cause trouble."

"I think your significant others may have been responsible," Leah murmured.

"True." Mason inclined his head. "We're not looking for drama. We're done with that."

"See, that's a problem." Scott leaned forward and rested his elbows on his knees. "No drama equals no free publicity, which then means Grander has to hand out more money to promote you guys. Money that currently isn't in the budget."

The room fell quiet under the threatening tone. Ryan looked to Sean for guidance, who glanced to Blake, the domino effect hitting each band member until they were all staring at Leah, silently asking for permission to put this asshole in his place.

"I would've thought our ticket sales gave us the luxury of more paid publicity." Her words were tight, clipped, yet her enticing lips were still curved in that friendly charade. "The tour's almost sold out."

Damn, he admired her. She always knew how to act—what to say or what to do—to make people pay attention and take her seriously.

For the duration of his marriage, it had bothered him to contemplate her qualities. He'd already been committed to Julie when they met, and thinking of another woman didn't feel right, no matter how platonic. Now things were different. So devastatingly different his chest reacted whenever they were in the same room. His wife was gone, or soon would be, and he no longer harbored guilt for admiring Leah the way he'd wanted to for years. She deserved his appreciation. Only problem was, she'd made it clear she didn't want it.

"Yes, you're right," Scott agreed. "Tickets are almost sold out. But Grander has decided those sales aren't as high as they could be."

"Greedy much?" Blake drawled. "The sales are through the roof."

"And the label wants more."

"How much more?" Ryan asked.

They hadn't pulled the tours dates out of their ass. A lot of Leah's blood, sweat, and cursing had gone into determining a schedule that would fit in with each band member, along with the venues. The most important requirement had been working around Blake and Gabi. The bass guitarist demanded the tour be wrapped up before the birth of his first child, with the rest of the band happy to oblige because they all wanted to be there, too. The two of them had already been through enough with the loss of their first pregnancy. More tour dates wouldn't keep them apart; it would only break Blake from the band.

"We want more publicity. More hype. More sales. We want you to reach your potential."

"Let's cut the crap." Leah strode forward. "Seeing as though you were unsuccessful in convincing the guys to re-sign, you're trying to bleed them dry before their contractual obligations are over."

"We made Reckless into what it is today. We deserve a substantial return on our investment."

Mason's eyes widened in fury. The lead singer had a low threshold for label bullshit after what his fiancé, Sidney, had been through. She'd been dumped and discarded from her contract after a public scandal involving a highly viewed sex tape. Ryan had no doubt the situation was a main contributor for Reckless choosing to go indie for the next album.

"A substantial return—" Mason spat.

Leah held up a hand, cutting him off. "What are you suggesting?"

"We've already thrown around a few ideas." Scott rested into the sofa, smug. "We want you to create a talking point. Even a scandal. We need you to milk the free publicity train as much as possible."

Ryan chanced a cautionary glance at his best friends. Free publicity was rarely a good thing. Not emotionally, anyway. Free publicity meant a reporter could pick and choose what information they gave to the public. It meant spinning and twisting facts. It meant opening your soul to the devil and hoping they didn't expose something you'd prefer to keep quiet, like a drug scandal or a cheating claim. Free publicity was fucked, and they all knew it.

"I was thinking a feel-good interview with Gabi and Blake about the pregnancy," Scott continued. "We all want to know what's going on with the little bub."

Blake glared. "Are you fucking kidding me? Gabi has been—"

Leah raised her hand again, the simple command enough to cut Blake off with a grunt. "Gabi is off limits."

All of them would be united in her declaration. There was no disputing Blake's wife had already been through enough turmoil lately, along with moving her life from Australia to the US. The further Gabi remained from the spotlight, the better.

"That's non-negotiable," Leah continued. "So what's your next suggestion?"

Scott turned his focus to the lead singer. "How about leaking a date for Mason's wedding?"

"No way." Mason slumped into the sofa across the back wall. "I put a ring on it. That's all Beyoncé said I had to do."

Scott released a bark of laughter. Nobody else encouraged the humor. "Then maybe a staged proposal from our most recently attached band member."

"Pass." Sean's scowl spoke louder than words. He hadn't been with his choreographer girlfriend, Melody, for long. They were still in the smitten, can't-breathe-without-speaking-to-you stage. There was no way the drummer would let her take a bullet. "*Hard* pass."

"What about you, Mitch? Do you have any news that could stir some free publicity?" Scott didn't pause. "We need something."

"I've got nothing for ya," Mitch grated through clenched teeth. His wife, Alana, was the official band photographer and the longest standing woman on the tour apart from Leah. Even though more shows would affect their relationship the least, Alana would probably be the worst equipped to handle public scrutiny due to her secluded upbringing.

"I guess that leaves it up to you, Ryan. Which is perfect, really, seeing as though you're now the only single member of the group. Our publicity team already had an idea in place, but with the pending divorce I thought your friends would be more willing to take the limelight."

The weight of the room fell on Ryan's shoulders. Everyone stared at him with vastly differing looks—one with cunning, others in horror or rage. Leah merely took him in with the unaffected stare she'd perfected. *Almost* perfected. He was sure he glimpsed the slightest hint of panic in her blue eyes. "I've never taken the fall before. It's only natural I do it now."

He spent years honing his reputation. He was the gentleman, the one who vowed to honor his marriage, and more importantly, his wife. And that's the way he'd wanted the world to see him. He refused to be another celebrity cliché surrounded by sex, drugs, and rock 'n' roll. He'd only ever indulged heavily in one, and it definitely wasn't the sex or the drugs. In fact, he'd never tried an illegal substance more than once, and he'd been the only one enthusiastic about polishing the family jewels for a damn long time.

"What's this idea you're talking about?"

"Well, there are a few options." Scott's lips curved in a gradually building smile. It was sinister. Repulsive. "We can focus on your divorce. The legal battle has already dragged on for months, so it's not like it's a secret that you and Julie can't come to terms with the settlement..."

"No." Not an option. He wasn't going to do anything to poke his ex's already accomplished bitchiness.

"Or we can kill two birds with one stone and hook your newly single ass up with the lead singer of your opening band. Slicker isn't building the media presence we'd hoped for, so placing the two of you together with a few dates in public places, maybe a scandal here and there, will boost both your popularity and theirs."

"You want us to waste our time promoting another band?" Mason placed his hands on the top of his head, his knuckles white, his waning restraint evident. "This is ridiculous."

Ridiculous? Yes. But Ryan was still stuck on the unfamiliar concept of dating. He hadn't been through those early relationship stages since he was a teen. "What happens if I refuse?"

"Then we'll recoup our losses with more tour dates."

"Fuck off," Blake spat. "We planned those dates for a reason. I'm not going to miss the birth of my child if the tour gets extended."

"We could fill the spaces in the schedule first." Scott pushed from the sofa and stood. "You've got vacant two-day blocks in there that can house more concerts."

"Those two-day blocks were arranged to allow Blake to get back to see his wife. Not to mention we're legally obligated to give the crew and bus drivers a break." Leah was the voice of reason. The classy, professional calm that kept them from tearing this guy apart. "They also give Mason and Sean the opportunity to catch up with their partners."

"We can get more crew members." Scott waved away the claim with a lazy hand. "And fly the wives in for a few nights."

"Gabi can't fucking fly, asshole." Blake tensed his fists. "We won't place any risks on this pregnancy."

"And I won't place any regard on the love life of my artists. I'm not here to facilitate your libido. If the demand is there, we'll be scheduling more shows wherever the hell we want them."

Blake inched forward, closing in on trouble. "You can't do that."

But they all knew he could. When they'd first signed as an unknown band, the label had put them through hell more times than Ryan could remember. Spite from their camp wasn't new. It was merely a distant memory since they'd begun making millions.

Scott raised a brow. "You might want to re-read your contract."

A chorus of profanity erupted. There were threats of violence, clenched fists, friends holding friends back from committing murder.

"Calm down." Leah raised her voice. "Just *calm down*."

Ryan swallowed over the building anger while the vicious snarls took moments to die, leaving the room saturated in palpable fury. Scott remained smug, the power firmly in his grasp because he still had a contract hanging over their heads until the tour was complete.

"More concerts are impossible." Leah raised her chin and crossed her arms over her distracting chest. "You need to give us more options."

"You should've thought about that before declining our last offer."

"Fuck you." Blake's curse reverberated off the walls like an avalanche. "This is bullshit."

"It's OK." Leah placed a hand on his arm, guiding the bass guitarist back from the brink with a mere flash of her lashes. "Go to the hotel and let me deal with this."

"No. I need to know what's happening. I need to know what I'm going to have to explain to my wife."

Leah leaned in and whispered in Blake's ear. The guy winced at her words and the fight left his shoulders. There were brief seconds where the two of them were side by side, the entire room watching, waiting for the final response that came in a succinct nod, stormed footsteps across the room, and finally a slam of the door in Blake's wake.

Ryan had been there before. He'd been the one in his friend's shoes, the one prepared to rip his hair out for the sake of the woman he loved. And just like now, Leah had always pulled him back from insanity and made everything peachy again. She was Wonder Woman, only better, and a hell of a lot sexier, too.

"This is pretty fucking rough," Mitch muttered.

Ryan nodded at the understatement. Over the years, the industry had fallen to shit at their feet, while Reckless continued to grow and make Grander millions. They'd done their part. They'd paid their dues. They shouldn't be punished for wanting a better contract next time around—one that Grander refused to give.

"I'll do it." He glared at Scott and hoped the guy had a clear picture of his disgust. He hadn't wanted to open his mouth and take the fall, but their choices were vanishing like booze at an after party. He was the only single member of the band. His friends all had loved ones waiting at home, and he was well aware of how tour headlines could mess with a relationship. Hell, they'd probably mess the shit out of his divorce, but what was the alternative? "I'll date this woman and help lift her profile, but you need to back off on the tour."

"Grander will want more than a few dates. We want results."

Ryan chanced another look at his friends. Mason was minutes away from needing police intervention. Mitch was pale with worry, while Sean was gazing into space, his nostrils flaring. Then there was Leah. Beautiful, protective Leah. She was focused on him, her emotions hiding under the full-time professional façade.

"And you'll get them." He turned back to Scott. "I can put her on the paparazzi radar, and the rest of the guys can help build hype on social media. It will skyrocket their visibility. You can't put a price on that sort of early publicity to a band's career."

"I agree." The smirk was back on Scott's face. "But if you're unsuccessful, we'll have the extra tour dates on standby."

"Nope." Ryan stood tall, adamant, determined and oh-so-close to telling this guy what he really thought. "I won't do it with that hanging over my head. If I'm risking everything and I have to fake-date someone during the middle of a divorce, I want assurances."

"Then I guess we're at a standstill." Scott shrugged. "Grander won't be happy with a vague pledge that you'll build hype."

"*Make* them happy with it." Mason dropped his hands to his sides. "You need to think long-term instead of instant gratification. Of course we can fill more tour dates. Nobody will dispute that. But once we're gone, we ain't comin' back. Take this opportunity for us to create your next big name, otherwise it could be years before you get another chart topper on your list."

"Could you commit to making Slicker a chart topper?" Scott's focus switched from Mason to hit Ryan head on.

That was a huge ask. God-damn monumental. The market wasn't what it used to be. The influx of indie artists and the inexpensive marketing of social media meant anyone and everyone was an up and coming star. Even with their substantial fan base, they couldn't click their fingers and create a new worldwide sensation.

Mason narrowed his gaze, inclining his head almost imperceptibly. No matter how improbable, they would commit to this. They had to.

"Yes," Ryan announced. "We will."

"Great." Scott leaned to the side and pulled a piece of paper from his pants pocket. "I'll take the information back to the team and see what they say. If they agree, I'll call. But while you wait, here are the suggested changes to the tour."

Ryan snatched the document and scoured the highlighted dates. *Shit.* Eight more shows that extended the tour for two weeks. He glanced at Leah, his jaw stiff, his anger coursing between them. The slight convulse of her throat was the only indication she understood his silent message.

This was bad.

This was fucked.

Her features continued to tighten, her frown deepening and deepening until everything froze and a calculated look of understanding washed over her.

"Nice pretense, Scott." She narrowed her stare on the representative. "I can't believe we almost fell for that."

"Hmm?" Scott quirked a brow.

"We're already a month into the tour and you expect everyone to be on board with new dates—the band, the crew, the venues? I call bullshit. You knew how adamant we were about the schedule. What you came in here for was the boost to Slicker's profile. That was the goal all along, not the tour." She cocked her hip and scoffed. "You start by threatening us with suggestions you knew the guys would never agree to—Gabi and the pregnancy, Mason and a wedding date. When the whole plan was to get us to promote your failing band."

Scott waited for her to continue. When she didn't, he pushed to his feet. "This is about taking what we can from a band who snatched everything they could from us before they decided to cut and run."

"Go to hell," Sean growled. "It's not our problem you're delusional in thinking we'd sign another shitty deal. Get over it and move on."

"I don't have to. Not while we still have your current contract in play."

Mason shoved to his feet. "Do you know what I do to guys who—"

"Good night, Scott." Leah stepped in front of Mason, taking control, her presence a warning to the lead singer and anyone else in the room who wanted to voice their opinion. "We'll speak again tomorrow."

"You're such a good leash." Scott chuckled. "You're the only woman I know who can bring five grown men to heel."

Ryan tensed. Every muscle, every limb. The reason they responded to her instructions wasn't because of authority or superiority. It was plain and simple respect. She'd earned the ability to pull them up on a dime because she'd proven her perspective was always clearer than theirs. It was what they relied on her for. That damn Wonder Woman thing, and she just proven it again by seeing through Scott's bullshit.

"And you're such a good lap dog." She beamed a smile at him, her eyes flashing in supremacy. "Now get out of here and let me deal with this."

Everyone remained silent as Scott sauntered from the room. There wasn't a sound. Not even the asshole's footsteps breached the heavy rush of blood in Ryan's ears. Then the door slammed shut and the space erupted into a vocalized dog fight.

"He can get away with this, can't he?"

"Yes." Leah met Sean's concern with a cringe. "History has shown that record labels can do whatever they like. Hell, they could even slip you a roofie and rape your ass and you'd still have to fulfill whatever contractual obligations they deem necessary."

She wasn't exaggerating. Behind the glitz and glamour of the music industry was a threatening relationship fans weren't privy to. The artists held all the talent, and yet the label held all the power.

"I didn't see this coming." Mitch slumped onto the sofa and cradled his head in his hands. "I honestly thought we'd walk away from Grander amicably."

Ryan nodded in agreement, but Leah didn't mimic the movement. The guilt in her eyes said she'd anticipated this. She'd known it would happen.

"Scott would've been under pressure to re-sign Reckless." She released a defeated breath. "And now that he's failed, Grander is grasping at straws to get whatever they can before you're out of contract and no longer under their dictatorship."

"So what do we do? How do we fight this?" Mason knitted his hands back above his head. "It's hard enough being away from Sidney, but Blake has to deal with a hell of a lot more. And I'll be damned if I pimp out a band I hardly know."

"That's the problem. We have no power. We can't fight this. What we have to do is give them what they want in the easiest way possible and get out as soon as we can."

"Are you kidding?" Mason glared. "No fucking way."

She turned on him, five and a half feet of gorgeous fury bearing down on the lead singer. "No, I'm not kidding. You have no idea what it's like to be under the label's control. You've slid by on impressive sales and side-stepped all the drama because your income frees you from the back-stabbing. But believe me, this is what most artists have to deal with on a continuous basis. This is what the industry is like for everyone below the top ten percent. You wanted to decline signing the contract they offered, now face the backlash."

Ryan itched to cut in, to back her up no matter how clueless he was on the topic. Only she didn't need it. Mason held up his hands in surrender and returned to his position on the sofa. "Sorry I spoke."

"Don't be sorry. Be realistic. Their logic is clear." Her voice was softer now, the edge of defeat heartbreaking. "They want to create a new Reckless Beat. At least sales-wise. Having us promote Slicker and gush over their songs will be one thing, but instigating a story fans can follow and become emotionally involved in will be bigger and better. It happens all the time. Celebrities get involved in scandalous relationships mere months before an album release. The process has become a routine for some artists."

Ryan didn't doubt it. He just wasn't sure what he was getting himself into. He'd barely spared Slicker a sideways glance in the last month. They were a fledgling band assigned to the tour by Grander. The two men and two women group had no pulling power in regard to ticket sales. They had no tour experience at all. They were a heavy weight that nobody in Reckless had the time to coddle. So Ryan had chosen to give them a wide birth in an effort to hide his resentment.

It wasn't hard. Things were frantic on the road, not enough sleep and too much adrenaline. It helped when Reckless now stayed in hotels and the up and coming group had to slum the nights in their tour bus. "So dating this woman will save our asses?"

Leah wouldn't look him in the eye. She looked everywhere *but* him. "If you're comfortable doing it, then yes, it would be the easiest option. Then again, if you're not willing, we'll work around that, too. I don't want this to affect your divorce."

His thumbs throbbed with the need to smooth the furrow of her brow. "No, I'll do it. It's no skin off my back." He'd do whatever he could to take her stress away. He'd do it for Blake, too. And Mitch and Sean and Mason.

"Then all we can do now is wait." She focused her attention on Mitch. "Can you go and check on Blake for me?"

"Yeah, of course." He walked past her and rubbed her upper arm. "Is there anything else I can do?"

"Get some rest." She gave a sad smile at his touch and then glanced at Mason and Sean in turn. "You've got another sold out show tomorrow, then we're back on the road."

"Yes, Mom. Let us know as soon as you hear something." Mason accompanied her to the door, Sean and Mitch following after. "See you tomorrow."

"Good night." She held the door open and watched them leave. Even after their footsteps faded, she didn't look at him. "Are you going to hang around here for a while?"

"No. I just wanted to make sure you're all right."

"I'm good."

She lowered her gaze to the hallway floor, killing him slowly with her disconnect. They couldn't be alone in the same room together anymore. He wasn't sure if she thought he was going to steal another kiss, or do something else equally moronic, but it was clear that returning to the way they once were wasn't easy for her.

"I need to get going, though." She shot him a millisecond glance. "I've got some research to do on your new girlfriend."

He winced. He wasn't interested in dating a stranger, fake or otherwise. "I'll let you go."

Yep, the same stilted conversation they'd been having for months. One uncomfortable sentence after another. Curse him and his senseless mistake. He missed her. He missed the conversation and the friendship. He missed the laughter and the reliance.

He strode to the door, trying to ignore the slight tense of her shoulders on his approach. "Don't worry about this mess, OK?" He'd do some pretty crazy things to be able to move closer, to pull her in for one of the hugs he'd grown to rely on. "I'll blow this chick out of the water."

She gave a derisive laugh. "I don't doubt it. But I'm also sure she'll blow you, too. It'll be a great way to get back on the horse."

He wasn't looking for a damn horse. Apart from an end to the divorce bullshit, all he wanted was Leah's forgiveness. He needed his best friend back. And now, he was certain this situation with the lead singer of Slicker would send his 'right time, right place' progress back in the opposite direction.

Leah hadn't slept in days. Not that it was common to notch up a lot of slumber hours while on tour. Finding a pleasing hotel resting place was an unfavorable lucky dip. You never knew when you were going to score sound-proofing and a good mattress, and you certainly had no warning when there would be paper-thin walls and a chorus of sex noises from the room next door. And that was on the favorable nights when she wasn't on the sleeper bus, traveling from location to location with a crew who snored loud enough to damage her hearing.

The insomnia had allowed her to spend the last two nights online stalking Felicity 'Flick' Knight and prepare how to tackle the latest Reckless disaster. The woman was drama-free according to the Internet. She was also too scarily stunning, too talented, and too fucking flawless to not have more than a few skeletons hanging in her perfect closet. But there was no getting around the relationship charade. Grander had agreed to stop riding their asses if this stunt went to plan, and the termination of said ass riding was on the top of her to-do list.

Ryan was due to arrive at her suite any minute now. A discussion about his responsibilities would be had. She'd then formally introduce him to the squeaky-clean singer and they could be on their merry way to fake Fucksville.

Yippee for a job well done.

Only it didn't feel like she'd succeeded this time. Her insides churned as if she was approaching failure. Failure of what, she had no clue, and no matter what she did, she couldn't shake the sensation.

If anything, she should be relieved. Since their kiss, and the subsequent escape to Vegas, she'd been on the edge of anxiety, wondering if her professionalism would slip again, shoving her into another fantastically inappropriate embrace in his profoundly muscular arms.

This situation should be her saving grace. Her buffer. Ryan's occupation with another woman would give him less time to obsess over their fractured friendship, and maybe give him someone else to rely on, seeing as though she'd successfully kept her distance from him for months.

Yep. It was a win-win. Any minute now gratefulness would kick in. Any. Damn. Minute.

Fortunately, the knock at the door saved her from trying to awaken an emotion she wasn't prepared to welcome.

"I'm coming." She stood, sucked in a breath, and straightened her calf-length skirt. Sweat coated her palm as she pulled open the suite door and found a handsome face she hadn't been expecting. "Blake? What are you doing here?"

"Ryan said he was meeting with you and Scott. Do you mind if I sit in?"

"Is that a good idea?" He was still temperamental from the first showdown. Being away from the woman he loved was far harder for him than Mason and Sean. Not that the others were dealing. They just had a thick layer of pride that didn't allow for pining in public.

"This is a meeting about Ryan and Felicity. At the moment, the additional tour dates are on hold, and you know I'll keep you informed if that changes."

"Yeah, I know, but I still want to be here."

He wiped a hand down his face and his fatigue pulled at her heavily guarded heartstrings. She rarely let the Reckless men lead her to make emotional decisions. Apart from Ryan, Blake was the only one near capable of manipulating her rarely seen non-professional side.

"Come in." She released a defeated huff and side-stepped to open the door wider. "Ryan should be here any minute."

She glanced down the hotel hall, double-checking the man of the moment wasn't already on the way before she closed the door and walked to Blake. "Spill." She rounded the small glass dining table and sank into a seat opposite him, the manila folder full of her research placed between them. "Why do you need to be here?"

"I guess I feel guilty. I won't agree to more tour dates because I can't go for months without seeing Gabi. But it also doesn't sit right to let Ryan slut himself out for me."

"It isn't specifically for you." She ignored the slut comment, because frankly, it fit. Anyone with a brain and a healthy libido would realize this type of arrangement would end with the fake relationship turning into real sex. "We all want to be finished with the tour when the baby comes."

"I know." His knee began to pulse—up down, up down—as he tapped his foot on the carpeted floor. "And I'm well aware that Ryan needs to get laid, but not like this. Not when it's staged and under a microscope."

She bit the inside of her cheek, unprepared for the brutal truth.

"What he needs is a woman who will unapologetically screw Julie out of his system," he continued. "A cheap and nasty groupie who will—"

Leah held up her hand. "I get the picture." The visual was like a machete to her sex-drive. "Ryan needs to get laid."

"Speaking of getting laid, when was the last time you got busy?"

She screwed up her face in the most unladylike way. "Unless you're offering your services, that's none of your damn business."

He grinned, his bad-boy charm surpassing the everyday male and moving into god-like territory. Thankfully, she was immune. "I'm only asking because you were determined to take more time for yourself after you returned from Vegas, yet you're still the work-obsessed woman you've always been."

Another knock sounded at the door, a welcomed reprieve from the unwanted conversation.

"Gabi's pregnancy changed my priorities," she lied, pushing to her feet. "I need to work harder now to make sure everything syncs with the birth."

In reality, she'd come home from Vegas and taken an additional two nights off from the usual Reckless mania to try to regain some of the social life she'd once had. All she'd scored were rejection texts from old friends who were now too busy to catch up, and innumerable hours spent obsessing over her mistake with Ryan. So she slid straight back into the breakneck pace of working twenty-four-seven and became addicted to the distraction.

"I'm sure you can cut back on a few things to make more time for yourself."

She headed for the hall, not looking back. "Are you offering to take some of my duties?"

His non-answer wasn't surprising as she flung open the door and came face-to-face with a walking, talking heart palpitation.

"Ryan," she greeted.

"Hey." He jerked his chin at her, his smile lazy and sweet.

Even with tired eyes he was profoundly handsome. It was the one thing she couldn't ignore—his physical appeal. Her thoughts could be smothered, her dreams stabbed and incinerated, but his gorgeousness was always there. Always an insistent reminder.

"Come in." She swung an arm toward the dining table. "We've only got a few minutes before Scott and Felicity arrive."

He strode before her, making it impossible for her gaze not to latch on to the tight stretch of his biceps against the material of his T-shirt. She hated those muscles. Loathed and despised how mouth-watering they were from years of guitar play.

"What are you doing here?" Ryan directed to Blake.

"Being a good pimp." He gave a girlie smile and winked, the expression in complete contrast to his lethally spiked hair and the harsh tattoos inking every inch of his arms. "I wanted to make sure your first act of prostitution was done right."

"Nice," Ryan muttered, settling into the seat beside his friend. "I think I can handle the logistics on my own."

"Maybe." Blake shrugged. "But it's been a while since you fucked something warm-blooded."

"Assh—"

Leah held up a hand, and like always, her men complied. "Are you two done?"

Ryan glared. "I was about to tell Blake to go fuck himself, then I would've been finished."

Blake's lips twitched. "And I would've replied with, 'I will, and I'll think of you while I do it,' and then the conversation would've been over."

Leah clutched the back of her chair and gave them *the* look. The one she'd honed to perfection.

"Sorry," Blake muttered.

He certainly would be if he continued with the bullshit. She currently lacked the patience to put up with their non-stop smack talk.

"We need to get started." She sank into her seat and flipped open the folder. "Here's the information I pulled on Felicity."

Researching Ryan's next bed partner was akin to a chili sauce enema. Unfortunately, she hadn't paid the woman enough attention before the Grander bombshell, and being unprepared wasn't an option.

"She grew up in a small town in Michigan. Didn't go to college but had good grades in school. She's played everything from piano to guitar to violin." She spread out the pages, exposing black and white images of the dark-haired, light-eyed beauty. "I couldn't find anything on past boyfriends or scorned lovers. No connection to drugs or alcohol abuse. In fact, there was nothing juicy at all. Nothing exciting. Nothing memorable. It doesn't add up, but then again, who am I to judge a straight-laced rocker?"

"Nobody came out of the woodwork when they signed with Grander?" Ryan sat forward and shuffled through the information.

"No. There wasn't any dirt at all." Not a single thing to give her reason to stop the charade and keep another woman from setting claws into her rhythm guitarist. The *band's* rhythm guitarist. "From what I can tell, she's drama free."

"She's also fucking hot." Blake picked up one of the pictures, his eyes wide with appreciation. "She's got the goth, rock goddess thing going."

Leah cringed and both their gazes fell upon her as if the reaction had been audible. *Fuck,* had it been audible?

She couldn't refute the woman's beauty—full lips and flawless skin framed by sleek blue-black hair, boy short at the back, chin-length at the front. Add the slim waist, perky breasts, and what seemed to be a firm butt, and the woman became a walking erection dispenser.

"Just keep it in your pants for the duration of the meeting," she muttered. "I don't want Scott thinking this arrangement is anything more than a huge pain in my ass."

Blake smirked and she anticipated his filth before he opened his mouth and said, "If Ryan's lucky, it might be more of a pain in Felicity's ass, right, my friend?"

Ryan didn't bite. There was no humor. No reciprocated perversion. "Are you sure this is a good idea?"

Leah shrugged. "Fucking her in the ass is probably something you should discuss with—"

"That's not what I'm talking about and you know it."

Yeah, she knew, but like Blake, joking away the uncomfortable squeeze in her chest was a crutch. She still couldn't shake the feeling that this situation was all wrong when it should've been all right.

"Yes." She shuffled the pages together and closed them inside the folder. "If we're successful in boosting Slicker's popularity, it should be enough to placate Grander."

"And if it isn't?" Blake asked.

"I honestly don't know." Scott had made thinly-veiled threats over the past two days. Threats that couldn't be ignored when Reckless wasn't in a position of power. "Your current contract states the number of tour dates should be determined by buyer demand, not band availability. Even though Grander signed off on this tour being shorter than previous years because of the baby, it doesn't mean they can't change their mind. And we all know they only agreed because they were hoping to sweeten you up for another contract."

"If only there was another way to go about it." Blake stared at the closed folder, a hint of humor in his tone. "We need to boost this chick's reputation and sex appeal, but we're relying on a dude who hasn't used his dick in ten years."

"Don't worry about my dick," Ryan muttered. "Gabi seems to think it works fine."

"Whoa." Blake choked on a laugh. "When did you turn into a smart ass?"

Leah pressed her lips tight to fight a grin.

"I guess your taint has finally rubbed off on me." Ryan turned his gaze to her, freezing her heart with those soulful eyes. "And now that I don't have an ungrateful wife nagging me about my image, I can finally relax and not give a damn."

"At least once this charade is over, anyway." He shouldn't have to wait. He deserved the world and everything in it after putting up with Julie for so long.

"I know." He inclined his head. "It's only a matter of time before I get what I want."

She stiffened, inside and out. There was a warning in his tone. A threat. *Fuck.* Maybe it was a promise. *No.* She shook off the stupidity and pulled her professionalism back into place. Clearly, she was hallucinating. Blake hadn't even noticed the tension she seemed to think was clogging the air. He was still smiling at Ryan's comeback, oblivious to her skip down Daydream Lane.

The last awaited knock sounded at the door, breaking the silence and tearing a pathetic gasp from her throat. *Motherfucker.* She needed to stop being a temperamental Nancy around him. One kiss shouldn't have the power to shake foundations. Not when she'd successfully ignored the topic for this long.

"Let's do this." She shoved back in her chair, more aggressive than necessary. "And please, for the love of god, think before you speak."

She made for the entrance, trudging her grumpy ass forward, feeling Ryan's stare follow her for the duration. With a heavy yank of the knob, she swung the door wide and glanced at the unwanted guests in turn.

"Scott..."

The Grander representative gave a smug grin.

"Felicity..." The woman, on the other hand, was subdued. Her smile was in place, yet her eyes were filled with scrutiny. Judgement. For someone who had been given the golden goose to skyrocket her career, she definitely wasn't showing a worthy dose of excitement. "Come in. Take a seat."

Leah hung back as her guests shared nauseatingly merry greetings and made themselves comfortable around the dining table. This was it, the moment where Ryan jumped from one bad decision to another. One unworthy woman to the next. All for the sake of the Reckless Beat family.

"I gather you've informed Felicity on the publicity stunt." She pulled out the chair at the head of the table and took a seat.

"Yes." The woman nodded. "But please, call me Flick. Only my mother calls me by my real name."

"Sure." How cute. She focused on Scott, ignoring the way Ryan and Blake eyeballed the singer. "So, what's the plan?"

"You tell me. As far as Grander is concerned, we have nothing to do with this. It's all on you."

"Right... So you're demanding this publicity stunt take place but refuse to be a part of it?" *Yippee fucking ki-yay.* She couldn't wait to add Fake Relationship Facilitator to her resume.

"I don't think we need our hands held," Ryan said to Felicity. "Do you?"

The woman cringed. "God, I hope not. I feel embarrassed enough already."

"I'll try to make it as painless as possible."

Ryan grinned at his future conquest, fucking grinned. It was such a sweet, gentlemanly gesture that made nausea and discomfort tag-team in Leah's chest. He didn't even know her, couldn't trust her, and yet, here he was, diving in head first. If he wasn't careful, this would be another divorce waiting to happen.

"We'll be in Atlanta tomorrow," he continued. "After the show we can hit a nightclub and let the paparazzi take it from there."

Felicity turned a lighter shade of pale as she nodded. "OK."

Was the woman morally conflicted over the thought of a fake relationship? She certainly wasn't this timid on stage last night when she was screaming her enthusiasm to the audience and gyrating against the microphone stand.

"Leah?"

She snapped her attention to Ryan. "Yeah?"

"I asked about how we will get the paparazzi involved."

"We'll leak it somehow. Don't worry, they'll swarm as soon as they hear word you've moved on from Julie."

"You really think they'll swarm?" Felicity's voice was panicked, her ruby-stained lips tight with disbelief. "What happens if I can't make this look plausible?"

"Then you try harder." Scott stole the words from Leah's mouth.

This woman still had celebrity training wheels, her cluelessness evident for everyone to see.

"You've got nothing to worry about," Blake answered. "The paps will want this story as much as we do because it sells. They'll wait for the money shot and they'll consider any unrealistic behavior as puppy-love nerves."

"And between now and tomorrow night, we can get to know each other." Ryan gave her another one of those consoling smiles. "I'll make sure you're comfortable."

"Can I suggest taking a few photos on our terms first?" Leah grated through a clenched jaw. She didn't want to pussy-foot around this woman's apprehension. It was bad enough her men were already fawning over her, jumping through unnecessary hoops. Felicity was supposed to be a rocker, an upcoming star. If she couldn't handle a small dose of media manipulation, she didn't have the skills to be in this industry.

"What do you mean?" Felicity met her gaze.

"Mitch's wife is the official Reckless photographer. We can get her to take some staged shots and leak them under an alias. That way you're assured you'll look good—" not that this woman could ever appear anything less than fuckable, "—and you'll be prepared for the first wave of craziness."

"That sounds good."

Curse her and her appreciative smile.

"Are you good with that?" Felicity focused on Ryan in hope.

He nodded. "I'm happy with whatever puts you at ease."

Gagging noises filled the room, or maybe it was only in Leah's head. This situation was becoming more unbearable by the second. She could only imagine what it would become once the two fake lovers were nauseatingly familiar with one another.

"Great. I'll call Alana and—"

"No." Ryan spoke over her. "I'll do it. You'll have enough on your plate trying to organize the PR team and track the success of this stunt."

He was dismissing her? She'd never been relegated to the back seat when it came to publicity. This was her domain. Her job.

"We're good." He looked at Felicity. "Right?"

"Yeah." The woman shrugged. "I'd actually prefer fewer witnesses. I'm not the best actress."

"You won't need to act, sugar." Blake ruffled Ryan's hair, receiving a scowl in return. "You'll happily succumb to this guy's charms within minutes."

Felicity smirked, the first unscripted reaction of the day. "We'll see."

The rest of the meeting was dedicated to how Grander would deem this a success. A social media explosion was expected. There needed to be an influx of followers and friends and tweets. Paparazzi and news outlets had to recognize Felicity as an up and coming celebrity. And the clincher, Slicker was required to hit a chart on at least one major online retailer for this nightmare to be over.

There were also stipulations on the type of attention they were aiming for. Even though any publicity for Felicity would've been welcomed, Scott made it known they were only aiming for favorable hype. Meaning—if someone had to take the fall for a stunt gone awry, it would be Ryan. *His* reputation would be the one tarnished in the event of a social media backlash. *His* hard earned gentlemanly status would be ruined. And *his* future happiness would be at stake.

"Like I've previously stated," Scott drawled, "if this doesn't work, we've already got staff and venues on standby for the additional shows."

"Yeah," Blake grated. "You've mentioned that once or twice already."

"We understand the terms." Leah didn't require a caustic tone. She made sure her stare was enough. "I'll just need them in writing."

"No problem." Scott pulled a folded piece of paper from his jacket pocket. "The terms plus the standby dates."

She didn't move to claim the offering. "I want it in an email." What she really wanted was an evidence trail.

"You don't trust me?"

"I don't trust my mother." She'd learned to cover her ass early in her career. Nobody had loyalty when money was at stake. And morals were in short supply when the industry thrived on greed.

"I'll send the email. But leaking this information won't be in your best interest."

She ignored the threat and smiled. "I'm well aware of what will happen if this gets out."

Fans didn't like to be manipulated, even though PR teams bent them over and did exactly that on a daily basis. The majority of trending scandals instigated by artists were more prevalent than those that were unexpected.

Tina Costintia caught buying a pregnancy test two days before her album release—*staged*. Jensen Peters snapped half naked on a secluded beach the day his latest award nomination was announced—*staged*. Baby photos of Hillary and Jackson Miller's baby leaked as their celebrity status slowly dwindled into obscurity—*staged*.

If an artist wanted to put their career in the spotlight, it was far easier to create a scandal than it was to earn hype on the merits of something legitimate. But on the flip side, if you were caught, it was a sure-fire way to kiss a bright future goodbye.

"I guess we're done." Scott stood and made his way to Leah's side. "Here's your list. And I'll email you a copy later."

"Thanks." She stood, unable to tolerate him peering down at her, and took the paper from his hand. "No doubt I'll be in touch."

"I'm looking forward to it."

She glared at his back as he strode to the suite door.

"I better go, too." Blake pushed to his feet and came to her side. "I need to call Gabi and pack my bag." He squeezed her close and planted a kiss on her temple.

"Thanks for the reminder." And the excuse to kick the remaining two out of her room. She turned to Ryan and Felicity, maintaining her professionalism with an amicable curve of her lips. "Do you lovebirds need anything else from me?"

"No, I think we're good." Ryan's stare bore down on her, drilling holes into her soul. "We'll talk somewhere else and leave you in peace."

Goodie. She couldn't wait to start planning someone else's love life when she didn't have one of her own. For the first time, it seemed like she was unqualified for her position. "Have fun." She strolled for the bathroom, baited breath and all, as she waited for them to leave.

"Hold up."

She stopped at his command and wished his voice couldn't control her more than her own mind.

"Flick, can I meet you in the lobby?" he asked. "I want to speak to Leah for a minute."

The unintentional seductress pushed to her feet. "Sure."

Leah remained immobile as Felicity's footsteps trekked to the door, the latch clicking shut seconds later. Her heartrate increased. The slightest hint of claustrophobia settling in with the thought of being alone in a room with him. But like always, she had to maintain the professional persona. She had to hike up her chin, straighten her shoulders, and face Ryan like he was any other band member. "What's wrong?"

He moved closer, the few steps done in a gradual assault. "You're not yourself. I want to make sure this situation isn't stressing you out."

"Me? I'm fine." She placated him with a laugh. A fake and delirious laugh. She had this shit under control. Everything was peachy in her world. "You're the one who offered to sell yourself like a hooker. I should be asking you the same thing."

"It's a small price to pay, I guess."

"Maybe, if it all goes well. But if it doesn't..." The possibilities were endless. He'd never tasted the bitter filth birthed from Internet trolls. He wasn't used to drama. "I know the guys appreciate you taking the bullet on this one."

"And what about you?" He took another step, creating havoc on her nervous system. He was close. Unprofessionally so.

"What about me?" Her voice grew in pitch.

"Do you appreciate it?"

Jesus. How did she answer that? Lying wasn't an option. She couldn't say she loved how he'd put his reputation on the line, because he'd know it wasn't true. She would've much preferred anyone else to take the fall. He was too vulnerable. "Why does my opinion matter?"

Another step. Another dose of fear to add to the growing pile. "It's always mattered. You know that."

Don't. The demand shoved to the forefront of her mind, begging to be set free. "I should start packing." She slid backward, putting necessary space between them.

His eyes were killing her. They didn't focus on her in friendship. They looked at her as if she instigated the start of world peace.

"Leah..."

He took another step, breaching personal space and snapping something painful inside her. "Stop."

His face fell, his agony heavier than a beach-load of sand. "What's wrong?"

She tried to recover, tried to pull her shit together and fake a brilliant smile. "I'm busy. That's all. You should go."

"No." He stood firm, his agony turning to anger. "What have I done?"

Everything. Nothing. And neither answer made sense. "Please, I've got a thousand people to call before the end of business today."

"Right… So Blake can hug and kiss you but I can't get within two feet? I thought we were trying to get back to the way we were."

And there it was. The confrontation she should've prepared for. "We've been trying for months. Obviously, we're going nowhere."

"No." He shook his head, his stare narrowing, shrinking her. "*You're* going nowhere. I'm more than happy to revert to normal and forget that kiss ever happened."

But it *had* happened, and now her lips would be forever haunted with his affection. "It's not that easy for me."

"Why?" He straightened, preparing for battle.

She had to shut this down, extinguish any chemistry or attraction, or whatever the hell made this situation unbearable. This had to end. Now. "Because you carelessly risked my job with that kiss."

He recovered from the verbal slap quicker than anticipated. "And now you think I'm going to smack one on you whenever I get within arm's length?"

"No. It's not that."

"Then what is it?" His voice softened. "I need to make this right somehow. We both know I messed up. But it's time you let me fix it." He inched closer. "I need you. This divorce and the stress with Grander is killing me without my best friend to talk to."

Three big cheers for the fucking friend zone.

He smiled, a curve of lips so sad and small, yet so monumental. "And having to rely on Mason for advice has brought me to a remarkably new low."

"Ouch." She chuckled despite her best intentions. "That is pretty low."

"See?" He spread his arms wide in temptation. "I'm a mess without you."

No, no, no, no. She wasn't going to risk her job again. She wasn't going to fall victim to temptation. To desire. To longing. She'd successfully suppressed that shit long ago.

"Can't we just hug it out?" he asked, as if the question resembled, 'Would you like ketchup on your fries?' When in reality it hit her ears to the tune of, 'Would you like a lobotomy with a side of disembowelment?'

"Hard pass." She repeated Sean's latest catch phrase to combat the burst of adrenaline scorching her veins.

"Why?" He chuckled. "I give the best hugs."

He did. He really did.

"No, you don't." She screwed up her face to back up the lie. They were fast approaching ground zero and there was no way she could return to the destruction of her body against his. Not now. Not ever. "I need to pack." She side-stepped. "Is that all—"

He grabbed her around the waist, his devastating grip tugging her into his chest in one fell swoop. Two seconds. That was all it took for her to go from struggling to manage her composure, to complete and utter devastation.

An apocalypse had nothing on this moment. And all she could do was stand there, her hands on his shoulders to keep herself vertical, while her heart went through a shredder at a snail's pace. She mentally clung to her professionalism, not letting the platonic squeeze slip into fantasy territory.

"See. It's not so bad," he murmured into her hair.

Not bad? Really? She held her breath to fight a groan. "Ryan, I need to get started on my workload."

"Is my erection making you uncomfortable?"

What. The. Fuck? She pushed him, her eyes wide, her jaw practically scraping the floor while every nerve in her body sizzled as if she'd been burned.

"I'm joking." He snickered. "Too soon?"

"*Yes*, too soon." She shoved at his chest. "*Way* too soon."

He continued to laugh, the delicious mirth contagious. "The look on your face…"

"This look?" She pointed to her flaming cheeks, trying to contain a smile.

"This is the look of a woman who never forgets."

"Believe me, I know." His eyes turned somber. "But it was worth it to see you smile."

"I'm not smiling." She kept her lips thin, the edges lifting without her permission. "And just remember that next time you ask for a hug and I refuse."

Christ. She'd never felt more delirious. With one brief embrace he'd short-circuited her brain, rewired her pulsing nerves, and slaughtered her professionalism. She was in meltdown, and unfortunately her body was loving the destruction.

"Noted." He inclined his head and backtracked toward the door. "Next time I won't ask."

RYAN DISCONNECTED THE CALL TO ALANA AND SCANNED THE LOBBY. MITCH'S wife was going to meet him in the restaurant in fifteen minutes, just enough time to find Felicity and get inside that mind of hers.

"Looking for me?" The Slicker singer came up behind him, matching his lazy stride across the reception area.

"I sure was." He shot her a friendly smile, faking comradery because he had a feeling she needed all the support she could get. "We might get some privacy if we do this in the dining area."

"Sure—"

Her response was cut off by a high-pitched squeal that had him swinging around to face the culprit.

"Ryan Bennett?" A blonde in her late teens rushed toward them, her curly hair bobbing with each step. "Can I get a picture? *Please*? Oh, god, I can't believe it's you." She was bouncing on her toes, her eyes wide, her cell clutched in her hand.

"No problem." He gave the approaching security guard a dismissive look and swung his arm wide to let the woman sink against his side.

"I can take the photo if you like." Felicity held out her hand for the phone.

"No." This was a perfect opportunity, one that would ease them into the charade. "Why don't you get in here with us?" He gave her a pointed look and reached for her with his free arm. "Have you heard of Flick from Slicker?" he asked the fan.

"No." Her mouth gaped. "Are you famous, too?"

Felicity chuckled. "Not nearly as famous as this guy."

Her palm pressed against his chest, the warmth a comforting feeling after months spent in emotional isolation. He smiled at the camera, the click encapsulating the first moment in this crazy new nightmare as Felicity's softness leaned into him.

"Thank you." The woman beamed him a look of awe. "My mom won't believe this." She squealed again. "Neither will my friends."

"Make sure you tag us on Twitter and we'll share it around, then they'll have to believe it."

"Oh, I will. I'll do it now."

He kept Felicity at his side with a firm hand as the other woman became engrossed in her cell.

"Nice to meet you," he murmured in farewell and started for the restaurant.

"Is it always like that?" Felicity was rigid, not an ounce of relaxation in her lithe body.

"Sometimes." He didn't want to point out the heavy presence of hotel security keeping them buffered from the crazies. "It'd be different if Mason was here. Blake, too. Panties seem to disintegrate when they're around. No man, woman, or child is spared."

She scoffed. "And you're not a panty dropper?"

"Nah. I've been married for the duration of our success. I'm practically the decrepit uncle in the band hierarchy."

"I don't believe that for one second."

Maybe she should, because from his point of view, this thing between them would run smoother if she knew his lack of seduction skills. She might be monopolizing the nervous-as-hell market at the moment, but he was the one likely to do something inappropriate, all in the name of cluelessness.

It didn't help that Mitch, Blake, Mason, and Sean were his only knowledge base. He was pretty sure the tactics his friends used to score their women had nothing to do with gentlemanly wooing and everything to do with sexual prowess—a skill he wasn't sure was still in his arsenal.

They strode into the restaurant, declined the lone waitress's offer of service and helped themselves to a secluded table at the back of the room. The place was empty. Not a soul in sight.

"I don't think the restaurant is open," Felicity answered his unspoken question and sank into her chair. "It's mid-afternoon. Right in the middle of lunch and dinner. I'm pretty sure the waitress should've turned us away, but there was that glazed gleam of recognition in her eyes."

"It must be my lucky day." He sat across from her, not sure whether he should be flirting to break the tension... Not sure how the hell he was supposed to flirt at all. "So, what's bothering you most about this situation?"

She sighed and brushed the light wisps of hair back behind her ears. "Where do I start?"

"Wherever you want."

She lowered her gaze and fiddled with the polished cutlery. "I have a lot at stake with this."

"We all do." He made sure his face matched the seriousness tightening his throat. "Not just me, but Reckless in general. All the wives of the bandmates, too."

"True." She sucked in a deep breath and slumped in her chair. "I guess the worst part is the humiliation that comes with acknowledging Slicker's lack of success. And Scott..." She shuddered. "That man is a jerk. He's taking pleasure in rubbing in our failure, and has made it perfectly clear I have no choice in this charade. Either I participate or there won't be another album."

Her reluctance made the situation ten times worse. He'd never forced himself on a woman before... Oh, wait... He guessed he had. And look how that situation panned out. "Making you miserable is going to kill me. But the harder we drive this home, the quicker our goals will be accomplished. Then we can part ways and pretend like this never happened."

"You think it will be that easy?"

"Yeah," he lied. "A few public appearances at romantic venues. A kiss here and there..." Her cringe pulled him up short, even though he hid the same reluctance deep inside his chest. "I'm not your type, am I?"

She laughed and gave him an apologetic look. "Sorry. I didn't mean the knee-jerk reaction. This is just happening a lot quicker than I expected."

No biggie. It wasn't like his ego hadn't already been pulverized by his ex. He could take a few more hits before he was out for the count. At least he hoped so.

"Please don't take it personally," she continued. "You know you're gorgeous. You've got the rugged appeal and those hypnotizing eyes. It doesn't help that this is forced."

He scrutinized her, from her cynical gaze to the droop of her pouty mouth. She wasn't offering an ounce of enthusiasm. "This doesn't leave me reassured for our success." The happiness of the five most important people in his life relied on this woman and her delirious amounts of apathy.

"I'm not backing out." Her lips parted and her already pale skin seeped of color. "*Shit.* I'm sorry. I was only complaining. I'm completely dedicated to this. I promise."

Completely disgusted, humiliated, and freaking out at the mere thought of kissing him, but yeah, totally dedicated.

"How's it all going?"

He relaxed at the familiar feminine voice and looked to his side to see Alana smiling bright, her camera bag resting over her shoulder.

"Hey, sweetheart." He pushed back in his chair, thankful for the reprieve. "Alana, this is Flick, she's the lead singer in our opening act."

"Yeah, I know." She gave him an incredulous look. "I've seen a performance or two. You've got a great voice."

"Thank you. And I've heard you're a mighty fine photographer."

Alana blushed. "I sure hope so. It allows me the best job in the world."

"Here, have my seat." Ryan made to stand and was shoved back down by a surprisingly strong hand.

"If I need to sit, I'll pull up another chair." She placed her camera bag on the floor. "So... Do you have any ideas about how you want to do this?"

"I'll leave that up to Flick." He was already growing tired of being the positive force. If she had a long list of reservations and compounding moral issues, she could pick where they started.

"No, Ryan, you should make the decisions." Felicity shook her head, her features still filled with apology. "I'm new to this, but I'll do whatever needs to be done."

Jesus Christ, did she think he was a pro at media manipulation?

There was a pause as Alana glanced from him to Felicity and back again. "Can I suggest something?" she asked. "Eola Lake is right around the corner and would be the perfect setting. It would allow me to capture an image with a bit of distance to it. We don't want to slap your fans in the face with something obvious. We want them to create a talking point, to question whether it's really the two of you together. Because if they talk and argue online, it'll give us a better chance to get this romance trending."

"That's brilliant." Damn it. Why hadn't he thought of that?

Alana blushed again. "It was actually Leah's idea. She called me a few minutes ago and gave some suggestions."

Of course she did. He'd tried to distance her from the drama set to drive a bigger wedge between them, but that woman was stubborn. She would force herself to the front line no matter what.

"I bet she picked out the perfect spot, too."

"You know her well." Alana grinned. "Come on. I'll show you."

Ten minutes later, they were in a secluded area beside the water, Felicity's back against the trunk of a wide tree as he leaned into her.

"How are you feeling?" His thigh was between her legs, his palm plastered beside her head. The position gave him whiplash. Days ago he'd been struggling to assimilate to single-status; now his body was entwined with a complete stranger, and he wasn't enjoying that either.

"I'm perfect."

He snorted. "Do you really think you can bullshit me?"

She wove her hand around his neck, the softness of her skin delicately brushing away his solitude. "Put up or shut up, right?"

That pretty much summed up their situation. "Yeah, but if I'm making you uncomfortable I want to know about it."

"Nah." She smiled, the first genuine curve of lips he'd received from her. "I'm settling into this like a pro."

Thank Christ. Although he'd been used to a certain level of sterile disconnect in his marriage, he didn't want to relive it with Felicity. One woman striving to make him feel inferior was enough for now.

"I need you to keep talking to me, though." She tickled the back of his neck with her fingernails. "What do you do for fun?"

"There isn't much fun flowing through these veins at the moment. I've got an ex who's prepared to bleed me dry and a label determined to make my life hell."

"And here I am, making it even more difficult."

She placed her other palm on his cheek, stoking the emotion for Alana who was hiding somewhere in the distance with a lens pointed in their direction. They'd been instructed to act casual—loving yet playful. They didn't want the pictures to have a sleazy vibe. Not yet. Apparently, the money shot was somewhere between flirtation and hot 'n' heavy.

"We're through the worst of it." He leaned in and winced when she stiffened. "I'm only going to nuzzle your cheek," he whispered in her ear. "You can tell me to back off whenever you like."

"I'm still good." She lowered her hand to his waist. "Just warn me next time. I'm jumpy because the camera scrutiny is new to me. I don't usually get this much attention."

"I find that hard to believe."

"There's nothing but honesty here."

He still wasn't convinced. Blake hadn't been exaggerating when he'd called her hot. Felicity had a non-stereotypical appeal. She wasn't dainty with her heavy boots, black tight jeans, and the thick eye make-up which enhanced eerily bright eyes. She rocked her own set of rules with her harsh exterior, and leveled it with a soft interior which was poking his intrigue.

"But you smell really good." She inhaled deeply. "Your aftershave is intoxicating."

"Darlin', you smell mighty fine yourself."

She hit him with those baby blues. Hit him hard. "Thank you."

There was a moment of silence, an awkward expanse of seconds where his heart panged for another woman. "Do you think Alana's got enough by now?"

"I don't know." She pulled a face, an expression caught between humor and discomfort. "I still feel like the worst actress in the world."

"You're doing fine." Too damn fine.

His cell rang in his pants pocket and he palmed the device to see Alana's name staring back at him. "Hopefully this is good news." He hit connect and lifted it to his ear.

"I have the best shot. You're going to love it."

"So we're done?"

Felicity looked at him in hope.

"Yeah. You're so done. This is absolutely perfect. You're going to be breaking hearts all over again."

He should've been relieved. Instead, his chest pounded with a rhythm of an entirely different beat. He didn't want to be comfortable with Felicity. Falling into easy conversation and breaking personal space barriers within hours wasn't an achievement. It was a liability. He was lonely. He was heartbroken. And this beautiful woman was smiling up at him, mimicking his apprehension in her own little way.

"OK. I'll meet you at the hotel." He disconnected the call and made to back away.

"Wait." Felicity's grip tightened around his neck. "Do you want to get this kissing thing over and done with?"

He froze. "I can say, with complete honesty, that that's the least enthusiastic proposition I've ever had."

She jabbed at his chest in a way that sparked memories. It made him think of someone else, someone who had once smiled up at him with a similar playfulness in her eyes.

"Your poor defenseless ego," she cooed. "But I'm not joking. I'm finally relaxed and I think we should get it out of the way. It'll make it easier for when we need to do it in front of an audience."

The logic was tight. Too bad every inch of him was in protest. He didn't want to kiss her. He had major hang-ups. He had skeletons. He had a shitload of issues destined to multiply once his lips touched hers.

"Let's leave it for now." He stepped back. "Think on it. Fantasize about it. And when you're at the point where you can't take another breath without kissing me, *then* I'll blow your mind with my skills."

She threw her head back and laughed. It was a brilliant sound—loud and rambunctious. It wouldn't be difficult to lean forward and give her what she wanted. To practice what they eventually had to do for show. But it wasn't merely a performance for him. He'd only kissed two women since he was a teenager, and he was still undeniably in love with one of them.

Divorce or not, single or not, kissing Felicity would mark the first step in an unwanted direction. And unfortunately, it was inevitable.

"Come on." He turned away and began walking for the hotel.

She was still chuckling when she lifted his arm and snuggled into his side. "I think we're going to get along just fine."

He looked down at her, at the gorgeous face, the easy smile, the enticing body. "Yeah. Me, too."

That was the problem.

Four

RYAN SLUMPED INTO THE SOFA AND PLACED HIS CELL DOWN ON THE COFFEE table. He was supposed to be somewhere. With someone. But he couldn't think. Couldn't move past the feeling of his life being tipped upside down and all the goodness shaken out.

Back in Orlando, Rockin' Gossip had snapped up the opportunity to share the exclusive photos of him and Felicity. Hours later, his world was under a microscope. The Internet had been smothered with the image of him smiling down at his 'newfound love.' And the happy snap taken in the hotel lobby—the selfie with the young woman—was all the evidence Reckless fans needed to lose their minds over the relationship story.

The 'practically unknown lead singer of Slicker' was now amassing followers along with sales, the number gradually building with every passing hour. He, on the other hand, had received tweets, comments, and emails questioning his morals. *You're not even divorced yet. Give your wife a chance to move on.* And another—*So much for the dedication to your marriage. Did you even think about how Julie would feel? #player #typical #growup.*

He'd frantically blocked or deleted all the slander in his timeline, completely unaware of how to react to the negativity. Maybe he was meant to ignore his reputation going to shit. Leah hadn't mentioned the nastiness.

Neither had his bandmates.

The worst part was knowing exactly how his ex would feel, and it had no reflection on the response she posted on Twitter claiming heartbreak and disappointment. Julie would be pissed he'd moved on before she did. End of story. And evidently from the call he'd just received from his lawyer, she was trying to use the information to manipulate the divorce negotiations.

"Ryan."

He stiffened at Felicity's call from the hotel hall and picked his phone up off the table. "*Shit.*" That's where he was supposed to be. Not in his suite taking midnight calls from his legal team, but out with Felicity creating more speculation and hype about the fake relationship.

He jogged to the door and swung it open. "I'm sorry. I got caught up in a phone call."

"Bad news?"

"My lawyer."

She cringed. "Shit must be getting real if he's calling after midnight. Do you want to postpone going out?"

Yes. Permanently. "You know we can't."

Her cringe remained. "I know." She offered him a sad smile. "Are you ready?"

He looked down at himself and remembered the five second shower he'd had and the quick change of clothes. "Yeah. I guess." He yanked the room card out of the holder and pulled the door shut behind him.

"You look exhausted." She strode by his side, refreshed and picture perfect after the night's performance. "Are you having second thoughts?"

Every damn minute of every damn day. "Nah. I'm good. I'll kick out of the adrenaline detox soon and be back to normal."

Truth was, he'd been dreading every breath inching him toward the imminent kiss. It didn't matter how many texts he received from Felicity, or the amount of effort she was now putting in since the overnight increase in popularity. The act was a necessary evil. One soon to be unleashed.

"How about you?" He pressed the elevator button. "Are you dying to kiss me yet?"

She rolled her eyes with flair. "I can barely restrain myself."

He wished it were the truth. Kissing a willing woman, even though his head and heart weren't engaged, would be far better than forcing himself on someone who wasn't interested. Again. "Good to know. I'll make sure I don't disappoint."

He entered the hotel elevator and rested against the back wall. The mirrors surrounding them reflected a publicist's dream—two young and talented people with the world at their feet. But what loomed over him was a building nightmare. He'd deflected paparazzi for years, now he had to embrace them. He'd safeguarded his private life to maintain his sanity, now he had to plaster it over the Internet.

Everything had changed. There was nothing left to cling to. His friends were paired off. His wife was no longer around to bring comfort. Not even Leah was willing to help him through the turmoil. He'd wanted to talk to her about the Internet trolls who were popping out of the woodwork. Hell, he would've given anything to hear her voice, even in anger, but her cell kept cutting straight to voicemail.

"Hands?" Felicity reached her fingers toward his. "That was the plan, right?"

"Yeah." *The plan.* He joined their palms, the softness of her skin brushing his. There was no comfort in her touch, only a double-dose of shame. "Ready?"

"Ready."

The elevator doors opened and he led her into the lobby. Lights glistened from every angle, sparkling off marble and glass. Then the flash, flash, flash of cameras blinded his periphery.

"They were here when I arrived." Felicity jutted her chin toward the entrance. "Hotel security had to usher me inside."

A white limo was parked out front, the centerpiece to the small crowd of people waving posters, banners, and Reckless T-shirts behind a rope barricade.

"I tipped them off."

He swung around at the sound of Leah's voice and dragged Felicity along for the ride.

"They're not aware of your destination," she continued, her business suit far sexier than Felicity's midriff top and tight jeans. "But if they don't follow you to the club, let me know and I'll send Alana along to take some snaps."

"I don't think we'll need it." Felicity nestled into his side, maintaining the charade with a little too much devotion. "Since the original photos were leaked, I haven't been able to blink without someone posting it on the Internet."

"Good." Leah's attention dropped to his hand, the fingers entwined with Felicity's.

His chest tightened, waiting for a glimpse of pain, even a slice of distaste. Not that he craved her torment. All he wanted was the slightest affirmation to keep him hopeful for their future. A future that kept seeming further and further away.

Right time. Right place.

"The public has never seen you lusting over a woman." A heavy swallow was her only reaction. "You always kept it private with Julie. This will be the first opportunity to give them a taste."

"Give them more ammunition to troll me online, you mean?"

She finally met his gaze. "No. Not ammunition. Validation. Your fans are shocked. I'm sure they'll have a change of heart once you convince them you're happy."

Happy? Was she kidding? He was a mess, barely able to break a smile, let alone persuade anyone he was enjoying himself. "Leah, this—"

"I'm going to make sure the driver is ready." She began backtracking, her pantsuit tailored to cling to every curve of her body. "Club security expected you ten minutes ago."

His world darkened, the final glimmer of light being snuffed. She kept fleeing from him. Over and over. The default setting morphing from annoying to unignorable. "Wait."

She paused, a questioning brow rising.

He begged her with his eyes, begged for her friendship and forgiveness, begged for one glimmer of what they once had, or what could still be. "I think I need to ditch the club."

His sense of failure intensified. He couldn't handle a crowd right now. Not the people or the loud music. What he wanted was to tell her how this situation was tearing him apart. To explain to his best friend how much he loathed being this man—the one the world was growing to hate. And he needed, more than anything, for her to listen and say, "I know," because she did. She *did* know. She knew everything about him, and seeing her act like this situation was just another day and just another task was brutal.

"What?" Felicity dropped his hand and moved in front of him. "You don't want to go out?"

He kept his focus on Leah as she approached. "I don't think I can fake it in front of the cameras tonight."

"But you've been doing a great job." Leah slayed him with her curiosity. "I thought you were starting to enjoy this."

Enjoy? She was definitely kidding. "I'm tired. I'm in a hell of a mood. And I don't have the energy to play happy families."

"Then don't." She hiked a thumb over her shoulder toward open glass doors. "Go to the bar and keep it real. Talk. Drink. Be yourself."

"What about the photo op?" Felicity asked.

"I'll speak to the limo driver and tell him his services are no longer needed. I'm sure the crowd will ask what's going on while I'm out there. I can let them know you've decided to have a quiet night at the bar instead." Leah gave a halfhearted smile. "They'll follow. They always do. And the bar windows aren't tinted, so if you pick a seat that isn't entirely secluded you'll get the publicity."

Felicity turned to him, her gaze earnest. "Ryan?"

He could see the worry in her eyes. The concern for her career. She couldn't lose momentum now Slicker was finally gaining attention. They both needed to keep this story moving.

"I can handle something quiet."

Leah nodded and headed for the entrance without another word. He watched her leave, watched every single step until she was outside working her magic on the shouting crowd.

"Come on." Felicity grabbed his hand. "This'll be painless after you've got a few drinks under your belt."

It had taken two, but that was merely to dull the edge of his self-loathing as photographers snapped pictures of them through the windows of the bar. Another two drinks in quick succession had him in a state of painless lethargy.

"I can't handle this."

"Huh?" He glanced up from his scotch and didn't like her defeated expression. "What can't you handle?"

"This." She waved a hand between them. "The knife's edge. The anticipation. I think we need to expedite the journey a little."

"Expedite?" He took a sip of his drink. "That doesn't sound like you."

"We're on a tight schedule. We don't have long to build this career-saving hype that's supposed to make Slicker a worldwide sensation."

He narrowed his gaze, scrutinizing her. "From someone who couldn't withhold a flinch whenever I stepped within two feet, you've sure changed your tune."

"I've been trying to focus on what matters. Before, I thought I was hurting people unnecessarily. I've since realized the publicity is working, so they'll have to deal with it. We're finally gaining traction on our music."

Again, it didn't sound like her. Not when she'd been messaging him last night about her anxiety. "Who have you been talking to?"

"No one." She broke eye contact and stared toward the bar. "The sooner we get this over with, the better, right?"

"Was it Scott? Did he tell you we need to move this along?"

She raised her wine glass, took a slow sip, still not meeting his gaze.

"It is, isn't it? He called you and told you to speed things up."

"He has a point. Nobody cares if we're holding hands or chatting. They want the juicy stuff. They want headlines and scandal." Her eyes were distraught as she turned to face him and gulped the remainder of her wine. When she raised to her feet his chest concaved, the pain tightening on her approach. "Let's give them what they want."

"This isn't you, Felicity." He held his breath, his muscles tense while she straddled his lap. All he could think of was Leah, how he was betraying his feelings for her, how her consciousness was nudging the back of his neck.

"No, it's the bottle of wine." Her grin was weak. "But once this is over, I'll be able to sleep at night."

He wasn't so certain. He'd be happy to put it off for as long as possible. Hell, he'd be happy to fake the whole kissing thing and hope photographers took advantage of deceptive angles and bad lighting.

"It'll also get the hurt over and done with." She placed her hands on his shoulders, the delicate touch harming more than it helped.

"The hurt?" He grazed his thumb over her cheek, not because he needed to keep up the act, but to sooth the pain emanating from her.

"People I care about." She focused on his lips, his hair, his beard. "They don't agree with what I'm doing. The sooner they realize this is a strategy, nothing personal, the better."

"Are you sure?" He heard the click of a cell camera, then another and another. People inside the bar were taking photos, lapping up his demise and capturing it for eternity.

"Are you?" she countered, meeting his gaze.

"I don't think I have a choice. I can't let my friends down."

"And I have no choice either." She leaned in closer, the scent of sugary sweet breath sinking into his lungs. "Let's just do this."

She repositioned herself, her crotch brushing his cock. He stiffened, waiting for a spark, a reaction from places down south… Nothing. His dick was in hibernation. Out cold. But it wasn't like everything inside him was dead. He cared for her. Just not in a way that compared to anything he felt for Leah.

"This doesn't feel right." She paused, her lips an inch from his.

No shit. He chuckled, because what else could he do? "I don't think it ever will." He pressed his forehead to hers, not sure if he'd prefer things to stay sterile, or if it was best to move on, at least temporarily, to keep his mind off the massive piles of crap surrounding him.

"I don't like hurting people."

Me either. "I'm sure this will be painless."

She nodded, her hair tickling his cheeks. "OK."

"OK?" Shit. He wasn't prepared for acquiescence. He was still reeling, teetering on the edge of stupidity and obligation.

"OK," she whispered.

The closer she came, the harder his chest pounded, the thicker his blood clogged in his veins. Breathing became a struggle under the drowning thoughts of another woman.

She was everywhere.

She was everything.

"I can't do this." He tilted his face, diverting the course of Felicity's mouth to his cheek. His eyes were shrouded in her hair, her perfume sinking into his lungs. She smelled good—sweet, clean, and familiar. But nothing changed inside him. There was no glimmer of warmth. No lust. No excitement.

No Leah.

Hell.

"Then what do we do?" Felicity's voice was shaky, the hint of rejection hitting him square in the conscience.

"Stay close." He cradled the back of her head, letting his fingers slide through her hair as he nuzzled her cheek. Her breasts were against his chest, her crotch right where any hot-blooded man would want it. But he wasn't hot-blooded. He was cold. Made of ice. "I'm sorry."

"Don't be. We both knew this wouldn't be easy." She exhaled a breath and pulled back. "Are you still in love with your wife?"

He could've scoffed, or laughed, or set her straight with innumerable words to paint a vivid picture of his loveless marriage. Instead he nodded. Because nodding was easier than admitting the truth.

"I thought so." She slid onto the couch beside him, her legs now draped over his. "Do you have kids?"

"No." He shook his head. "But I wanted them." Badly.

Her eyes were kind, the pity soul deep. "If it's any consolation, I think the vultures enjoyed the show. Men are smirking like they witnessed a lap dance."

"Perception is everything." He finished the remainder of his scotch and placed a firm hand around her knees while he rested the glass on the table. He couldn't take much more of this. Months of waiting for the right time and right place had taken its toll. Maybe it was time to start thinking realistically—with his head, instead of the heart that had already steered him wrong once before.

It wasn't like Leah was swan-diving for the chance to risk her job to be with him. Sucking face with Felicity and praying a spark would miraculously ignite might be exactly what he needed. He just didn't need it here, in the open, with assholes taking notes. "Should we leave?"

"Yeah... But first." She leaned in, her lips briefly kissing his cheek. "Even though tonight didn't go to plan, thank you for being the lone gentleman in a sea of assholes. You're a great guy."

Everyone kept telling him that. He was a gentleman. He was kind. He was nice. Yet, for all his so-called awesomeness, he was in his 30s, single, and playing chicken with his reputation. It wasn't a winning combination from his perspective.

"I'm sure things will work out for you in the end." She slid her legs from his lap and pulled out her phone. "Do you know the cab company's number?"

"Don't even think about it." He gave her an incredulous look. "You're not catching a cab by yourself at this hour. You can crash in my bed and I'll take the sofa."

"Can't bring yourself to kiss me, but still expect me in your bed? The man's got game." She chuckled and glanced down at her phone. Her face slowly morphed, from happiness to confusion.

"What's wrong?"

Her gaze snapped to the empty entrance of the bar. "Umm." Her focus flew back to her cell screen, her fingers rapidly typing. "I... um..." She glanced back at the door. "Hannah is here."

"Hannah?" He frowned through the lack of recognition. "You'll need to be more specific."

"My bass guitarist."

He remained clueless until a leggy brunette strode toward them from the entrance of the bar, her form-hugging dress worthy of a New York runway. Her hair was loose around her shoulders, her lips dark red and dragging the attention of men and women alike.

"Great," Felicity muttered. "She's drunk."

Ryan scrutinized the guitarist, only gaining a faint hint of intoxication from the barely visible wobble in her step. "Don't worry. You're supposed to stay wasted on your first tour." Reckless had. He'd partied hard and drank even harder. At least until Julie found out and reined him in.

"She's not drinking for fun. She's drowning her sorrows in liquor again." She stood and greeted her bandmate with an arm around the woman's waist. "What are you doing here?"

"Ending my search to find you." Coffee eyes met his. "Apart from a few words in passing, we haven't formally met."

He shook her offered hand and then indicated the free space on the booth seat. "Are you joining us?"

"No." Felicity spoke to Hannah. "We talked about this. You shouldn't be here."

"We talked, but we didn't agree. In fact, I'm pretty sure I argued the hell out of this stupid stunt that puts you in the limelight while the rest of Slicker sits in the dark."

"*Shh*." Felicity's panicked gaze cut to him. "We really need to leave."

"Sure." He shrugged and stood. "Are you still coming back to my room?"

"Your room?" Hannah's lips parted as she sized him up. "Am I cock blocking?" She switched back to Felicity. "You were about to leave with him?"

"I offered to sleep on the sofa so Flick could get the bed. I didn't want her traveling to the bus on her own." And now he didn't want the two of them leaving together because a drunk beauty in a gorgeous dress like that was bound to draw unwanted attention.

"And you were going to take him up on his offer, weren't you?" She ignored him. "You should tell Scott. He'd be proud of his little puppet."

Felicity sighed. "It's a clean, comfortable bed after weeks of a wafer-thin mattress on a noisy bus with Trent and Carl snoring. You would've taken up the offer, too."

"Would I?" Hannah looked back at him and cocked her head in scrutiny. "He's not my type."

"You're being ridiculous." Felicity met his gaze and winced. "Ryan, do you mind if she crashes, too? The two of us could share your bed."

Instantly, two pleading stares were on him. A million hell-yeah thoughts could've gone through his mind but he only had one—how the heck was he going to explain to Mason that two beautiful women had slept in his bed and left the next day untouched? Or did he bite the bullet and dive back into the dating pool with a threesome under his belt?

"Sure." He cleared his throat. "It doesn't bother me."

Hannah frowned. "Really? This wasn't a booty call?"

He stepped forward, summoning enthusiasm he didn't have, and leaned into her. "If I had plans to sleep with Flick, they would've been fulfilled hours ago." It was a bluff. A shield to hide his lacking skills of seduction and an inability to stop thinking about someone else.

"Aww, you're such a gentleman." She patted him on the chest, her eyes turning seductive.

"That's the consensus," he muttered. "Now let's get out of here."

Five

THERE WERE NUMEROUS DEFINING MOMENTS IN LEAH'S LIFE. SHE WAS THE manager for one of the hottest bands on the planet, for Christ's sake. She *owned* defining moments. She had a long list of phenomenal days that shaped her into the professional, hard working woman she was today, and she wouldn't change a thing. Not a week went by without reminiscing on one of her achievements. At least that was the case until her recently acquired defining moments came with negative effects.

First there was the kiss. A delicious, fantasy-filled brush of lips that sent her spiraling. She'd always known her dreams couldn't turn into reality. It wasn't plausible to have Ryan *and* her career. So the choice to commit to Reckless hadn't been something she could regret. The band members were all she had, and there was no regret over the decision she made. She wasn't whimsical or unrealistic. A relationship with Ryan simply wasn't an option. End of story.

But the kiss had shaken her nonetheless. She'd had to work hard to suppress the remembered taste of scotch on her tongue and the feel of his hard chest against hers. That glimpse in time had changed everything, no matter how hard she tried to believe otherwise.

Then came the images of Ryan and Felicity together. Although somewhat less devastating, she'd had to swallow down an uncomfortable tightening in her throat over the dreamy way they looked at each other.

Even worse was the story behind the pictures.

"These were staged," Alana had pointed out, tilting the camera viewer in Leah's direction. "But these..." Her friend's fingers had scrolled across the screen, increasing the discomfort, making Leah awkward in her own skin. "These ones were captured after I told them I'd taken the final shot."

Those images were still burned into her retinas. His hands had been on Felicity's body, his lips so close to her ear. The tightness in her throat had sunk to her chest, then her stomach, squeezing everything inside her until there was no way to deny the reason for her discomfort. Yep, she'd been jealous. But that reckless emotion had quickly been snuffed by her determination to move on from her pathetic infatuation.

Until now.

Turns out, she didn't snuff much of anything, and the discomfort from those images was merely a taste of displeasure in comparison to the all-encompassing pain currently pushing its way through her bones.

Staying in the lobby, replying to emails and analyzing sales while Ryan had his first official fake date had been a mistake. She'd stupidly told herself she was on standby in case they needed her assistance. If he drank too much, or stalker types slipped through the hotel doors, she'd have to intervene. But as time ticked by without drama, she had to try harder to convince herself of why she remained in place.

Fuck. This had nothing to do with being on standby and everything to do with stalking his new relationship. Years of suppressed emotions were unraveling inside her. Jealousy fought with spite and desire. She should be the one in the bar enjoying his company. She should be the one making him smile and breathing in his familiar aftershave.

Damn it. The tour was messing with her head. Insomnia was turning her into a train wreck. *Grow a set and get out of here.*

She stood, grabbed her laptop and notepad, then froze at the sight of him at the bar doors. On instinct, her body reacted like it always did—hunger and anticipation mingling in her blood to create a lethal combination she always ignored. His hair was tangled, the shoulder-length waves brushed back from a face that housed a wickedly sexy grin.

It took a moment to realize what created his happiness. The briefest pause in time to grasp that his mirth wasn't for her and instead came from the women at his sides. Not one, but two sickeningly seductive females who seemed intent on a plan she couldn't determine.

With naïve relief, she began counting down the seconds until the end of the charade when the threesome would part ways. She even moved forward, focused on meeting him at the elevator doors to get the inside scoop on what they'd been doing for the past two hours.

But their charade didn't end.

They didn't part ways.

In sadistic fascination, she watched them walk toward the elevator, the unmistakable promise of sex following along behind them.

"No." The plea whispered from her mouth as she shook her head. "Don't do it, Ryan."

With each progressive step, her heart clenched a little harder, pumped a little faster. She tried clinging to her band manager role, attempting to disguise her heartache as professional intuition, and failed miserably.

This was personal.

It was about intimacy she craved and feelings she could no longer suppress.

The man who had always been unobtainable due to marriage was now single. He was within reach. An unlikely possibility, however, a possibility nonetheless, and she'd just thrown away the opportunity without a backward glance. *Hell*, she'd facilitated the transition into a new relationship by bowing to Grander's heavy hand.

"Ryan, wait." She wasn't sure where the words came from, the sound shooting across the empty lobby like a reverberating gunshot.

The trio paused, all of them turning to face her from the elevator doors.

She clutched tight to her belongings—her laptop, notepad, and elusive sanity—then shuffled quickly on her toes to make her way toward them.

"What are you still doing awake?" His tone was filled with a comforting concern.

"I've got work to do and I needed more breathing space than my tiny hotel room." Lies, lies, lies. "Are you calling it a night? Do you want me to organize a driver?"

"No, we're good." He had the sense to look guilty. "I'm, umm..."

"Too modest to admit you're a gentleman who won't let us travel to the sleeper bus on our own." The newest member to the fake relationship patted Ryan on the chest, her long red nails scratching into the fabric. "He offered to let us crash in his room."

"Yeah. Such a gentleman." Leah swallowed over the bile coating the back of her tongue. "I'm sorry, I know we've met before but I can't place the name." It was another lie. She knew exactly who the femme fatale was as she offered her hand to shake. The ploy was a last ditch effort to dint the woman's perfect smile.

"Hannah." The woman's grip was strong.

"She's with Slicker," Felicity offered. "My bass guitarist."

Yep. *Hannah Olsen.* A woman with absolutely everything in common with Ryan.

The elevator doors opened, helping to increase the bile production and the painful pound beneath her ribs. There was nothing she could say to stop him from moving on. There was nothing she could do to make these women leave.

Not without her humiliation playing a major role.

"I'll...ahh...let you get on with it, then." She stepped back—from him, from her feelings, from an unobtainable future. How had she slipped so far? She was stronger than this. More realistic and practical, too.

Shark week must be approaching. Yeah, that had to be it. She was being undeniably psychotic because the lining of her uterus was instigating a mass evacuation.

"Enjoy the rest of your night." She waved them away, a merry little cheerio she wanted to end in a middle-finger salute.

"I'll catch you tomorrow?" Ryan's gaze held a plea. Maybe even an apology.

She ignored both, pretending this was another booty call like all the others she'd witnessed from Mitch, Blake, Sean, and Mason. "Yeah. Of course." She nodded and jerked her thumb over her shoulder. "I'll get the next elevator. I think I left my pen on the coffee table."

She held his focus as the heavy doors closed, sealing his fate. Sealing hers, too.

"Whoa." She exhaled a shaky breath. "That was intense." An out of body experience. One minute she was working like a good little band manager, the next she was trying to throw her career under a bus. A big bus. Huge bus.

"Fuck you, uterus."

Her legs moved without thought as she maintained the pretense and headed back to the sofa. For some reason her chest was still aching like a mofo and her limbs were increasingly heavy. Maybe she was having a heart attack. It would explain a lot.

She sank into the squeaky leather cushions and tried to laugh off the brain fade. Tried and tried and failed. This was a good thing. The obtainable was now back to being beyond the bounds of possibility. There was no more temptation. No more bait to lure in her nonexistent sex life. No more snare to entrap her curiosity.

Ryan was officially back to being out of reach.

Fanfuckingtastic.

So why wasn't she celebrating? Why wasn't she doing a happy dance to rival all previous happy dances? Why?

Probably because she felt like she'd just let any chance of happiness slip right through her fingers into the waiting hands of someone more willing to appreciate the prize.

Six

Washington, DC

S HARK WEEK HAD BEEN A BITCH. IT HAD ALSO BEEN A THANKFUL EXPLANATION for losing her mind over something she should've had under control.

But just to be safe, Leah had kept her distance from Ryan, and the band in general, for eight days. Choosing instead to communicate via email and text message while she focused on online sales reports and securing more promo opportunities.

Apart from poking her head into the dressing room or catching up with Mason, Mitch, Blake, or Sean when they were apart from their rhythm guitarist, she'd spent most of her time sulking in numerous hotel rooms, gorging on chocolate and coffee. Even the crew on the sleeper bus had been smart enough to keep their distance. Nobody dared to poke the bear. Not when her head was always stuck firmly in her laptop or her cell was plastered to her ear.

The alone time had given her a chance to regroup and beat herself into a bloody pulp over her stupidity. Now she was fighting fit and ready for battle.

"Nice of you to join us," Mason drawled, his unimpressed glower eating up her approach.

"I thought it was time to stop working myself to the bone and see if you guys are actually pulling your weight." She approached the portable table near the front of the empty stadium, Mitch, Sean, and Blake turning their focus from Ryan on stage to greet her with various non-verbal responses. "Do you have any news for me?"

"Nope. We're all good."

She quirked a brow. "That's not what I'm told." The end of shark week wasn't her only reason to come back into the land of the living. "Some of the crew have messaged me with concerns over Ryan's performance."

Mason glared. "He's hitting home runs at every show."

"I'm told he's late to every sound check, which would explain why he's the only one on stage at the moment."

One message she could ignore. Two was something she took on board and held in consideration. But three, four, and five meant she had to start asking questions.

She chanced a look at the man of the moment and suppressed the pang in her chest with Olympic gold precision. There were heavy bags under his eyes, his usually warm skin pale beneath his beard, his adored guitar almost seeming like an unwanted weight in his hands.

"He's struggling." She hadn't wanted to believe it. If he needed nurturing, she'd have to be the one to give it because the men surrounding her didn't bear an ounce of emotional intuition.

"Yeah." Mason snickered. "Struggling to keep up with a healthy sex life."

She winced, immediately regretting her journey out of hibernation. "I'm not joking." She turned her back to the stage and crossed her arms over her chest. "Why didn't you tell me he's been late to the last three sound checks? Clearly, his mind isn't on the tour."

"Maybe because you've been MIA."

She gave a derisive laugh and pinned him with her trademark scowl. Men with smaller egos had withered under that look. "Have you not seen me every day? Have you not received email updates on an ongoing basis? Have I ever rejected any of your calls or made myself unavailable?" She raised her brow, waiting for a lie or an apology.

It wasn't surprising he gave neither.

"Moving on," she purred. "Has he spoken to any of you about how he's handling his private life?"

A myriad of non-committal gestures were made—a shake of a head, a shrug, a mutter.

"Not one of you has had the sense to check up on him? Not even once?" Her stomach dived under the weight of guilt.

"This isn't happy hour at the shrink society, Leah." Blake rolled his eyes. "Not all of us like to share the shit that drags us down."

Mitch whacked his best friend in the arm and then met her gaze with regret. "Alana said he's spending a lot of time with Felicity and Hannah. They seem to be tight."

Sean snorted.

"I meant their relationship," Mitch grated. "Not the women."

Leah didn't appreciate the humor. Nor did she enjoy the mental image. "So I guess the fake relationship has inspired polygamy."

"The media hasn't latched onto Hannah yet, but they're certainly eating up his time with Felicity." Mason grinned at her, the expression taunting. "And that's all that matters, right?"

"Yep." She nodded, determined not to bite.

Unless Ryan's private life started interfering with the band in a more detrimental manner, who he slept with wasn't any of her business. Just like it hadn't been her business throughout his marriage to Julie. And just like it wouldn't be if he was single and sleeping his way through the millions of groupies wishing to get laid.

Ryan—his heart and cock included—wasn't her concern.

"Don't worry. I'll mention something to him." Sean moved close and gave her a hip check. "I don't want his drinking to get out of hand either."

"Drinking?" She should've shut her mouth and walked from the stadium like a manager on a mission to get more exposure. But no, she had to ask. She had to open her damn mouth.

"He's not drinking that much." Mason scoffed. "We all need to cut him a break."

Sean nodded. "I agree. But drinking while on stage or during practice has always been a no-go."

The look on her face must've said it all.

"I said don't worry." Sean gave her a half-hearted smile. "He's not drunk. I think he's merely taking the edge off a little more than usual."

She looked at Mitch, Blake, and Sean in turn, noticing the concern she hadn't seen before. "Has he taken the edge off this morning? Do you know if he's been drinking today?"

It was already after lunch. Mid-afternoon was an acceptable drinking hour for most, but not when your days started at noon and ended after midnight. This was early morning for them, and the fact they weren't meeting her gaze meant they knew how concerning it was.

"Let it go, Leah," Mason warned. "He's earned his stripes. He deserves to fuck up every now and then. We'll pull him into line if we need to."

That wasn't good enough. She wasn't going to entrust Ryan's safety into the hands of Mr. Manwhore and his posse of merry men. "Why doesn't your leadership fill me with comfort?"

"Maybe because you've got more of an invested interest in Ryan than you should."

Fuck. Me. Where the hell had that bitch slap come from? "Excuse me?"

She'd kept her 'invested interest' to herself. The way she was acting was no different from when Blake or Sean or even Mason himself had gone off the rails. It was her job to be invested. Her duty to care.

"Ahh..." Mitch took a step toward the stage. "I'm gonna go see what Ryan's doing."

"Yeah, I'm coming." Blake followed.

Then Sean bailed, too.

She waited until she was alone with Mason, his smug grin increasing her fury to an apocalypse-inducing level. "Have you been spending time with Scott?" she asked. "Because he seems to be rubbing off on you."

"That's a low blow."

"Well, you'd know what it takes to make one." She rested on her hip and tap, tap, tapped the toe of her shoe on the stadium floor. The desire to kill him was clogging her arteries, no more than it usually did when he was an asshole, but the subject matter on this occasion was uncalled for. "Do you want to explain why you're being such a cu—"

"Whoa. I can't believe you were about to say the c-word."

"And I can't believe you would be so fucking rude."

"I'm being rude?" He pointed a lazy thumb toward his chest. "Because here I was thinking you were the one disrespecting us by hiding out in your hotel room and communicating through fucking email. Then you come back and try to work us into a frenzy over Ryan when there's nothing wrong with him."

"Oh, my god." She threw her hands up in the air. "Are you kidding me?" She didn't know where to start. Didn't know whether she should verbally chop him down at the knees or end this argumentative dance by punching him in the face. "I've got a whole new workload now that I have to babysit Slicker's sales. And not only do I have to ensure the tour is perfect, I also have to put out my feelers—" she made quotation marks with her fingers, "—because you want to see what other labels have to offer before you consider starting one of your own."

He opened his mouth but she shoved a finger at his sternum.

"And you think there's nothing wrong with him turning up to sound check drunk? Are you insane?"

"He's got a lot of shit on his plate. Don't expect him to eat it with a smile on his face."

"I don't. I expect him to hold the same work ethic he's had for years because any deviation is a sign there's something wrong."

"There's nothing wrong with him," he grated. "But maybe you should start scrutinizing things closer to home."

She balked, in complete shock that he'd be stupid enough to keep slinging fighting words at her.

"You're the one everyone is worried about." He glared. "You're the one who fucked up, Leah. Not Ryan."

He wasn't joking... But he had to be, otherwise she was going to hurt him. Permanently. "Watch where you go with this, Mason. I've taken enough of your bullshit already."

"Noted." He inclined his head and turned to walk away.

"Where the hell do you think you're going?" Her voice rose. "We're not done."

He shook his head and glanced over his shoulder. "No, we're not. But now's not the time. Pull your shit together and we'll talk about this another day."

Pull her shit together? Her hands shook, her face heated. How dare he accuse her of not succeeding in something she'd worked too damn hard on, for too damn long?

Every day she pulled her shit together. Every fucking minute she had to gather strings and ribbons into a massive bundle to maintain the professional façade they all thought came naturally. They didn't understand the difficulty in shoving down emotions that refused to be silenced. They didn't know how badly she wanted to go back to a devastating kiss she should've forgotten the moment it ended. A devastating kiss that resembled bliss in hindsight. Because that kiss, no matter how disturbing and punishing, had been sublime perfection. Even if she couldn't have it again.

Fuck. Mason was right.

She'd completely lost her shit.

"Hey," Ryan shouted as he jumped off the stage.

She remained quiet with his approach while Mason stared her down, warning her to keep her mouth shut.

"What's going on?" Ryan wiped his wrist over the sweat on his brow.

"Nothin'." She held Mason's gaze. "My friend here was merely playing his favored asshole role. You'd think he'd be sick of it by now."

"And you'd think you'd be sick of standing in the wings after all this time, but clearly we enjoy what we're good at." Mason backtracked, giving her a checkmate smirk as he fled.

Asshole.

"Are you two fighting again?"

She closed her eyes briefly, the hit of his voice punching harder than normal. "Yes. Again."

It seemed her years had been built on the foundation of battle. She was either fighting with Mason, Grander, her boss, the tabloids, the obsessed trolling fans, or her love for him. Always her love for him.

"What's it about this time?"

You. She met his gaze and held her breath. *We're fighting over you.* "Nothing important."

"OK..." His brows narrowed, the slightest wrinkle forging its way between those beautiful eyes. "What's been going on with you? I haven't seen you in days."

"I've been busy tracking your success. Your dates with Felicity are gaining favorable attention." She wanted to fist pump for keeping her animosity in check. "Congratulations."

"Thanks." His frown deepened, his scrutiny keeping her pinned. "We're trying to make sure we're seen as much as possible."

"You're doing a great job." The Internet was currently smothered with images of his puppy-dog eyes and needy hands. Even her Facebook sidebar taunted her with ads containing his bearded face.

"Not everyone would agree. Hannah still has a problem with the project. She's not being openly aggressive, but her annoyance is there whenever we step into the spotlight."

"Jealousy?" Leah sure knew how that felt.

He nodded. "Maybe. And I don't blame her. Me and the guys know how it feels to be in Mason's shadow. It's part of the job." He jerked his head toward one of the exits. "Do you want to chat about this at the hotel? I need to get out of here."

No. She didn't want to be in a confined car smothered by his scent. She could barely look at him without being distracted by his beautiful lips, or the misery of knowing he'd paid homage to someone else with them.

Christ, she hated when Mason was right.

"I can't. I need to speak to a few of the crew before I leave."

"I can hang around—" The ring of his cell stopped him short. "Sorry." He pulled the device from his jeans pocket. "I better check in case it's my lawyer."

"Don't apologize."

Ryan scanned his screen. "It's Felicity. Do you mind if I take it?"

Another pang was squashed with Hulk precision. "Of course." She side-stepped to give him privacy but he gripped her around the elbow, stopping her progression.

"Stay," he mouthed, before greeting Felicity with a friendly, "Hey."

There was a beat of silence, then, "What's wrong?"

The pangs kept coming, the tiny stabs of envy peppering her internal organs. She smiled through the assault, the curve of lips turning into a snarl as she met Mason's knowing gaze.

"I'll be there in a minute." Ryan disconnected the call and pocketed the cell.

"You've gotta go?"

"Yeah. Something's up." There he went with another one of those apology-riddled glances. "We'll talk later?"

"Sure."

He stepped into her, curving his arm around her waist while he placed an excruciating kiss at her temple. She should've backed away. Instead, she found herself melting into him, sucking him deep into her lungs. His aftershave was rich, still prominent over the scent of sweat. But there was also the taint of alcohol, the briefest hint of scotch on his breath.

This was her fault. She hadn't been there for him. Couldn't be.

"Life has been tough on you lately." She slid out of reach, freeing herself from his heavenly arms. "Are you coping?"

"Why wouldn't I be?" His smile was halfhearted. "I'm living the dream."

"Don't placate me. Are you OK or not?"

His puff of laughter was callous. "Are you asking as my long-lost best friend or my band manager?"

She didn't know how to answer. He needed a friend and she needed distance. She no longer knew who to protect. "I can smell alcohol, Ryan. I'm worried about you."

"Worried enough to stop hiding from me?"

She swallowed over the confidence in his heated stare. "I…"

He waited, the seconds ticking by as her words remained tightly locked in her chest. "Fine. You want an answer? I'll give you two. First, to my band manager—I'll be honest and say it was one drink over breakfast. The girls were having Bloody Marys so I joined them with a scotch. No big deal." He shrugged. "The second response is for the friend I lost—you want to know how I'm coping with a divorce, a tour, and the bullshit of a morally crippling publicity stunt? Come find me tomorrow and we'll talk this out."

She clenched her jaw tight, caught between the role she wanted to play and the position she needed to maintain. It didn't help that she was focusing on one sentence. One word—tomorrow. Because clearly today was dedicated to Felicity.

"What time?" She breathed through the nerves in her belly, willing them not to take hold.

His expression relaxed, his tight brows falling to frame softer eyes. "I'll message you when I'm free."

"OK." She inclined her head, her heart in her throat, her ovaries somewhere in her chest cavity. "Tomorrow, then."

Seven

R YAN KEPT LOOKING OVER HIS SHOULDER, WISHING HE COULD DROP EVERY-thing to grasp the opportunity to speak to Leah. Tomorrow was a lifetime away, but obligation had his feet moving forward.

He was fading away from Reckless. All his friends had new relationships to focus on. They had calls and FaceTime and texts to deal with. They were immersed in their own lives and had no time for him.

Felicity and Hannah were growing to be his only companions. When they weren't traveling from city to city on the sleeper bus, they were in his suite, keeping him up until the early hours with their giggling and mumbled words from his bed while he slept on the sofa or fold out. The two women had a friendship that reminded him of what he previously had with Leah. A connection riddled with private jokes and uncanny intuition.

He felt obliged to come running when they needed his help. Being needed at all was a bonus when his world seemed to be turning against him.

His cell rang again, Felicity's name displaying on his screen.

"How far away are you?" Her voice was panicked, even more than it had been two minutes ago.

"I'm in the hall leading to your dressing room. Open the door and I'll be there."

The whoosh of air sounded up ahead, her head then peeking into the hall. She was pale, one hand gripping the door while the other latched onto the frame.

"Has something happened?"

"Nothing new, but we need to talk."

She backed into the room, opening the door wide to let him in. He followed, jutting his chin in greeting at Hannah who sat on the make-up counter, her hands clutching the wood beneath her, her back to the mirror.

"Spill." He eyed them both, back and forth as they stared at one another. They gave him nothing. No words. No expressions. Just overwhelming amounts of apprehension. "You're not going to tell me you're gay, are you?" he joked, even adding a chuckle to his voice to lighten the mood.

Neither of them laughed.

"Flick?" His pulse increased. The static in his head, too.

She met his gaze with a wince, then focused back on Hannah.

Oh, no. Hell, no.

He turned to Hannah, her fingers now holding the bench with a white-knuckled grip.

"You're gay?"

She bit her lip and nodded.

Bam. That sucker punch hit him in the gut, almost buckling him. Gay wasn't good. Not from his perspective. Not when they were trying to convince the world they were happily heterosexual.

"We've been together for almost a year."

Ba-bam. This verbal swing landed lower, right between the thighs with emasculating effects.

"Why are you telling me this?" Why now, when he no longer had the ability to save himself from the social media backlash?

Felicity came up beside him, her gaze pleading. "Hannah's been struggling to watch us from the sidelines. We've been fighting about it for weeks. We hoped telling you, and getting her involved, might make things easier."

He stepped back, needing space as he scowled through the mess otherwise known as his life. "What does that even mean?" How had he missed all the signs? *Christ.* They'd shared his bed for the last week and he still hadn't noticed. "*Fuck me.*"

He'd never been one to curse unnecessarily, but right now he wanted to shout expletives until he was diagnosed with Tourette's. He was going to go on a fuck-a-thon, otherwise it would be a drink-a-thon and Leah was already on his back about liquor.

He couldn't catch a break. He couldn't even catch his breath through the ongoing carnage.

"Why are you angry?" Felicity went to Hannah's side, the two of them huddling close.

"Why?" He started to pace, running his fingers through his hair and tugging on the strands in the hopes the pain would create clarity. "Have you looked at this from my perspective? Have you spared a thought on how brutal the media and public will be on a guy who couldn't satisfy his wife, then hooked up with someone else months later, only to turn her gay?"

"You didn't turn me."

"Does anyone else know that?" He spread his arms wide. "Because Leah did a thorough check on you and certainly didn't come up with the pussy preference."

They balked and he couldn't tell if it was from his word choice or his callous tone.

"I'll be forever known as the guy who turns women gay." If not publicly, he sure as shit wouldn't come out unscathed once his friends found out. "*Fuck.*"

"I'm sorry. I—"

He glared at her, resenting the confusion in her voice.

"Scott swore me to secrecy—"

The world stopped, alarm bells rang, and guilt suddenly lessened the anger. "Scott?"

"Sex sells," she blurted. "But apparently not when you're gay. He's the reason we're in this mess. We went to him with the information at the start of the tour in the hopes of coming out with a big bang. It didn't take long to realize he was homophobic."

Mother. Fucker.

"This publicity stunt wasn't purely about boosting your popularity, was it?" He dragged his feet to the counter and rested his ass against the cold wood. "He did this to hide your sexuality."

They both nodded, remaining silent as he focused on the carpeted floor. He felt like a dick. An inadequate, non-functioning, STD-riddled dick. All their muttered arguments made sense now. All the glances that held hidden meaning and the times Hannah had demanded every last detail on the dates he had with Felicity.

"I've always been gay. Flick, on the other hand, is bi. She has more experience with men," Hannah murmured. "And I know you thought I was being petty about her getting more media attention, but that was never the case. The attention that worried me was from you."

He hung his head and wiped a hand over his face. "You were never anxious about being with me." He tilted his head and focused on Felicity. "You were worried you'd upset Hannah."

Felicity nodded. "Neither of us wanted this. We had no choice. Scott made it clear our next album wouldn't see the light of day if we came out."

He scoffed. "And Scott always gets what he wants." The bastard had a knack for manipulation.

"I'm sorry, Ryan." Felicity walked toward him and nestled against his hip, wrapping her arms around him.

"Me, too." Hannah scooted from the counter and came to his other side to do the same. "We didn't spare much thought on how this would affect you." Her head rested against his chest, four arms holding him tight, two bodies keeping him warm.

"How do we make this right?" He spoke into her hair and wished he had the ability to fix this. But how could he when he couldn't even finalize his divorce or rectify his friendship with Leah?

"Don't worry about it." Hannah stepped back. "I'll get over it."

"No." He shook his head, his frown now cemented in place. "You said you wanted to get involved. What did you have in mind?"

She sighed, her glazed eyes blinking away unshed tears. "I want to be with you guys when you go on dates. I don't want to be constantly worried about Flick falling for yo—"

"She's not going to fall for me."

"Ryan, I don't think you realize how perfect you are. You've been nothing but a gentleman. You always put yourself last, have never, ever acted sleazy, and you're kinda gorgeous." She gave him a half-hearted grin.

"If you had a kitty, I'd be all up in that."

He spat out a laugh and wished he could hold onto the humor as it fled his system. "I'm done with being the good guy. It's starting to feel like an excuse instead of a moral compass. So let's shake things up a bit."

"And how do you plan on doing that?" Felicity straightened. "Nobody can find out I'm with Hannah."

"They won't." If Scott could play dirty, they could, too. It was time to stop being nice. "Grander wants a scandal. Let's give them a something they won't forget in a hurry."

Eight

"A THREESOME? ON STAGE? REALLY?" LEAH'S VOICE ROSE IN THE EMPTY silence as she stared at her computer screen and contemplated the need to run to the bathroom to retch. The video before her was from last night's performance. The crystal clear visual featured on the Rockin' Gossip website. Ryan was front and center on the Reckless stage, while Felicity and Hannah rubbed up against him, dry humping his thighs, clawing his shirt.

She had to give him props, though. He continued to play effortlessly through the duration, not losing his feel for the music even when Felicity kissed him on the cheek and then proceeded to saunter toward Mason to help him finish singing the song.

It was a phase. A juncture.

Sean said she had nothing to worry about. He'd promised. But Ryan had been committed to Julie for a long time. An outburst of sexual frustration was inevitable. An explosion of testosterone and lust had always been in the cards, and Leah had been destined to have a front row seat.

A knock sounded on her door, then the deep drawl of Mason's voice. "Open up, woman."

Perfect. A punching bag was exactly what she needed.

"What?" She yanked the door open with a snarl.

"Good afternoon to you, too, sweetie." He beamed a smile as his wavy hair tempted her to pull it from his unnaturally gorgeous head. "You always know how to make me feel special."

"Are you here to apologize for yesterday?"

His lips turned downward and he shook his head. "Nope."

She made to slam the door but he stopped the progression with his palm. He nudged into her room, assuming ownership, and made her suite his castle.

"What ya looking at?" He focused on her laptop sitting on the small kitchenette counter and pressed play.

"Apparently, it's Ryan instigating a live ménage."

Mason snorted. "Slight exaggeration."

"Do you still think that's normal behavior?"

"Who cares about normal? He was having fun."

"And so were you. I bet Sidney was happy to see you arm in arm with Ryan's not-so-fake girlfriend."

He nodded, his face contemplative as the silenced video continued to play in a loop. "She knows it was innocent, and that I wouldn't do anything to jeopardize our relationship." He made the two steps to her bed and sat on the edge. "She was also on the first flight out of New York just to make sure. ETA twenty minutes."

Leah smirked. "I'm glad to hear it."

"Don't pull the woman-code card. Sidney knows that no one else will ever compare to her. All that video did was give her an excuse to come here and get fucked into submission."

Leah closed her eyes and pinched the bridge of her nose. "Please don't mention your sex life in front of me again."

"Jealous?"

She glared. "No, I actually strive to have a healthy love life of my own one day, and I don't want to ever, *ever* have the unsightly images of you in my head."

"I'm sure losing me as a potential husband candidate will haunt you 'til your dying day."

"Get out." She pointed toward the door. "Just go."

"How 'bout we reroute the conversation back to Ryan instead?"

"Oh, for fuck's sake." She threw her head back and stared at the ceiling.

"You need to talk to him."

"I plan on it. We already spoke about catching up today. I'm merely waiting for his call."

"But you only have plans to talk about him. Not you." He lost the smug expression. "I know I'm an asshole most of the time, but I hate seeing you like this. When you look at him, we all get an insider's guide to the shit going through your head. We know how much you're swooning over him."

There were no words this time, only another adamant point of her finger toward the door.

"Don't play dumb, Leah. We've got your back on this."

No, they didn't. She was on her own. Always had been. Reckless Beat were a team. The five of them family. Yes, she had her own place within the hierarchy, but essentially, it was her job on the line if she breached the terms of her management contract. They wouldn't lose sales. Their fan base wouldn't even hear about her departure. The five of them would carry on, living the dream, while she lost everything.

"What exactly am I supposed to do?"

"Tell him you love him and all that shit."

"Get the fuck out." She jabbed her finger toward the door hard enough to hurt her shoulder. "I don't have time for you right now."

"I'm not moving." He reiterated the statement by lying back on the bed, hands behind his head. "I honestly thought the two of you would be a sure thing after that kiss. He was all broody and you were all meek and kittenish. It was a recipe for rough and dirty sex."

"I *was not* meek."

"Looked that way to us." He shrugged. "We finally thought you'd ditch the puppy dog eyes and latch on with both claws."

He was goading her, pushing, poking, so damn close to succeeding.

"You finished?" She placed her hands on her hips and stared him down.

"You ready to talk to him?"

She swung around and closed her laptop, prepared to ignore him for as long as possible. They'd only arrived in Cincinnati thirty minutes ago. Her bag was still packed and sitting beside the door. She needed to wash the sludge of travel from her skin and the tiredness from her eyes.

"I've got things to do. Including getting showered and ready for public consumption." She reached for the top button of her blouse and undid it, exposing cleavage.

"Go for it." He watched her, zero interest in his arrogant eyes. "I've got nowhere else to be."

"I'm undressing, Mason." She released another button, playing a game of chicken she was no longer confident of winning. "Sidney will kick your ass if she finds out you're here."

"Don't go assuming anything about Sid. She'd do anything for Ryan if given the chance."

"Really? She's on her way here because you got close with another singer on stage. Do you really think she's not going to care if you see me naked?"

"Seen it all before. You're just another one of the guys."

"Except for the double-Ds and vagina." She skipped the money-shot button and descended to the bottom of the blouse, flicking another open. "You know I'll tell her." She slowed her progression, running out of options.

"Do you mind if I take video?" He wove a hand from behind his head and reached down to dig his cell from his pants pocket. "Ryan might appreciate a bird's eye view of what he's missing."

"Oh, for fuck's sake, Mason." Stubborn, arrogant prick. "Get the hell out."

He chuckled. "I will when you admit you love him."

She looked him head on and would've tried to deny it if she could muster conviction. Alas, she was clearly lacking her usual feminine wiles. Instead, she raised her chin and sucked in a breath through her nose, flaring her nostrils.

"What's the big deal?" he continued. "Are you scared of being happy? 'Cause, believe me, I get it."

No, he didn't. He didn't realize this was about him. And Blake. And Mitch. And Sean. They were all the reasons why she couldn't be with Ryan. "I'm not going to ask you again." He didn't understand that losing her position was only devastating because in turn she'd lose her Reckless family. She didn't have a life outside the band. Without them, she had nothing.

"And I'm not going to let your contractual obligation bullshit fly anymore."

Too far. Way too far. He skipped straight past the mildly annoying status and hit the detonator for full-scale war.

"*Contractual obligations bullshit?*" She stepped forward and slapped his spread knees together. "I have a black and white document that stipulates I can't have any sort of sexual relationship, casual or otherwise, with any of my clients. It states in precise terms that I'll be fired, without warning, and I've seen it happen. *That's* not bullshit."

"We could get around it."

"How?" God damn, she hated his smug superiority. "You're not as almighty as you think you are, Mason. I thought you would've learned from the complete lack of control you have in the Grander situation."

"That's different."

"You're so naïve." Incredulity slid through her veins, through every inch of her body. "How is it different?"

"Because love prevails. Etcetera, etcetera."

"Of course." She waved a hand in the air. "Just like that, my troubles would melt away, all in the name of love."

"You know Ryan would do anything for a chance with you."

"Do I? He's not even divorced yet. And to me, it already looks like his ticket is full." She hiked a finger over her shoulder. "Do I need to show you the video again? Or tell you how I caught him taking those women to his room when we were in Atlanta?"

"You're not stupid, Leah. You know he feels something for you. Otherwise you wouldn't have wasted years of your life pining over him."

She wanted to deny him, to announce he was entirely wrong and needed to grow up. But as much as she hated admitting it, he was right. She hadn't been able to get Ryan off her mind for all these years because there had always been a reciprocated affection in his eyes. There'd always been a hopeful spark even though he never acted upon it.

"I know you're worried about keeping your position as our manager, but trust me, it's gotta work itself out. The five of us are here to look out for you if shit goes south."

There was no 'if' involved. There *would* be problems. Big ones. But her thoughts brushed over them, the slightest nudge of possibility edging its way into her consciousness after so long denying her fantasies. "I wouldn't know where to start."

"Talk. That's all it takes."

"And say what?"

"Tell him how you feel and see where it leads." He sat and pushed from the bed. "Come on. I'll escort you to his room."

"I don't need an escort."

"Then let me rephrase—please allow me to walk you to his door because you sure as shit will chicken out if I don't."

Not true...OK, maybe he had a point.

Her steps were cautious as she made her way to the door and retrieved her room key from the holder. Excitement and apprehension waged war inside her chest, both fighting for supremacy.

"You might want to do up your buttons." His gaze raked her body, from her face to her toes. "Unless that's the look you're going for. The skin show isn't doing any harm, that's for sure."

Shit. She clutched at her gaping blouse and cringed. She was shoeless and wearing crumpled pants, her make-up would be faded, too, and her hair a mess. All she needed was a belly rounded from pregnancy and she'd be a redneck's ultimate fantasy.

"I need to freshen up." She turned, prepared to postpone her stupidity and was yanked into Mason's side with a firm hand.

"Nope." He kept pulling her down the hall. "You've come this far. You're not going back."

"I've walked two steps outside my hotel door."

"Yep, and it's good enough for me."

Christ. This wasn't going to end well. The least he could do is allow her to look pretty when her life turned to shit. "You're not the most trustworthy person, Mason." She rebuttoned her blouse, keeping up with his steady pace. "I'm going to regret listening to you."

He met her gaze, his seriousness unsettling. "In this, I wouldn't steer you wrong. There's no Reckless without you. Just like there's no band without Blake if we need to extend the tour. We're a team, and once and for all we want to see the two of you together."

"That was awfully sentimental."

"I know." He screwed up his face. "I think I vomited a little in my mouth."

She laughed, but the humor didn't settle inside her. She was too anxious. Too nervous and apprehensive and hopeful. The overwhelming sensations only intensified on the elevator ride to Ryan's floor, each step toward his door a battle not to vomit.

Mason knocked hard below the room number and backed away. "My work here is done."

"*What?*" She grabbed his arm. "You can't leave me now."

"You expect me to hold your hand?"

She glared. *No.* She was Leah freakin' Gorman. But in this she needed something. Anything to stop her from running. "*Please*, Mason."

He sighed and gave a dramatic eye roll. "Fine, I'll help you out, as long as you know you owe me."

"I know," she muttered. And there was no way he'd let her forget.

RYAN WATCHED HANNAH AND FELICITY JOKE AROUND IN HIS HOTEL KITCHEN. Since the secret of their relationship had come to light, the women hadn't taken their hands off each other. They were always kissing or stroking or shirt-pulling. They were an extended version of puppy love he admired the shit out of. And every minute he spent with them was another minute where his loathing for Grander increased. He didn't know how anyone could begrudge their connection. It was archaic, and yet another reason why he was glad Reckless was cutting ties with them after this tour.

Accepting homosexuality wasn't enough, not when gay artists were judged for their sexual preference before being praised for their talent. But change wouldn't happen in Ryan's lifetime. Not when companies like Grander were controlling the industry.

"What's wrong?" Felicity sauntered from the kitchen, eying him with concern.

"Nothin', why?"

"You were staring into space with a disappointed look on your face."

"I was wondering how I didn't pick up on the gay vibe. It should've been a clear sign when you weren't interested in all this." He indicated his lazy sprawl on the floor with a wave of his hand.

"Come on." Hannah laughed. "The name of her band is S...licker, as in, slit licker."

"Oh." He exaggerated the epiphany with an eye-roll. "Now it all makes sense."

"And her nickname is Flick, like flicking the bean…or mine, to be more precise."

"Nice visual."

Felicity waggled her brows. "Feel free to watch any time."

"I'm good." He chuckled. "And what about your drummer and lead guitarist? Do Carl and Trent know?"

"Yeah, they know, and they're supportive. But our relationship is like a noose around their neck. Which is another reason not to rock the boat with the powers that be."

Both women adopted a somber expression, the weight of guilt clearly visible in their eyes. Ryan didn't know the men of Slicker. He'd barely spoken more than a few words with them, and still he didn't envy their shitty situation. Getting a big break in the music industry while also being at the mercy of a homophobic record label wasn't the best start to a career. "How did the two of you meet?"

Hannah came to stand in front of the sofa, peering down at him. "In a candy store on the outskirts of Dallas—"

"Han was reaching for the last packet of Pixie Stix—"

"A nasty fight ensued—"

"Really?" He wondered if they knew how cute it was to listen to them finish each other's sentences.

"No. Not really." Hannah winked. "I wasn't looking as I grabbed for the packet and our hands brushed."

"I told her to take it because it was only for my brother, but she insisted it was mine, even though I later found out she has a stubborn addiction to the stuff."

"An addiction to Pixie Stix?" He raised his brows. "That's hardcore."

"You better believe it." Hannah reached for her pants pocket and pulled out a straw-like, cylindrical tube. "I can't afford to pay the rent some weeks, but I've always got one of these with me."

Felicity placed a smacking kiss on her girlfriend's cheek. "She'd snort the stuff if she could."

Ryan reached up, took the straw from her hand and inspected the candy he hadn't seen since his childhood. "I'm surprised you haven't already."

Hannah smirked. "I'm game if you are."

"You want me to snort this?"

"Why not?" She grabbed it from his hand, ripped open the top, and maintained a mischievous grin as she tipped the contents onto the table. "How can I cut it?"

These women were crazy, and the best relief he could possibly have from all the fucked up shit he was trying to ignore. "Allow me." He grabbed his wallet out of his back pocket and pulled out a credit card.

As he cut the powder into lines she shuffled around the table and descended, making herself at home in his lap. There was nothing sexual about it. He didn't have the right appendages to make her happy. He knew, because she hadn't been shy in mentioning it over and over and over again.

There was a knock at the door as he wove his arm around her waist, enjoying the connection no matter how platonic.

"I'll get it." Felicity made for the door.

"I'm not sharing my haul with any more people," Hannah called.

Felicity snickered as she pulled the door wide, exposing Leah. The important parts of him responded, his lips curved into a smile, his chest thumped, and his dick slid from hibernation, too.

"Is Ryan..."

Her sweet question vanished under an expression of horror. Mason came into view at her side, the both of them focusing on the woman between his legs, then the white powder on the table.

"Oh, shit," Mason whispered, stepping inside.

Shit was right. He'd never seen that look on Leah's face before, the one pinning him with anguish. Hannah's continuous laughter didn't help either, or Felicity's snort.

"Sorry to interrupt." Leah backtracked, her gaze still darting between the misleading evidence before she fled from view.

"Damn it." He grabbed Hannah's hips and lifted her off his lap. Then he was jogging for the hall. "Wait."

Mason's hand slammed into his sternum, stopping him at the door. "Drugs, really?"

"No, dickhead. It's sugar from a Pixie Stix. We were fooling around." He shoved the hand away and continued after Leah. "Hold up."

She was already half way down the hall, her legs pounding out the distance, her posture lethal. "Not now, Ryan."

There was an edge to her tone. Not anger or frustration. It was something far worse, and he was the culprit.

She turned sharply and disappeared through a metal door—the stairwell entry. The heavy barrier closed between them by the time he got there and he shoved through to see her descending to the lower platform.

"You've got the wrong impression." He tried to back it up with a chuckle but all it achieved was a narrowed scowl as she continued to descend the opposite staircase. "It wasn't drugs. You know me better than that."

She didn't reply. Didn't acknowledge his presence.

He jumped three stairs at a time, over and over, until he caught up to her at the lower landing. "Hear me out." He slid in front of her, blocking her path to another staircase. "It wasn't drugs. It was powered sugar."

"Whatever you say." She was shaking as her gaze met his—her arms, her legs, her beautiful lips.

"Whatever I say?" They'd been best friends for years. They'd shared everything. She'd *become* his everything. And after months of ignoring him, she'd lost her trust, too? Something snapped inside him. He wasn't sure if it was his mental stability or his patience, but he lost his shit in a blink of an eye. "Now you think I'm a liar?"

"I can't be near you like this." She held up her hands and made to walk around him.

He gave a harsh laugh. "That makes a great change from the disappearing act you've been playing for a week now."

"I was giving you space," she grated. "You didn't want my help with this charade, remember? You kept shoving *me* away."

"Because I didn't want you seeing me with another woman." Jesus, how could she not see that? After all this time, how could she have misinterpreted his intentions? "My life has been circling the god damn drain, but all I've needed is you. I had to get through it on my own."

Her jaw ticked, his unmistakable Wonder Woman preparing for battle. "And if I had been there, I would've kicked your ass for all the shit you're pulling."

"And what shit is that?"

"You're always late to rehearsals. The guys say you're drinking all the time. You almost had a god damn three-way on the stage last night, and now this." Her voice cracked and her responding wince hit him in the chest. "Everything is escalating. Soon you'll go too far. Further than anyone can drag you back from."

"I'm not going anywhere." He pulled his frustration into check and softened his voice. "I've been late two or three times and it's always because of my lawyer. Julie has stalled negotiations and wants me back in New York for a face-to-face meeting. I'm doing my best to ignore her and let my legal team handle it."

"Why?" Concern furrowed her brow. "What does she want?"

Apart from his soul? "I don't know, and I don't give a damn." He grabbed the railing and gazed down. "And yes, I've been drinking more than usual." He glanced at her from the corner of his eye, those gorgeous depths placing an invisible hold on him. "But life ain't fun at the moment and I'm coping the best I can on my own."

She gave a derisive laugh. "The live ménage is a coping mechanism?"

Was she jealous? He scrutinized her, her cheeks turning pink under his stare. "Don't tell me you bought that crap. You were there when we set up the charade. You know being around Flick is all for show."

"I did. But you're awfully convincing." Her vulnerability lashed out at him. "And then you scored another lover who was never in the plan."

"I have nothing but friendship for both of them."

She scoffed and broke eye contact, focusing on the landing below. The silence stretched out, the awkwardness increasing with every second. Being with her would solve all his problems. Well, not solve them, but make them nonexistent. Nothing else would matter if he was finally with her. Nothing could drag him down.

But this place where he was—the spot between love and nothingness—was toxic.

"Leah?" He chanced another step, and reminiscent of the time when he'd backed her into a wall months ago, she retreated, maintaining the space between them. History was repeating itself, and this time he didn't have the luxury of intoxication to excuse what could be a huge mistake.

"I'm going to do something crazy..." He took another step, the nearness making her eyes widen.

"What?" Her voice was panicked.

"I'm going to tell you there's only one person I'm interested in. That there's only ever been one person capable of making me happy." He removed the last foot of space between them, backing her against the cement wall. "And you know it's you."

Leah didn't react. She didn't think she could. Her mind was too lost in thought to consider action.

"Leah?"

His voice was soft, so sweet and coaxing. She remembered how hard it'd been to get over the last time they were poised to kiss. She remembered the pain of suppressing her energized affection and vivid fantasies.

"Don't," she whispered. "I can't talk about this."

"If not now, when?"

He reached out a hand and she whimpered as his finger stroked her cheek. That one touch changed her life, her outlook and her reluctance, forever marking her skin.

"I was going to have this conversation once the tour ended," he admitted. "But that's too far away. I can't wait anymore. I don't care about the divorce or the complications. I want to be with you."

Her heart rallied, maintaining the arduous pace threatening to instigate a heart attack. He wanted her. And was prepared to take on anything that stood in his way. Yet, the world stood in their way. Their livelihood. The family they'd made within Reckless could be torn apart. At least, for her. She could be ripped from them.

"What about Felicity?"

"You're concerned about my gay, fake girlfriend?"

"Gay?" She balked.

He gave a mischievous grin, leaning closer, filling her with something akin to hope.

"Yeah. Her and Hannah. Apparently, this charade wasn't only about instigating hype. Grander doesn't want them announcing their relationship and making Slicker famous for homosexuality instead of their music."

She gave a slow nod, understanding, yet not entirely functioning because his body was pressed up against hers. All his places touching all of hers.

It wasn't like Scott's abhorrent behavior was a shock. The underhanded, manipulative schemes instigated by their label were more common than not. When it came to corporate greed, there were no limits.

"Talk to me."

She swallowed. "What do you want me to say?"

"I want you to say you'll give us a chance, and that you're confident we can find a way to make this work. I want you to tell me you'll let me take what I've been dreaming about for nights on end. I want to hear you say you want this with the same conviction I've seen in your eyes for years."

She sucked in a breath. "I want you..."

He opened his mouth to speak but she placed a finger over his lips, her heartache returning with vengeance.

"But trust that I've been thinking about this longer than you have. I've watched my employer fire numerous staff who became involved with clients." Her shoulders sagged as she leaned further into the wall. "They won't let me out of my contract either. Their commission for me working with you is too substantial to the company."

"We'll figure it out." He pressed his hips into hers and she groaned with the warmth. The perfection. "Trust me."

He leaned closer, their breath mingling, her heart latching onto his. She was a deer. A wild, brainless forest animal staring into the bright lights of an oncoming truck. Any minute now she'd be run through. Any damn minute.

"No." She placed a hand on his chest. On his hard, whimper-inducing chest. "I can't kiss you again."

His eyes met hers with gentle defiance. "Why?"

"Because there's no future in it."

"I disagree." He leaned further into her, his lips descending. So close. Too close. "Tell me I'm right in assuming you want this. Tell me you're not going to slap me this time."

"You remember?" Her words were barely audible as he crept closer, breathing her in.

"I remember every horrific second. You may not believe me, but I've imagined kissing you for a damn long time. I never thought, if given the chance, that I would've ruined it."

"You had a lot going on." She latched onto his biceps, holding tight. "You still do."

"Not enough to stop me doing this."

The bristles of his beard hit her first, a rough sweep before the smoothest of lips were upon hers. All she could breathe was him, the deliriously mind-numbing aftershave she'd phantom-smelled for months.

A mass of uncontrollable tingles took over her body and the ripple of his muscles under her palms made her moan. She could feel him everywhere. His hips, chest, hair. But nothing could beat the buzz of sensation that ignited when his tongue parted her lips, the gentle stroke devastating her foundations.

He kissed like a man in love. Like a man who needed to prove a point.

Then all her senses pinpointed to her pelvis and the unmistakable grind of his erection. She gasped against his mouth, her lips no longer kissing, his kiss no longer coaxing.

"Too far?" he whispered.

Was it? She didn't know. The only thing that made sense was sensation and the need for more.

"No." They were barely brushing the surface. They had so much further to go. Thousands of dreams to fulfil. Millions of lonely nights to make up for. She wouldn't be sated until this was body to body, skin to skin. "Not this time."

She gripped his shirt, her eyes on his as she tugged him closer.

His groan was her undoing, the sound defining her, making her strong in a situation where she'd always been weak.

"Kiss me."

He complied, this time without finesse or tenderness. This connection was harsh. Almost vicious in its hysteria. His hand found the hem of her blouse, his scorching fingers moving under the material to sear her belly. The trail of his palm was authoritative. His fingertips branding her with their abrasive grip, demanding ownership as they approached painfully hardening nipples. She'd always wondered what his touch would be like. Rough or smooth. Lustful or loving.

The strength in his hold dissolved her worries. The intensity of his mouth erased all concern. She was cocooned in a happiness bubble, each breath a double-dose of hunger. Nothing could tear her away from him. Nothing but the sound of creaking hinges overhead and the soft footfalls of someone approaching.

She broke the kiss and clung to his shirt.

"What is it?"

His words fanned her cheeks, his lips moving to her jaw, then her neck. His touch was still under her blouse, his exploration moving higher as her gaze caught hold of another pair of eyes peering down at her from the staircase above.

"Shit." She shoved at him.

"Sorry," Felicity called before backing out of view. "I didn't mean to interrupt."

There were rushed footsteps, another squeak of rusted hinges and then silence. Painful, arduous silence that slid panic into the place where passion had once been. The blood drained from her face, making her lightheaded as Ryan stared at her, his chest rising and falling with deep breaths.

"Don't worry about Flick."

"Don't worry?" She straightened her blouse, unable to look him in the eye. "You trust my career with that woman?"

"I wouldn't entrust your happiness with anyone. But I'll speak to her."

He reached out, and professional instinct had her backing away.

"I'll tell her to keep quiet." He straightened his shoulders, defensive. "Don't you dare pull away from me now."

"I'm not pulling away." Not really. Her body was still all up in his business, palpitating, shaking, coursing with adrenaline. Her head, on the other hand, was in reverse, trying to steer through the hysteria of an oncoming tidal wave.

"You're in panic mode. I've seen it before." He reached out again, this time encapsulating her wrist in loose fingers. "About three months ago, to be exact."

"Felicity found us together, of course I'm panicked." She pleaded with her eyes, trying to convince him of the obvious danger even though her anxiety was much more complicated. "Please go after her."

"I will. But then I'm coming after you."

No.

No, no, no. She needed to regroup, to find her misplaced sanity, and most of all, tear Mason a new one for talking her into something so addictive and destructive. She should've had a plan before attempting this career-suicide mission. There was always a plan.

"What's your room number?" His thumb rubbed back and forth against her skin, hypnotizing her into submission. Nothing compared to the lazy graze of his finger. She was being worshipped with the simplest of touches. He was reverence personified. "Your room number, Leah?"

"409."

"409," he repeated in a seductive drawl, making the three digits sound like an erotic password. "Give me a few minutes and I'll be there."

He smacked her with another kiss, then dropped the hold on her wrist and fled up the stairs, two at a time.

She didn't move, didn't even breathe until the door above opened and quickly slammed shut again. *Damn it.* Her limbs were tingling, her organs somersaulting. Her lady bits were salivating in the only way lady bits could.

"Idiot." She pushed from the wall and hurried out of the stairwell. She was barefoot, disheveled, and probably pregnant from the efficiency of that kiss. The professional, always immaculate Leah was lost, rushing into the elevator and down the hotel hall like a lovesick fool until she was safely inside the sanctuary of her room.

Her laptop taunted her from the kitchenette counter, reminding her of her job and the video amassing views from last night's show. Her slip couldn't have come at a worse time. There was the divorce, the tour, the supposedly gay fake girlfriends... The list described a circus program.

Her circus. Her monkeys.

How could she have stooped so low?

She strode for the bathroom, wrenched on the sink taps, and drowned her face in water to wash away the insanity. She could still feel his lips, could still taste him. But she couldn't let it linger. If it sank under her skin, buried itself in her veins, she wouldn't be able to regain control. And control was what she needed.

Stupid. Stupid. Stupid.

She'd been caught in a position the world could never find out about. Caught by a threesome-loving lesbian who had her mitts all over Ryan on a daily basis.

Stupid. Stupid. Stupid.

Her cell beeped over the sound of the running water and she ignored it. Ignored everything the universe had to offer because an apocalypse was gaining strength in her mind. This time she couldn't chalk the kiss up to unexpected psychosis. She'd gone to *his* room. She'd instigated the downfall.

Stupid. Stupid. Fucking stupid.

She shut off the water and dried her face on a towel, ignoring yet another message beep on her cell. Then it was her door, harsh knocks against the wood.

"Leah."

She closed her eyes briefly and exhaled the growing tightness under her ribs. She couldn't see him so soon. Her strength hadn't returned yet. Nor her sanity. So she tiptoed to the door, placing her hand and her forehead against the thick barrier between them.

"It's OK," his voice was loud, deliberately taunting her fear of him making a scene. "I can wait."

She peered through the peep hole and sucked in a breath at his carefree lean against the far wall of the hall. He was looking directly at her, his grin smug.

"How long do you think you're going to make me wait?" His lips curved higher. "Maybe I should get Mason to come keep me company."

"Jesus fucking Christ," she whispered. He was threatening her.

"I can hear you." He placed a booted foot against the wall and crossed his arms to look lazily down the hall. "I'm sure all the guys will come searching for me when I don't arrive at sound check. Then we could talk this through as a group."

Gorgeous bastard.

She sighed and opened the door a crack. "Did you speak to her?"

"I went back to my room, told her not to repeat what she walked in on, and then came straight down here."

"Ryan—" she nudged the door wider, "—you need to tell her why. This is important."

"I know it is, and I'll fill her in later. Right now, you're my main concern." He pushed from the wall.

"I shouldn't be." She shook her head. "Nothing happened." Her voice was frantic as she tried to erase the past. It was a mistake. She needed to keep reminding herself, otherwise her future was going to slide down the drain like boiling grease. And the way he looked at her. Gah! Those eyes. Those penetrating, soulful eyes.

"Bullshit." He approached, his authority growing before her. His confidence far more prevalent than she was used to. "Everything happened. Every god damn thing that should've been happening for years."

She swallowed, otherwise she would've whimpered, or mewled, or done some other pathetically weak thing to undermine her future as band manager. "Don't be like this."

"Like what?" He placed his hand against the door, his gaze gliding from her face, to her heating neck, and then back to her lips. He'd never looked at her like that before. Not like she was a woman and he was a man. It was always a friendly appreciation. A glance filled with love and kindness but amiable nonetheless. "Like a guy who's finally sick of being a spineless asshole all for the sake of a wife who never loved him. This is me, Leah. This is me demanding what I've wanted for too long."

Silence.

She had no words. She could barely breathe.

He took another step and she retreated as he moved into her room. She was always retreating. Always the weaker party when it came to him.

"What are you thinking?" he murmured.

She let her hands fall to her sides and concentrated on keeping her fingers still. "I'm thinking that I want you to leave."

"That's a lie."

"No." She shook her head. "It's not. I need you to walk out that door and pretend we didn't just lose our minds. *Please*, Ryan. For the sake of my job."

His lips lifted in a sad smile. "You know I can't do that. Not again."

She turned away, trying to determine what she could say to make him leave. She couldn't hurt him. Not anymore. But he couldn't stay either. Not when her fingers were tingling with the need to touch and her heart was pounding with yearning beats.

"I know you're scared."

Those words kept getting repeated. Maybe it was time to listen. She'd dropped her warrior status long ago and hadn't been anyone of strength for a while now. Not since Australia when she lost a part of herself. And definitely not since the news of his divorce.

"I'm petrified," she admitted. "I'm scared sick of what I might lose."

"Have you thought of what you might gain?"

"The fairytale of happily ever after?" She raised a brow. "Apart from me not being a fairytale kinda girl, I don't think your marriage, your girlfriends, and our careers will allow for it."

"It won't be easy, but you know I can make you happy."

Her heart clenched, trying to cling to his promise.

"Admit it, Leah." He remained near the door, not encroaching, not demanding, because his words did that all on their own. "If it weren't for external influences, we'd be perfect together."

Her lips wouldn't let her deny him, nor would she allow them to speak the truth. He was right. If life didn't exist outside this hotel room, she would be undeniably happy. But the world was there, on the other side of that door, simply waiting for its chance to strike.

"Take as long as you need to think about it." He leaned his shoulder into the wall, taking a casual stance. "I'll wait around until you're ready to admit it."

She released a breathy chuckle. "You're going to stand there until I surrender?"

"This isn't a battle. There's no surrender. You need to quit fighting and just acknowledge the truth."

She opened her mouth, prepared to give him the speech on contractual obligations, but he cut her off.

"You spend too much time fixated on problems instead of focusing on what you want and what we could have together."

"Believe me, I've focused enough on both." She threw her arms up in the air. "There. I admitted it."

He inclined his head. "Now prove it. Throw caution to the wind and give me a Leah-instigated kiss. Convince me I'm not alone in this obsession."

She shook her head. "Don't make me do that."

"I'd never make you do anything. But we both know the last thing you want to be doing is thinking."

"Thinking is constructive. Thinking is—"

"Safe. Yeah, I know." Hope left his features. "Do you really want me to go?"

Her stubborn mind said yes. Every other molecule in her body screamed no.

He sighed and reached for the door.

"Wait."

He straightened, chin high, shoulders rigid. Each glide of her toes along the carpet increased her rapid pulse. It was hard to breathe. Hard to strategize and scheme.

"Stop thinking."

"I can't." She was a thinker. It was her thing. Plan, plan, plan. "If I stop thinking, I'll never want you to leave this room."

"Then we'll both get what we want."

She encroached, coming toe to toe, thigh to thigh, and again, became sucked into the lascivious vortex. "Don't tease."

"Tease?" He flinched. "Working with you for years, knowing I could never have you, was a tease. This right here is the exact opposite. We can be together. We can work this out. Make no mistake, Leah, I'm all yours."

His fingers glided over her hip, gentle in touch yet jolting in effect.

"One kiss," she demanded. "No hands."

He held up his palms in surrender. "One kiss. No hands."

Her heart was beating too fast. Her palms were sweating. It was as if her world hung in the balance. Be careful or careless. Be selfless or sinful. She was dying to taste those lips and tangle with his tongue. She yearned to see his shirt on the floor, his jeans around his ankles, and his cock deep in the back of her throat. But... But...

"I'm waiting," he whispered.

"Give me a second." She needed to work herself up to this. To suppress her fears and anxieties. Her career... Her family... Her future...

She swallowed on her approach, knowing this was the end. She couldn't deny him. Couldn't hold back. He remained still as she tilted her head and brushed her mouth over his. She kissed him, slow and soft and sweet. There was no world. No Leah. Only lips and teeth and tongues. There was only comfort and relief. Necessity and instinct.

She was kissing Ryan—the man of her dreams. And he was kissing her back, increasing her fascination with the deft way he made her burn. It wasn't in a dingy stairwell, or in a drunken binge. This was a connection without risk, without harm. Until he gripped her hips and ground into her, sending an explosion of warmth to her pussy.

She found strength to wiggle from his grip. "You agreed, no hands." She glared at the laughter in his eyes and turned to walk away, only to be wrapped back up in his arms.

"Don't kid yourself. You knew I'd never hold up my end of the bargain."

His breath tickled her neck, his chest deliciously hard and warm behind her. She wanted to be annoyed, wanted to be able to muster a growl, only her smile was too rebellious. The happiness too intense. Ryan was here. In her room. His arms around her, inspiring perfection, bringing her dreams to life. But the higher he took her, the harder she had to fall, right?

"You're going to be late." She turned in his embrace and stared back at eyes that were idolizing her. "Again."

"Is that code for—I need time to obsess over what we just did?"

He knew her. Knew her so well. "Maybe."

His lips kicked. "You've got thirty minutes. We can catch a ride to the stadium together."

Thirty minutes wouldn't be enough. Thirty years didn't seem adequate. She needed to strategize and come up with an infallible plan to make this work. A plan she'd unsuccessfully strived to create for years, and now had to achieve within minutes. "I'll be there." As soon as she showered, changed, and found some Valium. "The lobby in thirty minutes."

"We can figure out how to tell the guys while we're on the road." He kissed her forehead. "Don't look so horrified. It'll be fine."

HE KNEW THIRTY MINUTES WOULD BE A LONG TIME FOR HER TO OBSESS. HE even expected her text—*I'm running late. I'll have to meet you there.* It was a typical Leah blueprint. Especially when he was involved. She wanted to keep her distance until she planned every single step in their path forward.

He didn't have time for that. She had her strategy, and he had his. Only problem was, his involved smothering her into submission. Which was why he ended up standing outside her door, waiting until she was ready to leave.

"Damn it, Ryan. What are you still doing here?"

"Waiting." He started down the hall after her, hanging back a little to take in the full effect of her tight pin-skirt. "I thought you were going to be late."

"I am." She glanced at her watch. "Two minutes."

He chuckled to himself. "You didn't think I could wait two minutes?"

She cleared her throat and continued to the elevator, pressing the call button harder than necessary.

"So where are we at?" He was teasing, which again, was all part of the plan. "Have we reached the pinnacle of anxiety, or are we still waiting on a lower wing?"

"I'm not anxious. I'm in work mode." She entered the opening elevator, rested against the back wall and met his gaze. "I'm trying to tally up my to-do list. For example, once I reach the stadium I have to have a stern discussion with the security team about who they let on stage during performances. And then I need to chastise the rhythm guitarist about arriving late to sound check. Again."

"Chastise?" He entered the elevator, left barely a foot between them, and leaned in to encroach on the perfection of her personal space. "That sounds like fun."

Her lips twitched. "Cameras, Ryan."

She stared him down, the barely visible flames in her eyes making it hard to concentrate. *Shit.* This was harder than he thought, especially in the groin department. After a lifetime waiting to get here, he was finding it difficult to focus on anything other than kissing her. Everywhere.

"Did you speak to Felicity?" She slid out of reach, her focus now on the elevator buttons.

"Yeah. Not before she told Hannah, but they're both going to keep quiet."

Her eyes closed briefly. "I hope we can trust them."

We. One word. Two letters. The statement was remarkably changing. They were a couple. At least as far as he was concerned. "We're holding a major secret of theirs, too. They're not going to want to risk discovery either."

"Fingers crossed." The elevator doors opened and she pounded out the distance toward the lobby doors, the authoritative tap, tap, tap of her heels seeming to strengthen her. Their escort to the stadium was parked outside. The black van with tinted windows kept company by the driver and one of their security team who stood at the open back door.

He ignored the few screamers as they walked outside and indicated for Leah to get in the back of the van before him. "Ladies first."

She rolled her eyes and lowered her head to climb in, giving him a phenomenal view. Normally, she sat in the front. He didn't think she realized her mistake until he was sliding along the back seat beside her. *Right* beside her.

"Would you like the window seat?" She drew out the words as if he had a learning disability.

"No, I'm good."

"Are you sure?" She glanced down at where his thigh rubbed against hers. "Because you're practically in it already."

"I'm keeping things close while I can." He brushed his hand over hers, entwining their fingers.

She sighed and rested her head against the window. "We need to cool it for now. I don't even want the guys to find out until I have my bearings."

He couldn't help smiling at her. He was already in freefall and she was still grappling for stability. "Sure."

"I'm serious, Ryan. Wipe the smirk off your face."

"Anything you say, boss."

"Stop it." A grin pulled at her lips. "This isn't a joke."

He leaned in as the van started, his mouth temptingly close to her ear. "I'm trying," he whispered. "But I've gotta admit, it's kinda hard to keep my hands off you now I've been given a green light."

She pulled her hand away. "There's no green light."

He shrugged. "Then maybe I should run the red."

There was another kick to those gorgeous lips. "Maybe you should move over and give me a little space. We need to figure out what to tell Mason. He was there. He knows you went after me. Felicity probably told him, too."

He skootched away, not for her sake, but for his. The crotch of his jeans was unbearably tight. It'd been months since he'd had any sort of sexual relief. "She didn't. He took off straight after I did, in search of Sid. He doesn't know anything."

"I'd like to keep it that way." She stared outside at the passing buildings, quiet in her contemplation.

The rest of the ride was done in silence, the barely audible drone from the radio seeping into the back seat. She continued to watch the scenery go by, while he stared at her, trying to read what was worrying her most.

He understood the troubles they faced. Some were bigger than others. Some external. Some emotional. Some revolved around his manhood and if it would work under the heat-of-the-moment pressure. But they were all manageable hurdles. Ones they were destined to leap, given a little practice.

He'd give her the chance to tell people in her own time. What he couldn't give her was space. He couldn't even allow a two-foot buffer as they climbed from the van and made their way through the staff entrance of the stadium.

She remained stuck in her own thoughts as they approached the sound of tuning instruments. Greeting the rest of the band wouldn't be easy. The news of the mistaken cocaine incident would already be a hot topic, and the alone time with Leah would be up for discussion. It was all part of the process. Part of the awesomeness that being with her was shaping up to be.

"We've got this," he whispered as they entered the main stadium, Mason, Mitch, Blake, and Sean all coming into view on stage.

She hit him with a frantic look. "Keep quiet and don't elaborate."

"Sure thing." He winked.

She winced, probably at his enthusiastic smirk, and turned away, outpacing him on their approach.

"Nice of you two to join us," Mason's amplified voice carried from all angles. "What's with the cocksucker grin, coke sniffer?" The question echoed around the empty outdoor stadium, attracting attention from the crew.

"Jesus Christ." Leah stopped and glared at him. "Stop smiling."

He tried. Failed. He couldn't quit the upward curve. "Can't help it."

She mimicked his smile, hers threatening. "Try harder."

"I will," he muttered. "I promise." It was a lie. The roll of her eyes announced she knew it, too. There was no point fighting the pull. The grin was there to stay. Unmovable.

She sighed and stopped three feet from the stage. "Mason, do you mind putting your immaturity on hold for a moment so I can give you all an update on the schedule?"

"Sure thing, captain."

The guys came forward, Mitch and Blake taking the temporary stairs, Mason and Sean jumping to ground level.

"I spoke to the stadium manager this morning. He wanted to make you aware of the water leak in your dressing room. Contractors will be going in and out during the day, so make sure you don't leave any valuables in there."

Mason focused on him, scrutinizing, making the curve of his lips kick higher. Then it was Blake, the bass guitarist frowning in confusion.

"Tonight's show is sold out, along with tomorrow," Leah continued. "The only problem we're currently facing is the lack of sales for Slicker. Their social media presence is increasing, but we're not getting the necessary traction on downloads. So if you're online, please think about retweeting or sharing to keep this ball rolling."

"Can do," Mitch offered, always the brown-noser.

"Everything else is on schedule... Oh, except—" She held up a finger and pinned him with a chastising look. "—Please be aware of the age demographic of your fans. Lurid simulations of sex shouldn't be part of the show."

He still couldn't quit the grin. Nope. It was cemented in place. Every show was filled with some form of perversion unsuitable for teens. That wasn't new. But this was—her jealousy. Her insecurity.

"Speaking of sex," Mason drawled, "are you going to fill us in on what happened earlier?"

"Earlier?"

He noticed the heavy contraction of her throat and couldn't help enjoying her panic.

"You got your panties in a twist and stormed off. I wanted a follow up on how Ryan may have untwisted them."

"My panties were fine, Mason. But thank you for your concern."

"We talked," Ryan added. "We're good."

"Seems you're more than good." Blake was still frowning. "What's with the joker grin?"

Leah shot him another for-god's-sake glare.

"Looks like a sex high to me," Mitch added.

"Bullshit." Sean started to scrutinize him. "I don't believe it."

"Could we all please focus?" Leah clapped her hands together. "Where's Sidney? Didn't you say she was flying in earlier?"

"Sidney, shmidney," Blake muttered. "I want to know why Ryan looks like he's just blown his load."

Damn. The guys were determined for answers. One sniff of gossip and they were ravenous. His neck started to burn from their inspection.

"*Focus.*" Leah failed to get their attention.

"He does, doesn't he?" Sean's eyes narrowed. "You either got laid, or spent some time with your favorite porn site."

"I didn't get laid." He glanced to Leah for approval, for help, for any damn thing to get these assholes off their scent, but she just stood there, eyes wide, lips parted, face pale.

"I think we're wearing him down." Mason snickered. "Did you get a knob job off the boss lady?"

Leah responded with an unhealthy gasp in the lead singer's direction. "Do I look like the type to get on my knees for any of you?"

Mason dropped his gaze to the body parts in question. "Normally, I'd say no..."

"Keep your voice down," she seethed. "You'll start rumors."

"You're awfully testy." Mitch switched his focus to Leah. "Panicked, even."

"The crew are waiting for you to do your job." Her foot tapped against the temporary outdoor flooring, only adding evidence to her nervousness. "Can we save the inquisition for later?"

There was a chorus of rejections— "No." "I don't think so." "Not until we have answers."

"Come on, guys." Ryan placed a comforting hand on her back and she startled.

"We kissed, OK? *Jesus Christ*." Her voice was viciously low. "Fuck the paparazzi, you guys are the real vultures."

Ryan froze at her admission, then did a visual sweep of the stadium to make sure nobody else overheard. Yep. All clear. When he turned back, his friends were all staring at her in disbelief.

"Do *not* look at me like that." She pointed a finger at them in turn, finishing with Mason. "This is your fault."

The lead singer shrugged. "I take no responsibility for your unprofessional actions."

She growled, the sound inappropriately sexy.

"I'm... shocked. I thought we were all joking." Mitch's eyes were wide. "After all these years..."

"Keep it down." Ryan made sure there was a warning in his tone. "This isn't something we want shared outside this group."

"This isn't something I wanted to share with anyone," Leah grated.

Mitch reached for her hand, giving it a quick squeeze before he let it fall. "It's cool. We won't tell anyone."

"Congrats, guys." Blake gave a friendly punch to Leah's shoulder. "Took you two long enough."

"Don't worry about anyone else." Sean backtracked to the stage. "We'll keep this quiet."

"Our little secret." Mason waggled his brows.

Then they were left alone, the world returning to normal as quickly as the carnage had erupted. But the damage had taken its toll. Leah was trembling, her invincible tenacity taking one too many hits.

"Don't panic."

Wide eyes met his. "What have I done?"

"They were going to find out sooner or later."

"If this gets out—"

"It won't." He pulled her into his arms and hated how she stiffened. "I've hugged you before. In public. This isn't anything out of the ordinary."

She nodded into his neck, her arms still limp at her sides. "I should go."

He clung a little tighter. "Can I see you tonight?"

"You're not going out with Felicity?" She leaned back, wounding him with her optimism.

"Only to make an appearance. I won't be long."

"We'll see." She moved from his arms. "Message me when you're done."

She walked away from him, her chin lifting with every step as she headed toward one of the exits. He shouldn't leave her alone. Shouldn't, but he also couldn't shadow her every second of the day. Facing her anxieties was one of their hurdles. All he could do was hope she didn't talk herself into hiding from him again.

"Hey, Leah," Mason's voice carried over the microphone again, taunting. "You can thank me later."

Shit. Ryan also had to hope Mason put a cork in it, stat.

She turned, a pretty smile on her face as she raised her middle finger to the sky. "Fuck you, Ron Jeremy."

RYAN PULLED HIS HOTEL DOOR SHUT AND RAN DOWN THE HALL. HIS LESBIAN fake girlfriends were in his bed, probably up in each other's ovaries by now, and he couldn't get away fast enough.

Leah hadn't returned his last message and it was late. Early, actually. The quick drink at a nearby bar had turned into a two-hour chat session with Felicity and Hannah's newly amassed fans. They hadn't been able to get away. Four beers later, he put his foot down and said he was leaving with or without them.

Now he was rushing toward Leah's room, praying she wasn't asleep as he sent one last message and then held his ear to the door to listen for movement.

"Damn it." She must've passed out.

He stared down the empty hall, arguing with himself over whether he should leave her be, or break the door down. Eventually, he chose a middle ground and rapped his knuckles gently against the wood.

Her throat cleared from inside, the sound sailing through his chest to nail him with arrhythmia. Every breath he took waiting for the door to open was akin to winning the lottery. He already had the lucky ticket, he already knew his prize. All he had to do was claim it.

The knob turned and she came to stand before him in a red silken nightgown. The straps mere threads, the hem falling to mid-thigh. She was a pin-up. A fantasy from the lazy blink of her eyes to her bare toes against the carpet.

"You were asleep." He wanted to feel bad, even a little remorseful. He couldn't muster either.

She rested her head against the door, her smile lazy. "I was watching TV and must have dozed."

"Anticipation really had you by the throat, didn't it?"

Her lips quirked and a sparkle lit the tired depths of her irises. "Anticipation of what?"

"Seeing me tonight." Description wasn't his strong suit, yet the words were a torrential flow through his head. All the things he wanted to do. All the places he wanted to taste. Not an inch of her would be spared or neglected.

"I see you all the time, Ryan."

The way she said his name with dreamy seduction made him rally not to slide past her and drag her back into the room. Coy was a thousand times better than standoffish. A million times better than dismissive. It was a blessing to finally be through with the distance they'd successfully built between them.

"And you wore my favorite nightwear."

Her chuckle was barely audible. "You've seen this before?"

"Yeah. I have." Once, when they'd been overseas touring and he'd made the mistake of walking by the window to her ground room floor. "But this is the first time I haven't felt guilty at the thought of stripping it off you."

Her breath hitched. Her sleepy lethargy vanished. He waited to be scolded or to receive the lecture on inappropriate behavior. Instead, she stepped back, pulling the door wide to give him free access to her room.

He couldn't deny the silent invitation scared the hell out of him. This was complicated. This was Leah. Success could have them sharing a future. Failure could land them in a place far worse than the aftermath of the Australian tour.

Slowly, he ate up the distance between them and walked inside. The atmosphere changed with the click of the lock as she shut them into the silent room bathed in the glow of a small television.

"How was your night?" Her words held a lilt he wasn't familiar with, a seductive quality that played havoc with the professional and friendly Leah he knew.

He came to rest against the kitchenette, his ass leaning against the counter. "Torturous."

"Hmm?" She raised a brow, every move enticing, every sound a push against his restraint. "What happened?"

"I spent the whole time thinking about you." Slight understatement. He'd obsessed over her, reliving their kiss and the reciprocated hope he'd seen in her eyes.

"I've had a lot of time to think, too."

That was never, ever a good sign when it came to this brilliant woman. "And?"

"You're still married." She raised her chin, some of her professional nature seeping back in.

"I've also scored two lesbian girlfriends." He reached for her, pulling her into his arms. "What's your point?"

She shook her head, denying his attempt at humor. "This situation is far from ideal."

"I know." He held her close, happy to do nothing but this for hours on end. No matter how much he looked at her, she seemed to grow more beautiful. More addictive. He could stare at her like this, no words, no movement, forever. "We'll figure it out."

"Do you mind sharing some of your optimism?"

"No problem. I've got enough for the both of us." He ran a hand over the softness of her cheek and trailed the delicate strands of flower-scented hair behind her ear. Her head moved into his touch, her eyes briefly closing. Her acquiescence squeezed the breath from his lungs and boosted his resilience. Everything inside him felt right. In place. At ease. There was no guilt over a fake relationship, or regret due to a failed marriage. After years chipping away at any hope for his future, it was hard to ignore how monumental this moment was.

"Did you kiss her?" Her eyes opened, an expanse of blue hitting him. "Or them?"

"No." He swallowed, the restriction in his throat making it hard to speak. "I guess it will have to happen eventually, though."

Her features didn't change, her lips maintained their sultry appeal, her lashes blinked in careless distraction. But he could feel her reaction, could sense the betrayal and animosity as if it were a physical entity she'd handed to him in a package with ribbon and shiny paper.

"I don't want anyone else, Leah." He released an arm from around her waist and cradled her jaw. "I'm here with you."

"I know." She tilted her face toward him, her mouth moving closer. "It's just that you've been committed for so long, I thought maybe you'd want to get a little crazy." She shrugged. "Ya know, like snorting sugar with lesbian lovers and such." Her straight face transformed into a beaming smile.

"I only want to get crazy with you."

"Promises, promises."

Bam. And just like that, with a flirty line and flash of her pearly whites, he was lost. Done. Completely sold on spending eternity with this woman. "Are you hinting for me to move this along?"

"I didn't want to be rude, but..." She nibbled her lower lip, the nervous reaction blindingly brilliant. Flirty Leah was now his favorite facet of this woman. Wonder Woman was profound; his best friend had been perfect. But this Leah, the one who made his chest throb and his libido surge was fucking phenomenal.

"I want to take this slow," he admitted. "I want to make up for those two forced kisses."

"Nothing was forced."

"But it wasn't what you deserved." He trailed his thumb along her jaw, to her chin, and slowly swiped back and forth below her bottom lip. Her mouth was the most tempting taste he'd ever craved. "I want a new first kiss."

He lifted her, placing her ass on the kitchen counter. "I want a proper kiss." He pushed between her legs, lifting the hem of her nightgown to the top of her thighs. "I want to take my time."

Her fingers tangled in his shirt, the slightest tug pulling him closer, dragging him toward the sweet scent of her. He leaned in, his nose hovering an inch from hers, his lungs dragging in her breath. She closed her eyes, her fingers gripping harder, her silent impatience making him burn.

"Kiss me, Ryan."

"I will." In time. First, he wanted to savor. He needed to memorize the hitch in her breath and the warmth from her skin. He had to study her. All the intricacies he'd never been allowed.

Her hand loosened in his shirt, her palm pressing firm against him as it made its way over his chest, his neck, and tangled in his hair. She opened her eyes, meeting his gaze. "Now."

She slanted her head, her approach unhurried. He felt her lips before they were on his, could sense the burn before the connection. The kiss was slow... barely moving... barely breathing. There was nothing hurried or rushed. Slight swipes of mouths, gentle brushes of noses.

She whimpered, the sound of surrender making him feel like he'd won a war.

"I've waited forever to hear that noise." He nipped her lower lip. "To taste it." He glided his tongue over hers, still slow, still barely moving.

Her legs lifted, her thighs encircling his waist as her hand descended from his hair and retreated to the hem of his shirt. She lifted the material, over his waist, his chest, to his neck. There was a split second of ice-cold separation as she yanked it over his head, then her mouth was back on his, meek and mild, gentle and coaxing.

He pulled her tighter against him as her nails slowly raked his skin, the trail painstaking in its leisure. Her touch inspired agony wherever it dragged, reigniting wounds from time wasted and years of misplaced affections. They should've done this long ago. He should've been with her from the start.

"We're not friends anymore, Leah." He spoke into her mouth, unwilling to pull away.

"I know." Another kiss. Another stroke of tongues.

"Don't let me mess this up." That was his worst fear. Losing her. Losing this.

She froze, her eyes still closed as she placed her forehead against his. "You won't. It's the external factors that will make this temporary."

Temporary? "Hey." He chastised her with a harsh smack of his lips. "This ain't temporary. Don't get cold feet."

"I'm not, but I don't want to get carried away either. If I have to make a choice—"

"Don't go there." He could deal with her hesitation for now. Anything else was static. "We're going to do whatever it takes to make this work." He dropped his hands to her thighs and dragged her into him, her heat against his cock. "Whatever it takes, Leah."

Thirteen

$\mathbf{S}$HE NODDED, HOPING SHE COULD COMMIT TO THE PROMISE. IN HER MIND, THIS was temporary. Disneyland for a day. A wish with a time limit. But with each touch, or kiss, or whispered word, she clung to the fantasy of more. She wanted to experience all of him before the fun was over.

She reached for his beard, let the harsh stroke of his whiskers tickle her palm. His mouth brushed hers again, then his teeth, and his tongue. It wasn't merely a kiss. It was a tease. A game. A show of affection and a promise of forever. It was everything. With his mouth alone, he'd made the beat of her heart thunderous and soaked her panties.

"Help me out of these." She wiggled back on the counter, giving herself room.

His gaze lowered to the join of her thighs and the small expanse of see-through material covering her mound. "Fuck."

The curse struck her belly. Hard. He wasn't prone to profanity like she was. Those words were only spoken at the best of times, or the worst of times. And she was a little giddy to be on the former column.

"Is this going to be weird?" She stared at his hands as they crept toward her underwear. She was waiting for the awkwardness to kick in, for the arousal to be tainted by years of friendship.

"Do you want it to be?" he murmured. "I can do something kinky if you like."

"Stop it." She lifted her ass to help him remove her panties. "You know what I mean."

He met her gaze, his fingers tangled in her waistband, his breath tempting her mouth. "Would darkness help? I can turn off the TV."

"No. I have to see you. All of you." She licked her lower lip in a nervous stroke, her breathing labored as he stepped back and pulled her underwear over her knees. "And I want you to know you're with me. Nobody else."

"I could never forget. I've waited a lifetime to be here with you, carrying the guilt of emotionally cheating on someone I'd fallen out of love with." He dropped her panties to the floor and convinced her with the intensity in his eyes. "You're everything to me."

She wanted to mimic the sentiment. He'd been *her* everything for far longer, after all. But layering this situation with vulnerability wasn't a good idea when tonight might be the only night they had. "Show me."

"It's all in the plan." His hands continued back up her thighs, creeping higher until he cupped her ass.

"You have a plan?" She tilted her neck, delighting in the tingled trail of his lips along her jaw, his fragile kisses leading up to her ear. "Impressive."

"One plan," he murmured. "Make you mine."

He pulled her close, causing her to gasp as his pants-covered erection aligned with her pussy. The hardness of him grated against the heat of her, the torturous tease making her mindless. She wanted to be his. Wanted nothing else as those kisses peppered her with affection.

She ached to tell him everything. To pour her heart out and explain why this couldn't be forever. But the words didn't come. They were stifled by pleasure. Suppressed under the weight of hope.

"I want you." Her voice was barely audible. The plea silenced from the blood rushing through her ears.

"Then tell me you're mine."

A palm trailed over her hip, his thumb leading the way toward her pussy. She held her breath as he encroached, held his shoulders, too. Then he was there, gliding the pad of his thumb over her clit piercing.

He froze, not moving, not coaxing. She wasn't sure if it was a torture technique. Then his head fell to her shoulder, the action almost defeated.

"What is it?" She panted through the torment.

"Nothing." He pulled back, only to smash his lips against hers, painful and punishing. His tongue took ownership of her mouth, his fingers staking claim on her clit. He slid his fingers lower, through the slickness of her arousal, and deeper.

She whimpered at the penetration, her pussy clamping down on pure, delicious fulfillment. Reality was lost for a moment. She closed her eyes and clung to him, tightening her grip with each thrust and swirl.

A hand glided through her hair, gentle at first, then tight, squeezing, demanding her attention. She blinked up at ferocity and ownership. There was nothing but him. He took her over. All her thoughts were his. All her breath. All her ecstasy.

He watched her with savage determination, not stopping the onslaught of his fingers or the manipulative tug of her hair. He was different like this, a stark contrast from the man she knew. There was nothing gentle in his features. No sweetness. No chivalry. The man before her was confident in his finesse. Calculated with his control.

She released a hand from around his neck to stabilize herself on the counter and began grinding into his strokes. She held his focus, matching his tenacity with her own. His fortitude built, those eyes becoming more adamant on her pleasure while her strength fractured under the skillful force of his fingers.

She kissed him, gasping into the connection. The grip on her ass shifted, nudging between her cheeks, gliding toward her pussy from behind. Everything inside her clenched. Bliss hovered.

"Fuck." She pulled back to suck in air.

"Soon."

He continued to work her into a frenzy, his kisses landing on her cheek, her shoulder, the top of her breast. Every time a sound escaped her mouth, he became attuned to the cause, pinpointing the pleasure-filled action and doing it again and again.

He stroked the wet flesh between her pussy and ass, then penetrated her core. He kissed her into oblivion. There was no respite. No pause to gain control. His teeth scraped her nipple. His beard marked her skin. His thumb rubbed her clit. Over and over. Her need building higher and higher.

Everything grew dark under the weight of rapture. She leaned down, delirious and searching for clarity as she placed her head against his shoulder, still rocking with his penetration.

"Fuck, you're gorgeous like this."

"Stop swearing," she panted, shaking her head to fight his hold.

"Why?"

"Because it's so fucking sexy." She couldn't take much more.

His low chuckle tickled her, burning her nerves and increasing his power.

"Wait until I start to fuck you." His voice traveled from the sensitive spot below her ear. "Wait until my face is between your thighs and you're fucking my mouth."

"Ryan," she warned. At least she thought it was a warning. In her head, she sounded stern. Authoritative. Yet, in her ears, the word had seemed oddly fragile. More like a plea.

"I'm going to fuck you until you know you're mine." He licked her earlobe and grazed the sensitive flesh between his teeth. "I'm going to make you come over and over until you're addicted to me, like I'm addicted to you. And between now and then, there's going to be a lot of therapeutic cursing heading your way."

She shuddered, head to toe, pussy to breasts. She never imagined him this way. Her fantasies were filled with gentle Ryan. Sweet, thoughtful Ryan. That man had been enough to make her wet on the darkest of days. But this guy, the one with the silver tongue and filthy mouth was going to kill her. One orgasm at a time.

"Stop. Talking." She wanted control. At least a little bit. Yet he tore it from her. He stole her sense and used it against her, his thumb now stroking over her clit jewelry like he owned it.

"Less talk, more action?"

He sucked her neck, hard, the skin burning under his lips. She dug her nails into his back, unable to stop herself from riding his fingers harder. She was close, so close. With each breath her pussy clenched, clamping down on him, threatening to take over.

"I'm…" Her orgasm hit, the fluttering overload creating senselessness. She made noise, made movements, all of them without thought as she clung to him, pulling him tighter and tighter into her chest. He whispered as she came, words with a lilt of love and affection. She struggled to understand him, tried to focus, but she was drowning. There was no escape until heaven receded and her gasps became proper breaths.

They remained silent as she gained control, her sense of self-preservation almost within her grasp when he removed his fingers from her pussy, clutched her ass, and dragged her from the counter.

She squealed—a girlie, weak sound.

"You're a squealer?" He led her to the bed, placing her down softly on the mattress, her nightie falling back into place.

"I am not."

He straightened, standing tall to stare down at her splayed before him. "I'm pretty sure that was a squeal."

She narrowed her gaze, ignoring the need to grin. "And I'm pretty sure your life will be over if you ever repeat what you heard."

He chuckled, his panty-melting smile killing her as he unbuckled his belt. "Duly noted." His erection bulged against his zipper, his length becoming more evident when he shucked his pants. She held her breath, swallowed, and gripped the bed coverings tighter in an effort not to squirm. He was truly magnificent. She didn't know how anyone could ever let a man like this slip through their fingers. It was stupidity. Insanity.

He met her gaze as he dragged his boxers below his knees and stepped out of them. The desire to lick her lips was undeniable. Everything inside her itched to lower her attention. To take in every inch of him. To lavish in all the parts of him she'd never laid eyes on. The need to stare at his nakedness a living breathing thing. Instead, she focused on his eyes, letting his confidence wash over her to smother all the reasons this shouldn't be happening.

"Go on." His voice was low, gravel-rich. "Look your fill."

Cocky bastard. But she did. She lowered her eyes and took in the sight before her, from his muscled shoulders, the defined pecs and trail of hair from his navel all the way down to his crotch. His cock stood proud, thick, the veins of his shaft bulging.

Yep, truly magnificent.

She clenched her thighs, unable to deny the need for friction. "Come here."

He complied, kneeling on the bed. He spread her legs, his attention on her face, not on the parts of her body he exposed as her nightie climbed up her thighs. "Take this off for me."

Her heart stuttered and she gripped the silken material to pull it over her head.

He looked her over, so slow, so leisurely, his gaze raking her as if she was a newly acquired masterpiece. Then he stopped, his head bowing as his eyes clamped shut.

"Ryan?" Her stomach turned as she waited for a response.

"Give me a minute."

Why? Was he caught up in thoughts of his wife? Felicity? Hannah? Christ, was he thinking this was a mistake?

When he finally lifted his chin, pure conviction stared back at her.

"I know you're worried," he started. "But I can't go back from this. I can't give you space anymore. Not even time. I just can't. I've wanted you for too long to ever return to friendship."

She nodded.

"No, you don't get it." He kept punishing her with his sincerity. "This is us now. We're together. You're mine."

She blinked to fight the burn. "I've always been yours."

His muscles bunched, pulling taut. "You've got no idea what it means to hear that."

"I think I do." She reached up, placed a hand around his neck and pulled him on top of her. "Because I feel the same."

His heavy body covered hers, the hardness of his chest pressing into her breasts. Arousal seeped from her core, the slickness of her pussy out of control. While one hand tangled in his hair, she ran the other between them and brushed her palm over his cock.

He hissed, the aggressive sound nirvana through her veins. He gyrated into her hold, working himself in a slow rhythm as he stared down at her, his lips close, his heart even closer. She could read his thoughts, the dirty ones making her shiver and the hopeful ones inspiring heart ache.

He wasn't holding back. She could see he wanted all of her, not just her body, not just her friendship. He'd ransack her soul if given the chance. And she wasn't sure she should let him. Not when being with him could mean the end of all the things that defined her.

"Don't think so loud." She squeezed the head of his shaft, delighting in another hiss.

"Then don't deny me," he growled. "Stop worrying. Stop obsessing over the negative thoughts."

He ground into her, her hand falling away as his cock nudged her entrance. She arched into the sensation, allowing him to slide into her, his length sinking deep. Her core contracted around him, another emotion-inspired orgasm already hovering close.

His palm glided over her waist, her ribs, to the curve of her breast. His thumb stroked lazily over her nipple, forward, back, forward, back, the slow tempo mimicking the way he began to move inside her.

His mouth found hers and their rhythm increased. The brushes of his thumb became harder, the glide of his tongue a lascivious swipe, the grind of his hips so painstakingly deep. Then everything stopped—sound, movement, pleasure.

"Shit." He withdrew and shoved from the bed.

"What is it?" She scrambled onto her elbows, tracking his movements as he lunged for his pants.

"Protection." He pulled out his wallet, his cheeks flushed with arousal, embarrassment or maybe even guilt.

"It's OK." She held out her hand. "Give it here."

He handed over the wallet and fixed her with a chaste grin. "I'm not used to…"

"I wouldn't want you to be." She didn't want him to finish his sentence. She didn't want Julie in this room, or anyone else, for that matter.

"It's in one of the side compartments."

He climbed back between her legs, paying homage with his lips to the inside of her thighs, her hip, her stomach. His attention was a delirious distraction as she ransacked his wallet, pulling out business cards and old receipts until she found her prize.

"Got it." The foil was scratched and crinkled, her fingers flicking over something rough on the other side. She flipped the small square and found a piece of paper stuck to the packaging. A tiny blue Post-It that read—

Enjoy the ride, bucko. Love Taiden.

"Does Sean usually leave love letters on your condoms?"

"What?" He paused, his lips poised above the curve of her breast.

"Yep." She held up the note and tried not to laugh as he squinted at the writing.

"Everyone's a comedian." He snatched the paper and threw it aimlessly. "God knows how long that's been there."

She wondered, too. Had it been days? Weeks? Months? "Make sure you thank him for the well wishes."

"Yeah," he grated. "I will."

His hand covered hers, the foil packet disappearing with his retreat. With a bite of his teeth, the wrapper was opened, the protection removed. Then he was gripping the base of his shaft in one hand and placing the condom over the head of his cock with the other.

She was embarrassed by her fascination as she watched him cover his length. He was so hard. So temptingly real.

"Want me to go slower to prolong the show?"

Bastard. "I could watch you do that all day." She met his gaze, smirked. "But then you'd never get what you want."

His eyes softened as he leaned down to hover over her, hip to hip, chest to chest. "I already have what I want."

She quirked a brow and jolted her pelvis. "So there's no need to go any further?"

"There's no necessity." He ground his erection into her, the head of his cock finding her entrance. "But there's definitely need."

She scratched her nails along his back and wove her legs around his waist. "I think there's a necessity to stop talking."

He brought his nose to hers, his smiling lips an inch away. "I'll never speak again."

The lush stroke of his mouth brushed over hers as his hips nudged into her. His cock breached her pussy, the penetration sinking further while his tongue coaxed a deeper kiss. He didn't break his promise when he pulled back. He didn't speak. But his eyes whispered compliments, the endearments making her moan.

He held her captive, surveying her as their rhythm increased. The grind of his pelvis became harder, his fingers clutching the bed coverings beside her head. The tendons in his neck tightened, his body glistened with a sheen of sweat. She leaned up to nip his shoulder, to lick and suck his salted flesh. Everything she did gained a response—a hiss, a growl, a harder thrust of his hips.

She clenched down on him and wove an arm around his, her nails digging into his bicep to hold on. The necessity to slow ate at her. She didn't want this to end, but she couldn't stop. Every grind against her clit piercing increased the insanity. Each peppered kiss along her skin stoked the need to come.

When his beard grazed the sensitive spot where her neck and shoulder joined, she lost hope. Her pussy fluttered. Spasmed. Her eyes clamped shut as she called out, the sound deafening. Then he was there with her, her name moaned over and over.

The friction built with his harsh thrusts, her receding orgasm coming back with vengeance. "Shit." She came again, her legs so tight around his waist she thought he might break. She was still coming when she opened her eyes and found love staring back at her.

The shocking image dissolved her pleasure, the seriousness dragging her into the real world where fantasies didn't exist. She'd never seen that look before. Not from any man. And not through all the years she'd seen him with his wife.

The affection he had for her was hers alone. A tangible emotion she would adorn like a treasured piece of jewelry. "How long have you imagined this?"

"All my life," he murmured, placing a kiss against her sternum.

She closed her eyes with a smile, allowing a few seconds of shameless bliss before she looked at him again. "Ryan, I'm serious." She tugged on the loose strands of his hair, demanding focus. "How long have you wanted to be with me?"

He kissed her shoulder, her neck, the delicious spot below her ear and whispered, "Forever."

Fourteen

LEAH HAD NEVER WOKEN UP HAPPY. SHE'D PREVIOUSLY ROUSED FROM slumber feeling content, occasionally even energized. But never happy, with tingles in her belly and a heavy throb beneath her ribs. Not until today.

Ryan's arm was wrapped around her waist, his chest spooned against her back.

"Morning, gorgeous."

"Gorgeous?" She turned in his arms, fixing him with a raised brow.

"Yeah, sweetie or pumpkin don't suit." His eyes were dreamy, this morning a shade greener than blue. "And although ball-buster was a great fit, I was looking for something more personal instead of a name the band, crew, and anyone in general would be likely to call you."

"That's sweet, Ryan. Really sweet." She shot him a playful glower and then nuzzled into his chest, wrapping her arms around the huge expanse of muscle. They'd stayed awake for hours, the darkness ticking away as they made up for lost time. "I never want to leave this room."

He ran his fingers through her tangled hair, letting his touch travel down her back with each swipe. Goosebumps awakened under his fingertips, his affection branding her skin like an iron.

"Still think this is temporary?" His lips were against her temple.

"I don't want it to be." The vulnerability was hard to admit. Painful, even.

"So how do we make this work? Do we come clean or keep it quiet?"

A breath of derisive laughter escaped her lips. They didn't even have that measly choice. "At the moment, there's no option but to keep quiet. We've got Felicity and Grander to think about. If this gets out, it'll jeopardize the publicity campaign for Slicker and inevitably extend our tour. Then there's your divorce—"

"Forget the divorce. I won't let Julie affect this in any way."

"There's also my boss. He can't find out. Not until I come up with some sort of leverage."

"What type of leverage are we looking for?"

She nuzzled further against his chest, wishing his heat and protection would work outside these four walls. "I don't know. I've been thinking about it off and on for years and nothing seems likely to placate."

"Talk me through it. What's the biggest hurdle?"

Her happiness was starting to vanish, the bliss of the night before being eaten away by reality. "Everything is a hurdle, and it all starts with my contract." She leaned one elbow on the mattress and faced him. "I'm para-phrasing, but the document says something like—any physical relationship with a client—casual or otherwise—will result in immediate dismissal."

"Contracts can be renegotiated. You know that."

"I do." She nodded, her lips unable to resist the temptation to kiss his pec. "But my boss won't renegotiate. Not without something in return."

"Like money?"

She fought to hide a wince. Putting a price on a newborn relationship wasn't something she was willing to do. Not only was she protective of her savings, but she was also aware of the heavy weight it would put on both their shoulders. "I wouldn't suggest it."

"I'd be happy to pay."

This time there was no way to hide the wince. It was there for him to see. "No." It wasn't like she didn't have the means to pay either. With no notable family, friends, or expenses outside of Reckless, her bank balance was exceptionally healthy. It was the idea in general, the Pretty Woman narrative that didn't sit well. "I'll think of something else."

"We'll do it together. You're not on your own." He finger-combed the hair back from her cheeks, his gaze lowering to her neck, his eyes widening. *"Christ."*

"What?" She sat up straight, her body on display as she tried to see what he was looking at.

"You've got a family of hickies along your neck and shoulders."

"What type of family? Conservative middle-class or devout Mormon?"

He cringed and delicately brushed her hair back to assess the damage. "Not funny," he murmured. "It looks like I attacked you."

"I'll wear something to cover it." She collapsed against him, her fingers trailing along the scratch marks and moon like symbols from her previously embedded nails. "You didn't get away unscathed either."

"I have battle scars?" His tone spoke of pride. "You can hide yours, but I'll make sure to wear something that shows mine off."

Her smile was a mere flash before her thoughts kicked in.

"What did I say?"

"Nothing." She sat up, gripping the sheet at her chest, and reached for her nightie. "I need coffee." She pulled the material over her head and flung back the covers. "Do you want some?"

"Sure. After I get a truthful answer."

She pushed from the bed, considering her response. It was jealousy, tainted with heartache and sprinkled with animosity. None of which he needed to hear.

"Leah?"

She heard the rustle of the bed, then the clink of his belt and the zip of his pants.

"I don't want to use threats to get you to talk."

"Threats?" She whirled around, getting caught up in his grin.

"I'll tell the guys you're a squealer." His grin turned to an unabashed smirk. "I'll tell them everything. Every dirty little detail."

She raised his smirk and countered with a sexy saunter toward him, stopping toe to toe. "You wouldn't dare. You're too much of a gentleman."

He shrugged, the confident response making her pussy clench. "Wouldn't I? Pretty soon the world is going to think I turn women to the dark side. Bragging about your orgasm tally will help to keep some balls in my court. And I'm sure Mason would appreciate finding out I was undoubtedly the biggest pain in your ass last night."

Her mouth fell open. *Don't say it. Don't say it.*

"Literally," he added.

"Oh, my G—"

He tugged her into his arms, pulling laughter from her in one movement. She knew he'd never rat on her. He was too kind. Too loyal. But he was certainly no longer a gentleman behind closed doors.

"Tell me." He smiled down at her, not relenting on his tight grip until she calmed and relaxed against him.

"It was nothing."

"Then spit it out."

She sighed. "I was only thinking that someone else will get the blame for the marks I left on your body. Photos will end up online and name Felicity or Hannah as the culprit. And even if I was held responsible, it would be evidence to ruin my career. So, either way, those marks aren't something I can laugh about."

There. The truth in black and white. Also the reality she hadn't wanted to face after such a fantastic night. She'd anticipated this moment of painful simplicity. The one which sucked the happiness out like a vacuum and replaced it with guilt and paranoia.

"I'll cover them."

She sighed and wiggled from his arms. This would be their routine from now on. At least until she found the much needed leverage to take to her boss. They'd have to hide, to sneak, to lie. Every moment would be tainted and juvenile.

"Stop worrying. We'll work it out." He glanced at his watch. "Damn it. I've gotta go. I'm supposed to be ready for that school motivational talk in half an hour."

Her gaze dropped to the bedside clock—midday. Wow. He was the cure to her insomnia. "I won't get a chance to see you before tonight's show."

"You can't fit me in?" He reached down to pick up his shirt off the floor, the betraying material moving over his head to cover a large expanse of gorgeousness. "Not even five minutes?"

"Five minutes would turn into ten, then twenty, and so on." He was addictive and definitely not a case where a five-minute fix would appease.

"I'll try to see you before you get on the bus."

"I guess that will have to do." He strode to her, one hand gliding around her cheek to cup the back of her head. "Until then." He pressed his lips to hers, once, twice, the connection fading before she had a chance to deepen it. "Be good."

Fifteen

Ryan: *Where are you?*

Leah: *Shit. Sorry.*

Ryan: *Where. Are. You?*

Leah: *Sidney may have led me astray. It was only supposed to be one drink at the airport bar but her flight was delayed...and more drinks were necessary. I caught the end of the concert but when I went to put my bag on the crew bus I must've got distracted.*

Ryan: *Distracted with what?*

Leah: *Sleep. I think I passed out. I don't remember crawling into my bunk.*

Leah: *Hell, I have no idea how I ended up in an old Korn shirt that isn't even mine.*

Ryan: *Are you joking?*

Ryan: *Leah?*

Leah: *It was Drew. Perverted little ass.*

Ryan: *You better be joking. Otherwise you'll have to explain to everyone why I had to beat the life from him.*

Leah: *Ryan Bennett is a lover not a fighter.*

Ryan: *Please tell me you're joking.*

Leah: *I'm joking.*

Ryan: *Are you lying?*

Leah: *Don't worry, he didn't see much. Nothing that he'll brag about anyway. He values his manhood too much.*
Ryan: *He's dead.*

Leah: *Why don't any of you have mechanic skills?*
Ryan: *I guess you heard about the bus breakdown.*
Leah: *Who do you think has to organize someone to fix it? I bet the sun will be up before I can find a mechanic. Get some sleep. You might be stuck in the middle of nowhere for a while.*

Ryan: *I'm not going to have time to see you before the show, am I? We're still an hour from Chicago.*
Leah: *No. You'll be lucky if you're not late ☹ And Scott tells me you already have plans with Felicity after the concert.*
Ryan: *Want me to cancel? You know I'd prefer to spend the night with you.*
Leah: *Go out. Have fun. I'll see you in the morning.*
Ryan: *Slip a spare room card under my door. I'll come back to you once I'm finished with Flick.*
Leah: *Spoken like a true player.*
Ryan: *Don't go there. You know I'd go public with how I feel about you if I thought it wouldn't affect your job.*
Leah: *I know. We'll make time for each other tomorrow. Promise.*
Ryan: *I expect your room card under my door. I'll see you later tonight.*

Ryan: *Why didn't you leave a room card?*
Ryan: *Leah? I'm back at the hotel. Are you still awake?*

Ryan: *I'm leaving the lobby in half an hour to have breakfast at a place called Bites and Beverages. It's around the corner. Meet me there. I mean it, Leah. I can't go much longer without seeing you.*

Leah rolled over and groaned at the unwanted necessity to get up. She'd fallen asleep while working on her laptop again. She was still in yesterday's clothes, the hem of her suit skirt around her waist, her blouse crushed and plastered tight against her boobs.

She patted a hand around the bed, coming up with her phone. The notification light flashed and she unlocked her screen, blinking against the bright light to read Ryan's messages.

Two days had passed without seeing him. Two torturous days where she would've given anything for him to find a way to her side. Instead, he'd given his spare hours to another woman. Her Google notifications a stark reminder of exactly how much time he was spending with Felicity.

But she still wanted to see him.

Be with him.

She threw back the covers, found some clean clothes, and took a quick shower. In thirty-five minutes she was dressed, make-up immaculate, hair done, and striding through the lobby like a woman on a mission.

"Can you please point me in the right direction for Bites and Beverages?" she asked the concierge.

He followed her to the door, held it open, and pointed to the left. "You won't miss it. I'm sure there'll be a crowd out the front."

She'd thought he'd been referring to the popularity of the food. She'd been wrong. As soon as she reached the corner, she found the mob of hungry paparazzi creating a barrier around Ryan, Felicity, and Hannah. The trio were snuggled close, the women framing Ryan as they all smiled for the cameras, lapping up the attention.

She continued forward, her feet carrying her to the edge of the crowd before she could contemplate the need to leave. It was stupid of her to think Ryan's invitation meant a quiet breakfast set for two. Instead, she'd been dragged into a publicity stunt, shoving what she couldn't have right in her face.

"Kiss her," a man shouted, raising his camera. "Give us something to put on the front page."

Her chest restricted as Ryan and Felicity chuckled. Hannah didn't hold their enthusiasm, but she stood tall, her smile waning. More calls erupted. A chant formed. "*Kiss her. Kiss her. Kiss her.*"

Panic seeped into Ryan's eyes, the same way Leah could feel it seep into hers. Felicity turned into him and blinked up at the man destined to place his mouth over hers.

Oh, no. Oh, no.

Leah dropped her head, unable to witness the carnage. *Shit.* She'd gone over this in her mind. Over and over. The kiss was inevitable. A forgone conclusion. The dedicated fans would take the relationship on face value. The highly intuitive would never believe. But those in the middle, the ones sitting on the fence, would need this push to send them into fanatic territory.

"Leah?"

Her chest restricted at his guttural call. She licked the dryness from her lips, pasted on a grin, and lifted her gaze to witness relief wash over him. He told her a myriad of messages in that look. She could see his pain, his guilt, and he hadn't even kissed the other woman yet.

"Have breakfast with us." His arm remained around Felicity, their bodies close.

The crowd parted, the vultures turning to capture her indecision with the snap, snap, snap of their cameras.

"No." She smiled, the expression awkward. "I only came to get a coffee to go."

"Don't be such a suit." This came from Hannah, her sure stride gliding forward. "Stay and have breakfast with us." She stopped at Leah's side and leaned in close. "We can get through this together."

Leah chuckled, pretending the whispered words in her ear were a sordid secret instead of mimicked heartache. "OK. But only for a few minutes."

The paparazzi repositioned their cameras, the click, click, click moving back to the happy couple. Questions were shouted as the four of them made their way inside, the non-stop flash following them to the counter manned by a wide-eyed waitress.

"Let the girls organize the seats." Ryan murmured over her shoulder. "I need to speak to you."

She frowned at the hand he placed on her arm and the assumptions it would bring from the people gawking at them. "Can't it wait?"

"No." He led her forward, his attention straying to the waitress. "We've got band issues we need to discuss. Do you have anywhere private we could talk?"

The young blonde looked between them, her words taking seconds to come out. "There's the bathrooms... Or the storage room, but staff will be coming in and out. Otherwise, there's only the covered parking lot out back. It's not entirely private but it's fenced in and you can't access it from the front of the building."

"Can you show us where it is?"

"No problem." The woman walked out from behind the counter, rubbing her hands on the apron tied around her waist.

"Are you sure this isn't something that can wait?" Leah slid her arm from his grip, well aware that even the kitchen staff were watching them.

"All I want is five minutes."

And all she wanted was to maintain a charade that was now harder to manage after witnessing his lips so close to another woman.

"Please," he added.

The fight left her shoulders and she sighed with defeat. Denying him was impossible, even when her career was in the firing line. She walked by him, following the waitress through a swinging staff-only entry into an empty hall.

"It's through here." The woman unlocked the deadbolt to the back door, exposing a carport filled with shaded vehicles. "You'll have to knock to get back in."

Leah nodded as she passed, descending the two steps to the asphalt.

"Thank you." Ryan followed behind, his voice still capable of sending a shiver along her spine. "We won't be long."

The door closed behind them, the clunk of the lock settling back into place.

"What's this about?"

He took the stairs in a lazy stride, his demeanor changing with each blink of her eyes. His anxiety faded, calculation taking its place.

"Ryan?"

His focus was on her lips, his teeth sinking into his own. "What, gorgeous?"

The compliment inspired goosebumps. It inspired a whole lot of unconscious bodily reactions. *Focus.* "Why are we alone in a parking lot?"

"For this." His hands found her cheeks, his mouth stole her breath.

She could've laughed with the predictability, but she didn't. Instead, she drowned in the taste of him, her lips brushing softly over his in a dance of affection. She didn't resist. Couldn't fight the instantaneous burn. She plastered herself against him, grasping what she'd gone without for days.

Like always, the world faded. Sense eluded her and nothing else mattered except for the anticipation of another press of his mouth against hers.

"I missed you," he murmured between kisses. "I didn't think you were going to come this morning."

"Is that why you started making a move on Felicity?" She winced as soon as the words hit her ears. "I'm sorry. I didn't mean it."

"It's justified." He stepped back, making her hollow. "I was hoping to get this bullshit with Felicity over and done with so it would stop eating me from the inside out."

"Don't explain. I could see how awful it was for you."

He turned from her, his hands in his hair, his head bowed. "It's even worse now that I know you were there. I feel like my asshole status has surpassed Mason's."

She chuckled, hoping to ease the tension. "That could never happen."

"Really?" He faced her, pinning her with his guilt. "Because I don't think he would ever sign up for the crap I'm putting you through."

"Hold up." She raised a hand. "I wasn't a blip on your radar when you signed up to help Blake out. And that's exactly what this is—*you helping Blake*...and the rest of the guys so there's no additional tour dates. This has nothing to do with me."

He looked up from under light lashes, his brow raised in disbelief. "You think you weren't a blip? Jesus, Leah, you've always been on my radar. If you only knew for how long, maybe you wouldn't consider me the great guy everyone keeps referring to. This has been going on well before my divorce was in play."

"You need to forget about me for a while and focus on why you're—"

"There's no way I could forget. Hell, I'd do anything just to get away from the jealousy, but it's impossible to ignore how I feel for you. Not until the end of the tour." He stepped forward. "Not for a week." He dragged her back into his arms. "Not even a day."

She stared up at him. "Why are you jealous? Is this about Drew? Seriously, you don't need to worry about him. Apparently, during my intoxicated binge, he decided he didn't want to go through my bag, so he shoved one of his shirts into my hands and pushed me into the bus bathroom to get changed. I dressed myse—"

"I'm not talking about Drew." His features scrunched. "Although, I'm damn relieved to hear it."

"Then why?" She placed her hands on his chest. "What's going on?"

He hit her with a sad smile, his gaze lowering, no longer meeting hers. His touch encased her wrist and he lifted her right hand between them.

"This."

He spread her fingers apart and she followed his focus to the tattoo exposed on the inside of her middle finger—three tiny black birds with outstretched wings.

"Do you think I'm not jealous of this?" His anguish hit her as their eyes met. "Do you think I haven't heard the stories about you and that guy in Vegas?" He dropped his hold and ran a weary hand over his beard. "He's all over your body, Leah. He's pierced you. Marked your skin. How can I not be jealous as hell over that?"

She closed her gaping mouth and swallowed. "I didn't think you—"

"Realized? Oh, I fucking realized. I heard the stories the weekend of Mitch's bachelor party. And when you took off after I kissed you, I knew you went to him. I could feel it." His Adam's apple bobbed. "Then you came back with his ink under your skin. The permanent reminder haunts me every damn time I look at you. And it's all because of my mistakes."

"No." She shook her head. "They're my mistakes. I was the one who couldn't handle the situation professionally. I failed. I could've stopped you from kissing me."

"Maybe." He gave a harsh chuckle. "But there was no way you were leaving that room without me making a fool of myself. That kiss was the only thing distracting me from opening my big mouth and telling you how I felt. Either way, I know you would've ended up running."

"I'm sorry." There was nothing left to say. Logan was a great guy, but he meant nothing to her. He'd been her catharsis during life's darkest days.

He'd been the needed distraction. And she'd made sure the heavily inked tattooist knew their connection was only physical.

"Don't be fucking sorry. We've both made enough apologies." He got in her face, his growl throaty. "All I want is for you to realize I will never hurt you. I can promise you that."

He warmed her, from the inside out. With his words. With his touch. With the hint of vulnerability in his tone that convinced her whole-heartedly of his sincerity. "I believe you."

"Good." His grin returned. "Because this wasn't what I came out here for." He cupped the back of her head, his forehead pressed to hers. "I missed you like hell."

She shuddered and closed her eyes. There was a reason why they shouldn't be doing this. But moving away wasn't an option her body or mind was willing to take. She wrapped her free hand around his neck and entwined their fingers with the other.

She'd thought she'd known this man, had believed all his secrets were hers. In reality, she didn't know the half of it. All those things she'd loved were far bigger, exponentially deeper. The reasons she'd fallen for him were now tenfold, and he'd already been irresistible.

"We should get back inside." She nuzzled into him, her nose brushing his as she closed her eyes. He smelled so good. Clean. Masculine. She sucked the scent deep into her lungs and released a tiny whimper with the need to exhale. "After one more kiss," she whispered, tilting her mouth over his.

She didn't hear his chuckle, but she felt it in the vibration of his chest, the renewed happiness ebbing from him to sink into her heart. His soft lips coaxed the connection to a new level, sweet and innocent turning into demand and hunger with deft flicks of his tongue. He loomed over her, his large frame backing her into the closest car, her ass sinking against the cool metal.

His erection nudged her pubic bone, causing another whimper. She was struggling to fight the need to strip him bare and have him right here in the parking lot. It wouldn't take long. Her pussy was already slick and ready to take him. The need for penetration may not even be necessary. The mere grind of his pelvis made her clit throb.

"If we don't leave soon," he panted, "I won't stop at a kiss."

"Then we should go..." It was hard to breathe, even harder to justify why this shouldn't go further. "But..."

He pulled his lips away, his gleaming eyes all she could see. "You want to keep going?" His hand seared her thigh, his fingers clawing higher, lifting her skirt with every inch.

Yes, she wanted to keep going. Yes, she needed to feel him inside her. Yes, oh yes, she ached for the orgasm already threateningly close. But...

She palmed his face, the prepared whisper of affirmation fading as self-preservation kicked in. "Tomorrow."

It was a promise, one that was denied with the firm shake of his head. "That's too far away."

"I'll make it worthwhile."

"Give me more than a day and I'll agree." He opened his eyes. "Give me the two days we have off between Kansas City and Tulsa. We can get some alone time while the rest of the guys are heading home. It'll be just the two of us."

"Tempting," she purred.

His hand climbed higher, reaching her panties. She gasped with the hard clench of her pussy and struggled to focus.

"Do we have a deal?"

One day she needed to learn a strategy to deny him. But today wasn't that day. "Yes." She nodded. "We have a deal."

He grinned, placing one last kiss on her lips before he lowered her panties in a flourish.

"What—"

"A souvenir," he explained, raising the material to hang between them. "Something to keep me company until I see you later tonight."

She pushed from the car. "And where's my souvenir?"

His grin turned to a smirk as he leaned back into her, the hardness of his shaft pressing against her. "This will have to do for now." His kiss curled her toes, the delicate sweep of his tongue along her lower lip in vast contrast to the high octane sex she was craving.

He left her in a mind-fog, so numb to anything other than pleasure that he had to tug her off the car to get her moving. They strode to the café's back door together, the tap of his knuckles nudging her professional mindset back into place.

"I'm not going to stay for breakfast." Seeing him with Felicity earlier was bad enough. She didn't want to have to witness their charade again on the way out. "I'll get a coffee and leave."

"I can't convince you to stay?"

"I don't want you to."

"You sure? I feel like we should be celebrating or something."

She snorted. "Celebrating?"

"It isn't a regular occurrence for me to almost make love in a parking lot."

She adored how he described it as love. Not sex. Not fucking. "Julie didn't enjoy spontaneity?"

"Julie didn't like much of anything." He gave a sad smile. "Suffice to say, I've never had any sort of sexual experience anywhere other than our home or a hotel room for years."

"*Bullshit.*" The denial came on an exhaled breath. "I don't believe it."

He reached over his shoulder and knocked louder on the door. "The lack of intimacy was never a warning sign because I had no previous conquests to compare our relationship to. Men always complain about a lack of sex, so I thought we were normal."

"Not wanting to have sex with you every second of every day isn't normal." She grinned. "In fact, it's damn crazy."

"Clearly." His lips curved. "I know that now."

The sound of footsteps approached from inside, her heart hammering with the upcoming conclusion to their conversation. She wanted to smash his sexual to-do list, signing her name against each sordid achievement. "What else haven't you done? I want to know it all. I want to do it all."

He leaned close, his lips brushing her ear as the loud clunk of the lock released. "I've never loved anyone as much as I love you."

Sixteen

RYAN STARED INTO THE ROLLING SEA OF PEOPLE BEFORE HIM, THE SWINGING overhead lights momentarily alighting parts of the moshing crowd. This is what he lived for—touring, music, inspiration—and yet the only sight he could see was Leah's image in his mind.

The two days apart had been a painful limbo. No matter how many times they messaged or spoke on the phone, he still couldn't convince himself she was in this for the long haul. He'd been on edge. Stressed. Annoyed. The usual banter from his friends had poked at his last nerve until he thought he'd snap. Then he'd seen her again. He'd kissed her. He'd almost taken her against a car in a café parking lot. And now he was on the other side of the spectrum. Thrumming. Adrenaline-filled. Pumped.

His final words at the café had made her blush. Those flawless cheeks had turned pink, her kiss-darkened lips had parted, and those gorgeous eyes widened. It was seconds of pure heaven before the waitress opened the door and stole the moment.

Now he was back to the emotional rollercoaster. Had he said too much, too soon? Was his time with Felicity likely to ruin his chances? Should he have taken her underwear out of his pocket before walking on stage? The damn material was burning a hole through his pants, the warmth sinking straight into his dick.

He was lucky the set list came naturally, otherwise Mason wouldn't think twice about shoving him into the waiting arms of a cannibalistic crowd. The woman was driving him crazy. Literally. He was analyzing everything like a love-drunk fool. Especially her last cryptic text message— *I'll be making an appearance during the show. Play along.*

He didn't know what the last sentence meant. Or the first for that matter. She didn't make a habit of watching their shows, and she certainly didn't stand side-stage...although the thought of her hiding in the wings made blood surge to inappropriate places that shouldn't be active while in front of an audience of thousands.

"...*Kiss goodbye to your heart, sunshine. It's time to make you mine,*" Mason sang the closing line to the third last song in their set, making the sea before them erupt. Usually Sean would fall into the fast tempo beat of their next song, but instead Mason sliced a hand across his throat, indicating for them to hold up as he turned back to face the crowd.

"How you feeling, Chicago? Enjoying the show?"

The usual cacophony of noise responded—screams, whistles, cries, the offers of first-born children.

"We're about to end the night with one of my favorite songs—" boos erupted "—but before we do that, I wanted to thank all those who helped our band manager with a special surprise tonight."

Ryan's stomach twisted. It didn't take much these days to wring him dry.

"Have you met the smokin' hot Leah Gorman yet?" Mason glanced side-stage and held out an arm for the flawless woman approaching with a huge wrapped box in her arms. "Come out here, boss lady."

Now his stomach was dropping, the hollow organ sinking to his feet. He couldn't stop himself from hungrily taking in the sight of her. His mouth dried in an instant as his focus glided over the black pumps accentuating muscled calves, to the knee-high charcoal business dress that fit her perfect body like a second skin, up to the perfection of her face adorned in light make-up. Had she taken the time to put on new underwear? Or was she bare, the smooth skin of her pussy easily accessible beneath her professional attire?

Fuck. He repositioned the base of his guitar to ensure the most enthusiastic part of his body was covered from all angles.

"Don't be fooled by her aesthetic appeal." Mason took the package from her hands to place it on the floor beside the microphone stand. "This woman can shrink a man's balls with the raise of a brow."

Leah inclined her head with a nod to the cheering crowd, unfazed by the taunts from the lead singer.

"You might also like to know this saucy lady has worked more stick than a NASCAR racer." Mason chuckled. "Ain't that right, honey?"

Shit. Ryan's pulse tanked, the excitement of his dick evaporating under the humiliation Mason was dishing out. He'd kill the bastard. He'd fucking slay him.

He reached for his own mic, determined to retaliate when a hand came around his shoulder. He turned to Mitch standing at his side and pulled out the ear monitor that was making it impossible to hear what was being said through the guy's moving lips.

"—your shit together. You're making your feelings pretty obvious by the look on your face."

Ryan turned his back to the microphone and glared. "He's making a fool of her in front of thousands of people."

"She can take it."

"She shouldn't *have to take it*," he growled, the harsh sound unfamiliar to his own ears. "This is bullshit."

"Thanks for the warm introduction, Mason," Leah commanded the attention of everyone in the stadium, her voice too damn confident and sexy to be broadcasted in public. "I'm not going to hold up the performance any longer than necessary. All I wanted to do was thank those who made their way to the special table we had set up near the main doors to the building. Your participation is appreciated."

Mason picked up the box off the floor and leaned into the microphone. "Blake, get your ass over here."

Ryan turned to the tattooed bass guitarist, focusing anywhere other than the man who was provoking the need for bloodshed. Blake eyed Leah skeptically as he took steps toward the front of the stage.

"As you know," she continued, "the first Reckless baby is due to enter the world in mere weeks, and all of us couldn't be happier." She held out a hand, wordlessly asking for Blake's guitar so Mason could hand over the package.

"What are you guys up to?" Blake handed over his instrument and took the box. "I don't like surprises."

"This is a present from our Chicago fans to congratulate you on your upcoming parenthood."

The man with harsh spiked hair and heavily inked skin seemed to fracture before everyone's eyes, his face crumpling like tissue paper. He bent over, tore the wrapping from the box and opened the cardboard to peer inside. A smile tweaked his lips as he pulled out a large teddy bear, the material of its body adorned in permanent markers of all colors.

"Wow." He glanced from Leah to Mason. "You guys are unbelievable." He placed the bear under one arm and pulled out another item from the box—a large, soft, green blanket.

"Fans had the choice to either sign their name on the teddy or have it embroidered on the blanket. A local seamstress has been working non-stop since the start of the show to get as many names as possible on there."

Blake shook his head, eying both the items in awe. "Fucking hell, guys." He sniffed. "You need to pre-warn me about this shit so I don't ruin my bad boy image."

Leah leaned close and pressed a kiss to his cheek. Whispered words were shared that no one else could hear while Mason reclaimed the microphone stand.

"Come on, Leah, his stick is already taken. And you don't want to make your Las Vegas lover jealous, do you?" Mason chuckled as he turned to the crowd. "A piece of Reckless trivia for you all—Did you know our saucy band manager had her clit pierced as a dare during Mitch's wife's bachelorette party?"

Leah stiffened, her spine jerking ramrod straight. Her gaze met Ryan's, a glimpse of regret hitting him head on as she began walking toward him. He didn't know what to do. Didn't know if he should show his cards and defend her. Or laugh it off. Or even encourage the humor to draw attention away from his cloying feelings.

Play along, she'd said. Was this what she meant?

She got within feet of him and Mitch, her eyes stark as she grabbed his microphone. "Mason, I'm sure the crowd doesn't want to hear about my past." She glanced over her shoulder hitting the lead singer with a lethal smile. "But maybe you could tell them about the time you fell for a cross dresser and almost became a bi-sexual without your knowledge."

The mic drop wasn't literal, but figuratively she threw the device to the ground and gave a checkmate smirk before stalking from the stage.

He watched her leave, the sound of his heavily pounding chest unheard over the hysteria from the crowd.

"She's OK." Mitch's voice barely carried over the insanity. "Focus on getting through the next two songs. You can kill him later."

Focus? He wasn't sure he knew how anymore. Leah seemed to strip the ability from him, making thought and sense impossible.

Ryan gave a jerky nod and placed his in-ear monitor back in place.

"I think that's my cue to get this show back on the road." Mason lifted his chin in Sean's direction, signaling the drummer to lead them into the next song.

"You sure you don't want to share the story?" Sean asked. "It sounds like they'd love to hear it."

"Start the fucking song," Mason growled, cupping the stand in front of him.

There was a chuckle and then the intro beat to *Devil Woman*. Ryan stood motionless, his fingers unmoving as the band played through the first chorus without him. He was numb. Lost to Leah's humiliation. Lost to his own. He didn't want the world invested in her relationship with another man. He didn't want their focus on something that ended months ago.

He wanted the acknowledgement Blake had with Gabi. Or Mitch with Alana. Mason with Sidney. Sean with Melody. He was sick of being left out. First, he'd been the only married guy surrounded by singles. Then the tables turned. Now he was finally on an even level, yet his feelings for Leah were ignored.

Mason shot him a look as he sang, the silent question answered with a hard glare. Ryan didn't hold back his frustration. It was clear for his so-called friend to see. The lead singer dipped his head, the small acknowledgement of the upcoming shit-storm taken without a pause in his voice.

Asshole. Fucking asshole.

Ryan should've walked from the stage. Should've, but didn't. Instead, he glided his fingers over his guitar strings and joined in with the chorus, trying to focus on getting lost in the music. Minutes later, the song ended without a dint in his frustration. The encore didn't calm him either. When the final note was strummed and the last lyric echoed through innumerable speakers, he strode for Jack, his guitar tech, dumping his instrument in the guy's hands.

"You'll have to share those stories about Leah," Jack joked as Ryan untangled the wires leading to the battery pack hooked on to his pants. "I'm not surprised about the piercing. She seems like the kinky type."

"Stupid, fucking Mason," he muttered under his breath, the words inaudible above the crowd's waning cheers.

The man in question walked by, entering the darkness of side-stage as Ryan handed over the ear-monitor equipment. This wouldn't end well. He knew it even before he started striding after him. Even before he caught up and opened his mouth to yell, "What the fuck was that about?"

Ryan still wasn't sure why he did it, but his foot came out without warning, shoving between Mason's legs as he continued forward. His friend stumbled, taking three steps to right himself as he ran into the backstage door.

"What the fuck was that about?" Ryan repeated.

Mason turned and grinned, appearing more impressed than annoyed. "I could ask the same fucking question. Did you just try to trip me? Like a five-year-old?" He reached for the door handle and pulled it open, slinking into the bright light of the hall leading to the dressing rooms.

"Fuck you." Ryan didn't do violence. He didn't want to be *that guy*. But clearly, what he wanted didn't play a part in the current situation. "Do I really need to threaten to break your pretty face before you'll take me seriously?"

"You couldn't mess with my prettiness even if you tried." Mason stopped inside the empty hall, the door easing shut behind them. "But it's nice to finally see some enthusiasm. I wasn't sure if you knew how to fight for a woman after all those pitiful years with Julie."

Fucker.

Mason was right. He was so right Ryan slammed his forearm against the asshole's throat and backed him into the wall from the humiliation of it. He *hadn't* been enthusiastic for years. There'd been no emotion, no excitement. And now it was all pressing down on him, tenfold. He couldn't breathe through the need to defend Leah. He couldn't think past the necessity to make Mason pay.

"Why did you do that to her?" he demanded.

The door opened behind him, Blake, Mitch, and Sean coming to stand at his sides.

Mason rolled his eyes. "She asked for it."

"She asked for it?" He pressed his arm harder. All it did was increase Mason's smirk.

"Back off, Ryan," Blake drawled, his voice lacking emotion.

"That's it?" Mason tipped his head to the side, glancing behind Ryan's shoulder. "That's all the help I get?"

"Pretty much," Mitch offered. "I'm kinda hoping he clocks you before Leah gets the chance. The lesser of two evils and all that."

"How did she ask for it?" Ryan pressed his free hand against Mason's shoulder. "What the hell could she have done to deserve that?"

"You don't get it." Mason snickered. "She asked for it. *Literally.*" He shoved at Ryan's chest, reclaiming freedom. "If you've got issues, you need to bring it up with her."

"What's going on?" The familiar feminine voice carried down the hall, her authoritative tone shooting up his spine like a firecracker.

For once, he didn't immediately turn to face her. He didn't want to see her. More specifically, he didn't want to be seen *by her*. Not when he couldn't control all the shit clogging his veins. It'd been so long since he'd had anything to protect. Anything to cling to. Fight for. He was becoming lost in the delirium of panic.

"Can you guys give us a minute?" Her question came from beside him, followed by mutters of agreement. "And don't think I'm not going to tear you a new one later, Mason."

The four of them started down the hall, Blake, Mitch, and Sean all bumping or throwing soft punches at the lead singer before they disappeared into the dressing room and closed the door behind them.

"Are you going to tell me what that was about?"

"You need to ask?" He didn't mean to snap. *Fuck.* He couldn't help it.

"You had an entire stadium laughing at you. Judging you. And now Mason tells me you asked him to do it?"

She remained quiet for long seconds. Not long enough to encourage him to drag his attention from the chipped paint of the cement wall.

"Our time alone this morning didn't go unnoticed. One of the gossip sites that ran the initial photos of you and Felicity, mentioned us hiding out in a back room. I didn't want any assumptions to be made. We can't risk someone latching onto the possibility and digging deeper until they find the truth. So yes, I asked Mason to help divert the topic of my promiscuity in another direction. And, as usual, he used creative license and took the request way beyond my instruction."

Motherfucking asshole.

"He needs to pay."

"No." She stepped closer, her slight frame taking up his periphery. "We all know what he's like. Mason deflects emotion. Instead of showing he cares, he turns his feelings into a joke. It's what he does. It's what all of them do."

"His bullshit attitude isn't a defense."

"Ryan." Her tone was guttural as she slid in front of him, leaning down to meet his gaze. There was something in her eyes, something that put him on edge and built his concern with every blink of her lashes. "This—" she waved a hand between them, "—is exactly why there's a clause in my contract. Your feelings for me can't get in the way of my position or your friendship with the rest of the band. This reaction, and ones like it, will be the reason why I have to walk away."

He stepped back, unable to mask the horror contorting his face. "So I quit caring and ignore how ten thousand fans are now talking about you and some tattoo artist from Vegas?" He squeezed his eyes shut. "*Jesus.* I need fresh air."

The after-show adrenaline was getting to him. The accompanying ton of emotional baggage on top of it was unbearable. He made for the end of the hall, not wanting to take his instability out on her.

"Please don't be angry with me," she called after him.

"I'm not angry with you." He stopped. "But I also can't pretend like tonight was a walk in the park."

She strode forward and lowered her voice. "Then take it out on me. It's my fault. Not Mason's."

A derisive scoff escaped his lips.

"Please, Ryan."

"Fine."

"Fine?"

"Yep." He threw his arms up in the air. "I'll take it out on you. But it'll be on my bus. Tonight."

She shook her head. "You know I can't do that. Especially not now."

"Then don't ask me not to take this further with the asshole who humiliated you."

"Let me get this straight." She cocked a hand against her hip. "You're trying to manipulate me to get me on your bus tonight?"

"On my bus. In my bed." He shrugged. "Either I take it up with you or I take it up with Mason. And I sure as shit won't be using the same techniques."

His angry expression subsided with the quirk of her lips.

"I don't like Mason enough to risk getting caught."

"Then I'll take it up with him. Let the fucker know I'll be waiting on the bus."

•••

Leah watched him walk away, her feet refusing to move until he turned the corner and vanished from sight. She'd never cared about the ire she'd previously earned from the guys when she had to make tough band decisions. But this was different. This was emotional and exactly what she needed to remove herself from ASAP.

She dragged herself to the dressing room door and knocked once, not bothering to wait for a response before she walked inside.

"Where's Mason?"

"Hiding in the shower." Blake rubbed a towel through his wet hair. He was naked from the waist up, displaying a new tattoo over his collarbone that read "She stole my heart but made me whole," in delicate font.

"Where's Ryan?" Sean sank into one of the arm chairs, a clean towel waiting in his lap.

"He said he needed fresh air."

Mitch winced. "He wasn't happy on stage. I thought I was going to have to hold him back from ripping Mason's head off."

It was her fault for not warning him. Her text message wasn't good enough. Then again, she'd never expected him to flip from the calm, caring man she knew, into someone overrun with aggression. "Can you please keep an eye on him? Let him know you're supporting him."

Blake tugged a clean shirt over his head. "To be honest, Leah, I don't think it's us he needs."

She winced, not appreciating the affirmation of her own thoughts. "I can't be enough for him right now. He's got the paparazzi all over him due to the divorce and this crap with Slicker. I should be keeping my distance."

"Is his old lady still stalling with the divorce proceedings?" Sean asked.

Mitch nodded. "I overheard him talking with his lawyer last night. She's not letting up and refuses to negotiate any further until she can see him in person."

"Seems like a dick move to me." Blake came to her side and gave her shoulder a squeeze. "It'd only make me more adamant to give her nothing."

She leaned into the embrace, thankful for the connection. "She must be working another angle."

The bathroom door opened and Mason stepped forward through a wall of steam, a towel wrapped around his waist. "A displeasure to see you, as always, Leah." He made for the duffle resting on the couch and pulled out a set of clothes. "Thanks for shoving me into a media nightmare. I'm going to have every vulture worldwide wanting the details of the cross dresser who tried to ram my dick down his throat."

"Tried to ram your dick down his throat?" Sean laughed. "I wonder how your hard dick escaped your pants in the first place."

"Let me remind you that you pushed first." Leah crossed her arms over her chest. "You should know by now that I'll bury you in return."

"Yeah, I think the upcoming year filled with bi-sexual headlines will firmly cement that in my mind." He glanced around the room. "Where's Bennett?"

"Getting some air. Nice job causing him more stress, asshole." Sean pushed to his feet and disappeared into the bathroom.

"This is my fault?" Mason dropped the towel, his ass on full display before he tugged on his underwear and jeans. "I was told to divert attention away from you and lover boy. In what way did I fail?"

"You didn't fail," Leah muttered. "I just wish you'd all realize how hard his life is at the moment. The only constant in his world is the four of you, and most of the time you're all too busy or preoccupied to consider how he's feeling."

"We're not too busy or preoccupied." Mason turned to her, fastening his belt. "It's a guy thing. We don't do deep and meaningful shit or bond over chick flicks. We decompress in other ways."

"For example?"

He pulled a collared shirt over his head. "We divert attention away from the crap he can't control. We play devil's advocate so he has someone to take his anger out on. We give him the freedom to lose his shit if he needs to. We don't hover over his shoulder and make everyone aware that he's struggling."

She sighed, knowing all the times he'd said 'we' should've been 'I.' "I understand that you're more comfortable saving the day by hiding under your Captain Asshole persona, but Ryan's not like most of you. He needs friendship. He needs someone to talk to. He needs—"

"Does he?" Mason raised a brow. "Or is that what Julie shaped him to need? Because I sure as shit remember him being one of us when we first started out. It wasn't until after they were married, and she sank her nails in, that he turned soft."

"He's not soft," Blake muttered.

"No, he's not." Leah glared at Mason. "You need to stop treating him like a leper just because he thinks and feels differently than you."

"That's where you're wrong. Am I the only one who remembers who Ryan used to be? Who he was before his wife changed him?" It was Mason's turn to hit her with a feral stare. "Yeah, he's always been the Romeo of the group—the charming son of a bitch who knew how to sweet-talk. But before he was shoved under the thumb, he used to party like the rest of us. He used to get into fights and swear like a trucker and not give a shit about upsetting everyone." He stabbed a finger at his chest. "I, for one, am not going to sit around and stop the old Ryan from making a comeback. You're too busy trying to keep him in the box Julie created, while I'm trying to help him escape that hell hole."

Leah blinked, once, twice.

As much as Mason drove her to insanity with his carelessness, he was far more emotional than he let on. And he was right, Ryan had been different back when she'd first met him. He was never the seducer or the egotistical manipulator. But he'd been more alive. More energetic. More like the man she'd spent time with over the past week—the man she'd originally fallen for. She just hadn't realized until Mason pointed it out.

"OK," she mumbled. "Then what would you suggest to make things easier on him?"

"It's simple. Give him what he wants."

She swallowed, remembering what his most recent request had been.

Mason latched onto the sight, his eyes narrowing, his lips quirking. "What does he want, Leah?"

Damn him.

His smirk grew with the knowledge in his eyes. "Leah?"

"He wants me on your bus."

"There you go." He dusted his hands together as if his work here was done. "An easy fix for tonight's drama."

"No." She shook her head. "It's not an easy fix. Not when anyone seeing me get on or off your bus will immediately make assumptions."

"You're thinking too much into it." Mitch grabbed a towel from the pile in the corner of the room and leaned on the counter beside the bathroom door. "You're our manager, of course you're going to spend nights on our bus when we've got business to discuss."

"What about the driver? I won't risk anyone else finding out, and it's not like Ryan wants me on-board so we can sing Kumbaya."

"Pat will be fine. He's signed a confidentiality agreement like the rest of the crew, and most of the time he has his earphones in to give us privacy." Mason lugged his duffle off the couch and moved to the corner of the room to grab another off the floor. "It's my own ears I'm worried about."

She shuddered. The thought of them overhearing anything intimate between her and Ryan wasn't pleasing to her either.

"I think it's a good idea," Mitch offered. "With Alana back at her mother's retreat until we take a break back home, it'll be good to have another female onboard."

"As long as you're OK with it, Lee-lee." Blake pinned her, his eyes asking innumerable questions. "Is this what *you* want?"

It was. She wanted to spend every waking moment with Ryan. To be unrestricted and unfazed by external influences. But there was something she wanted above all else. "More than anything, I want him to be happy."

"Then you've got your answer." Mason headed for the door, a duffle bag hanging over each shoulder. "Go get your shit and we'll meet him at the parking lot."

Seventeen

RYAN LEANED OVER, PEERING OUT THE BUS WINDOW. MASON AND LEAH HAD exited the stadium, the pair parting ways as they headed toward two different buses.

The cold shower had calmed him, at least enough to realize he owed her an apology. One that should come face to face, preferably with more material covering his body. For now, the towel would have to do. His suitcase was packed somewhere beneath the bus and his duffle was still in the dressing room.

He walked down the aisle, his attention now on Mason who had stopped in his tracks.

"*Leah.*" The Reckless front man's shout was loud enough to draw the attention of the nearby crew and stadium staff. "Hurry up and get your shit. We need to go over this contract before I can catch some Zs."

Contract? Ryan leaned over the small booth dining table, trying to catch a glimpse of the woman in question. No luck. She'd walked out of view, teasing his senses from afar. He was still snooping when Mason climbed onto the bus, taking the three steps in his stride before stopping at the start of the aisle.

"Let me have it." Mason spread his arms wide, two duffels swinging at his sides. "Get it off your chest."

Ryan straightened. "I've got nothing to say." Nothing helpful, anyway.

Mason gave a casual nod. "Fair enough." He lowered a shoulder and grabbed the duffle strap before it fell. "Peace offering?"

"Thanks." He accepted his bag and dropped it to the floor to go in search of clean clothes. "What contract do you need to go over with Leah?" He felt like a dick for asking, for snooping, but he couldn't help wanting to know everything where she was concerned.

"There's no contract." Mason stepped over him and shoved a duffle into the narrow storage cupboard beside the first column of bunks. "She said you wanted her on the bus, but she was worried about people asking questions. I just gave her an alibi."

"Thanks." The word was grated, not entirely forthcoming.

"Consider it another peace offering." Mason continued walking. "If you need me, I'll be hiding in the back, watching TV and hoping for temporary deafness."

Ryan fought a smile as he bundled a set of clean clothes in his arms and shoved to his feet. The rest of the band climbed onto the bus behind him, Blake, Mitch, and Sean trailing in a row.

"I need a drink." Mitch slid his duffle along the ground and pulled open the fridge. "You want one, Ry?"

"You guys aren't going to chew me out first?" Ryan tugged his underwear on beneath the towel, then his sweats. He'd find a shirt later.

"Chew you out for what?" Blake squeezed past. "Not taking a swing at Mason when you had the chance?"

"It was definitely a missed opportunity." Sean pulled the fridge door wider, sliding an arm past Mitch to grab a beer.

"I lost my cool," he admitted. "It shouldn't have happened."

"I hate to break it to you, bro, but you've never been cool." Mitch pulled two drinks from the fridge and closed the door with a nudge of his elbow.

More jokes. More laughter. Ryan supposed he should be thankful for the lack of accountability. He probably would've been if it didn't increase his guilt.

He dragged his feet to the storage cupboard, shoved his bag inside, and came back to take the beer from Mitch's outstretched arm. "Thanks." He twisted the top and took a long pull, his gaze straying to the beauty making her way up the bus stairs.

Sean temporarily blocked his view as he passed, making it impossible to anticipate what mood she was in. "I'll be out back with Mace if you guys need me."

Ryan nodded and cocked a hip against the bunks as Leah made her way toward him, her overnight bag on one shoulder, her handbag over the other. She wasn't smiling, wasn't glaring either.

"Do you still want me here?" her voice was soft, but it didn't offer them privacy, not when Blake and Mitch were sitting around the booth seat in silence and he was yet to hear the television turn on at the back of the bus.

"The answer to that will always be yes." He pretended they didn't have an audience, that his words were only heard by her.

She nodded. "Where do you want me to put my bags?"

"Anywhere. There's room in the storage cupboard if you want me to stack them."

"Let me get a change of clothes first. I need to have a quick shower before we get on the road." She lowered her bag to the floor and riffled through the contents, coming out with nightwear and a small beauty bag. "That should be all I need." She straightened, her belongings clutched to her chest.

Lucky her. His needs were far more extravagant. The post-show adrenaline demanded action. What action, he wasn't entirely sure. He wrapped an arm around her waist and pulled her close. "Forgive me for losing my mind?"

Her breathy chuckle brushed his lips. "Don't worry, I think mine is equally lost."

"Yeah?"

"Yeah." Her gaze lowered. "You being shirtless doesn't help."

"I'm happy for you to even the score."

Her laughter did crazy things to him. He wanted to sink into the sound. To bottle it and keep it with him forever.

"You don't think the guys would mind?"

"I wouldn't protest," Sean called out.

Her lips quirked. "We have absolutely no privacy here."

"Not an ounce," Blake confirmed.

She rolled her eyes and stepped back. "I'm going to have a shower."

Ryan extended his arm with her movement, not releasing his hold. "Need any help?"

"No." She reached for his beer and took a sip, the liquid moistening her lips. "But I'd love if you had a drink waiting for me once I get out."

"Can do." He dropped his hand, already hating the distance, and strode for the front of the bus. It was going to be a long night if he couldn't 007 some private time. There was no way Leah would be sleeping in a different bunk, but what they did in that bunk, while surrounded by eavesdroppers, was another question.

"We all set for Kansas City?" Pat climbed aboard and sank into the driver's seat. "Speak now or forever hold your peace."

"Yeah." Ryan slid into the booth beside Blake. "Just try and take the turns easy. Leah's about to have a shower."

"Leah?" Pat glanced over his shoulder. "Shit. I guess I've gotta stick to the speed limit now."

"I'll pretend I didn't hear that," she called from the bathroom.

The bus door closed and the engine burred to life. The steady vibrations coursing through the cushioned seat didn't help his surge in blood flow. The pulsation damn near killed him. He wondered how long he should wait. One minute? Two? Joining her in the shower was inevitable.

"Don't bother." Mitch placed his beer on the table. "I've tried getting some bathroom action before and it isn't worth it. You can barely turn in the shower, let alone swing a dick. Save it until she gets out."

Ryan glanced over his shoulder to Pat. The driver already had his headphones in place, the music loud enough for him to hear the garbled noise over the hum of the engine. "Don't forget we're trying to keep this under wraps."

"Don't worry. He can't hear a thing."

They were on the road in minutes, the cityscape going unnoticed as he kept his gaze trained on the bathroom door.

"So you're really doing this," Blake murmured. "Doing *her*, I mean."

He took another swig, and raised a brow. "It's a bit late to be askin', isn't it?"

"Don't get your cock in a twist." Blake landed an elbow to Ryan's ribs. "I just thought you and Felicity might be a thing..."

"No." He cringed. "Not even close."

"So you're all in with Leah?"

"If this is the lead up to warning me away, you can save your breath." He looked Blake head-on. "I have no intention of hurting her."

"It's not her I'm worried about. She's got bigger balls than all of us. I'm more concerned you've taken on a challenge you're not prepared for."

He glanced back at the bathroom door, willing it to open. "I can handle it." At least he hoped he could. Tonight wasn't a good indicator. His emotions were continuing to spiral, the excitement and frustration over being alone with her a building force. But there was Julie to think about. Grander. Felicity. The paparazzi. Leah's career. The list was endless.

"Don't bite off more than you can chew."

He smirked, an expression borne of determination, not confidence. "Don't worry. I'm a big eater."

The click of the bathroom door drew him to his feet. He grabbed a beer from the fridge, twisted the lid and slid back into the seat as she approached in a thin, loose sweatshirt and a pair of cotton shorts. Her hair was loose, her pretty face devoid of make-up. Casual, yet undeniably perfect.

Mitch patted the seat beside him and she sank into the offering, her gaze flittering from one man to the next. "What were you talking about?"

He smirked through another gulp from his bottle. "The weather."

"The weather?" She gave a coy smile. "Interesting." She grasped the beer in front of her and sipped, her tongue working her bottom lip in a slow sweep. "What's the forecast?"

Blake snickered. "I think it's going to get steamy."

"And wet," Mitch added.

Her lips twitched. "I find it hard to believe the two of you are in grown-up relationships."

"Uh huh." Blake nodded. "We get to see real boobies."

She rolled her eyes with a chuckle. "How is Gabi?"

"Round and glowing and absolutely beautiful." He grinned. "She's going to be a phenomenal mother."

"I agree. The two of you will make great parents."

"And what about you?" Mitch slid his arm along the back of the booth seat. "Do you plan on having brats of your own?"

"Not anytime soon."

Ryan swallowed over the spike in awareness. He couldn't deny the instinct to fill his woman with babies. If able, he'd give her a houseful of the little rug-rats. "You'd be a good mother. A hard-ass, but a great mother all the same."

She met his focus and took a pull of her beer. "I'm too selfish. It's different for guys. You don't have to contemplate the loss of a career, or income. Then there's the lack of freedom. I also like my body the way it is."

He lowered his attention to her neck, her chest, then back up again. "I like your body the way it is, too."

There was a beat of heavy silence before Blake cleared his throat. "This conversation took a sharp turn into fucking-awkward."

Her cheeks darkened as she took another long pull.

"Stop eye fucking," Mitch muttered. "You're making me uncomfortable."

Those high cheeks turned a deeper shade of pink. "I think that's my cue to call it a night." She pushed the half empty bottle of beer toward him. "Can you finish this for me?"

He jutted his chin in confirmation as she slid from the booth.

"Which bunk do I take?"

"Bottom left."

"That's the vacant bunk?"

He raised the beer to his mouth and did the opposite to Mitch's request—eye-fucking the hell out of her. "For the moment."

Her amiable smile turned seductive. A huge curve of luscious lips. That expression made his world stop. His thoughts quiet. Everything else was static. He wanted to wake up to that sight. To fall asleep to it. He wanted to be the cause of every curve of lips and devilish sparkle in her eyes.

"Good night, all." She started down the aisle and pulled the curtain across to shield the sleeping area from view.

It took five seconds for him to down the remainder of his beer. Another five to finish hers.

"I've got a spare pair of socks if you need them." Mitch slid from the booth, disposed of his empty bottle, and grabbed a new one from the fridge.

"Socks?"

"To shove in her mouth. You never know how loud they're gonna be."

He snorted, the bottle swishing into the plastic liner before thunking to the bottom. "She's not that loud… Only when I want her to be."

There was another pause, another contemplative silence.

"You two have already fucked?" Blake asked.

Mitch sat forward, resting his elbows on the table. "When the hell did that happen?"

"I don't kiss and tell."

"No shit." Blake's eyes were wide. "But come on, man, you've gotta give us something. Is she as high-strung in the sack? Or is she crazy good?"

The two speculated among themselves while Ryan mentally relived the first night he'd spent with her. Was she high-strung? Hell, no. Nothing was off limits. No place on her body went untouched, no expanse of skin untasted. He'd done things with her, *to* her, that he'd never done with anyone before. So, no. She wasn't high strung.

Was she crazy good? He chuckled to himself. He'd never been a guy who was owned by his desires. Not until that night. She'd taken his barely functioning libido and injected it with steroids. She made him daydream about dirty shit he never would've previously fantasized about. Leah had successfully found his switchboard and turned all the dials to heightened settings.

"Fuck," Blake was gawking at him now, his jaw slack. "She's kinky, isn't she?" He glanced at Mitch. "Check out the dazed look in his eyes. My boy's hooked a nympho."

Ryan smirked. "Like I said, I don't kiss and tell." He slid from the booth, ignoring their muttered curses as he strode behind the curtain. Each of the bunks was screened, the heavy material the only privacy.

"Try to keep it down." Mason called from the television area, his face alight from the glow of the screen. "Some of us don't want to be scarred for life."

"Some of us never have the choice when traveling with you."

"Retaliation is beneath you," Mason drawled. "You're better than that."

Better and more concerned about his bedpartner's reputation.

He didn't even think Leah would be up for more than a massive cock tease. Not that he'd complain. He was happy to abide by her professional boundaries. He wouldn't even protest if she wanted him sleeping in a different bunk as long as he got a few minutes one on one.

He flung back the screen to the bottom bunk, his train of thought flying away with the gesture.

Hot damn.

She was lying on her side in nothing but a black lace bra and panties, her hair cascading over a pillow clutched to her chest. She was beautiful. All perfect, creamy skin and curves he wanted to sink his teeth into. She was nothing short of the most mesmerizing sight he'd ever seen. And he didn't want to ruin it. He didn't want to climb in beside her and strip this moment from his life.

"How long do you plan on staring?" she whispered.

He gripped the bunk above, holding tight to the wood in an effort to focus. His dick was surging, the throb down south not even close to the pound in his chest. "As long as you let me." He crouched beside the bunk, sinking to eye level. "Knowing you're like this, for me, doesn't give me an incentive to rush."

She raised a brow. "Knowing your bandmates are mere feet away, listening, should encourage you to move faster."

"Point taken." He crawled onto the single mattress, hovering near the edge so he didn't crowd her. "You're beyond beautiful, Leah." He savored the sight of her, from the hair strewn across her shoulders, to the curve of her cleavage, the smooth waist, to her delicious thighs.

"You make me feel beautiful. And it's not your words that convince me. It's your eyes." The tender column of her neck convulsed with a swallow. "You make the world disappear when you look at me."

"That's because you are my world. You're everything." He raised his hand, letting his finger trail the same path his gaze had taken—hair, cleavage, waist, thighs. Goosebumps erupted over her skin, making all the creamy flesh pebble beneath his touch.

"I want to believe that."

"What's stopping you?"

Her slender shoulder budged with a tiny shrug. "There are a lot of things vying for your attention at the moment."

"And you're the only one I want to focus on." He leaned in, nipped her shoulder, and closed his eyes at her fast intake of breath before he lightly sucked the sting away. "Do you forgive me for flipping out earlier?"

"Mmm." She nodded, her hands finding his shoulders. "But it can't happen again."

He wouldn't make any promises. Not where Mason was concerned. "I'll make it up to you on our days off." He nuzzled her neck, her chin. "I have big plans to steal your clothes and hold you hostage in my hotel room."

Her muscles tensed. It wouldn't have been a noticeable reaction if he wasn't right on top of her, breathing her in, feeling every movement. "What is it?" He pulled back and released his tight hold on hope when he found her cringing.

"I can't spend the days off with you."

He inched further back, a little destroyed, a little humiliated.

"I need to go to New York with the rest of the guys."

"When did you decide this?"

Her fingers crept toward his beard, the tentative stroke leading along his jaw. "Two seconds ago."

He frowned, unsure what he'd done in the last breath to make her break their plans.

"I want to go back and tell my boss I'm in love with you." She swallowed again, deep and audible. "I'm going to beg to have my contract changed."

His smile was involuntary, along with the surge of affection pulsing through him from head to toe. "I'm not..." He shook his head, clearing the fuzz. "I'm not sure I heard you right. What did you say?"

Her cheeks darkened again, her blush returning to do unfathomable things to his self-esteem.

"I love you, Ryan." Her grin was bashful. "And I want to sort out the problems with my boss as soon as possible. I want to get it out of the way, then focus on doing the same with Felicity, so we can finally be together. Properly."

"Damn," he whispered. Damn, damn, damn. He'd been right weeks ago. He knew all his problems would dissolve if he was with her. He'd known, yet he never fully contemplated how freeing it would feel to have her love.

"What?" She chuckled. "You didn't think I was in love with you?"

"I'd hoped... I'd dreamed." He kissed her, a brief press of lips. "But no, I never thought I'd be lucky enough to hear those words."

"It's not luck." She closed her eyes, her words drifting into his mouth. "It's fate."

"You believe in all that?"

"I do now." She crept into him, deepening the kiss. First, it was the increased pressure of their lips, then it was their tongues. She nudged into him, their pelvises aligning, the hard length of his cock rubbing against smooth warmth as he teetered on the edge of the bunk.

Her fingernails trailed down his back, to his waist, then the elastic of his sweatpants. Her gaze met his as she tugged, wordlessly demanding him to undress.

"You sure you want to do this here?"

"This isn't the time for chivalry, Ryan." She smashed her mouth over his, her tongue parting his lips and delving deep. "Get your clothes off."

He couldn't remove them fast enough. He was wriggling, flexing, contorting, trying to get naked without elbowing her in the face. His sweatpants were around his knees when her palm grazed along the underwear covering his cock. He hissed in a breath, jerked, and felt himself tumbling backward, sliding beneath the curtain, his ass landing hard on the bus aisle before he could brace for impact.

Fuck. That shit hurt.

He climbed to his knees, and laughter carried over the blood pulsing in his ears. Loud, belly-shaking, masculine laughter.

"Have you got a license to carry that thing?" Mason spoke between gasps.

"Shit." Sean chuckled. "Be careful impaling her with that. You don't want to puncture a lung."

They were staring at the tent of his boxer briefs, not an ounce of remorse.

"Fuck you." He shot them the bird and shucked his sweats, leaving them on the floor of the aisle. He nudged back underneath the curtain and found Leah's face buried in the pillow, her body convulsing with mirth.

"Don't you start." He poked her ribs, unable to stop himself from chuckling even though his ass felt like he'd spent a week in prison.

She rolled to her side, her amusement coming in gulping hiccups. Yeah, she was laughing at him, but he'd never been more enamored. He'd never been more in love with her than he was right now, her body half-naked, her cheeks flushed, her smile wide.

"You need to laugh more often." He brushed the hair from the side of her face. "*I* want to make you laugh more often."

"You're doing a great job." She wrapped her hand around his neck and encouraged him forward. "Now kiss me before we call this quits."

Quits? Hell, no. "I gave you the opportunity to decline my services earlier." He smothered his body against hers, leaning her into the side wall of the bus, grinding his cock against the soft lace of her underwear. "No take backs."

She smiled against his mouth and nibbled his lower lip. "That was before you gave away what we were doing."

"Don't kid yourself, gorgeous. They knew what we were going to be doing before you even stepped foot on this bus."

"Yeah?" She quirked a brow. "And what if I said no?"

"It never would've happened."

"How can you be so sure?"

"I don't have an abundance of confidence with a lot of things, but your eyes tell me exactly how much you want me."

She arched her neck with a chuckle. "So your eyes speak of affection and mine scream with lust?"

"Pretty much." He pebbled kisses along her throat, to her shoulder, to her collarbone. Each connection increased her breathing and the depth of her nails digging into his skin. "I can already taste how wet you are." He ran his hand along her waist, over her hip to trail beneath her panties. Her musk scented the air, her desire seeping into his lungs, causing insanity.

He palmed her ass, then delved deeper, sliding his touch between her thighs from behind. Her heat increased the further he came toward her core, his fingertips being scorched as they trailed through the moisture of her folds. "You claim you could've turned me down. But I bet I could make you beg."

She mewled as he entered her, a lone finger sliding into her pussy. Her walls clamped down on his digit, her hips thrusting for more.

"Prove me wrong, Leah." His mouth closed in on hers. "Say no to me."

She shuddered, her nails scarring his shoulders.

"Come on. Say no."

She growled, fucking growled, as he pushed another finger into her heat. He didn't think she realized how loud she was. At least not until Mason cursed and the volume of the movie doubled.

"Don't taunt me," she demanded. "Not unless you want to learn that I can fight back."

"Not taunting, my love." He couldn't contain a smirk. There was no way she was denying him. No way in hell. "Merely trying to prove to myself that you do want me."

"You know I do." She shuddered with the next undulation of his fingers.

"I know now." He stared at her, at the way her teeth embedded in her lower lip and the lust-drunk sweep of her lashes. "But when we're not together I need to fight against doubt."

She paused, lucidity sinking back into her eyes. "Are you serious?"

He nodded. "You're too good to be true, Leah. I can barely believe it when I'm with you, let alone when we're apart."

She jerked her hips, making his fingers withdraw from her heat. "Then I need to try harder to convince you."

With his body still against hers, she wiggled out of her panties, then shoved his shoulder down on the mattress as she straddled him. She was crouched forward, the back of her head against the roof of the bunk, her sweet scented hair dangling in his face as she removed her bra.

"Fuck."

She glared. "I've warned you about swearing."

"Then stop doing shit to make me fucking crazy." He smirked, then held his breath as she descended, her body contorting like a pretzel as she came face to face with his crotch.

"Fuck." His pulse was a staccato beat. "Fuck." His balls were drawn tight. "*Fuck*." His shaft was throbbing. He could already feel her mouth on him, could already imagine how warm and wet she would be.

She peered up at him, the determination in her eyes rendering him immobile as she yanked his boxer briefs to mid-thigh. "Ready?"

He shook his head. He was *not* fucking ready. He was too hard, too hot, too fucking insane with the need for her mouth that he thought he might blow in anticipation.

She chuckled, the bursts of breath brushing his cock in a teasing caress. "Too bad." Her tongue came out, moistening her lips before swiping the head of his shaft.

He hissed. His hips bucked. And his throat was so dry he thought he'd die from the pain of it.

She turned her gaze to his dick, her attention moving from the pre-cum beading his slit, to his shaft and back again. "What do you like?"

"You..." He swallowed over razorblades. "I like you."

She chuckled again. "Maybe you'll like me even more in a minute."

Her tongue flicked the moisture from the head of his cock, once, twice. He had to clutch the sheet to fight the need to thrust. She was teasing the life from him, making his heart pulse so damn fast he wondered if it'd soon stop entirely.

He begged her with his eyes, begged more than his words ever could. "Oh, god, Leah. Please don't fuck with me."

"OK." She engulfed his length, her moist lips sucking him deep, blowing his entire mind with one simple movement.

He jerked into her and closed his eyes in an attempt to gain control. She worked him, up and down, over and over, pushing him to the brink. Little moans escaped her lips, the vibrations tormenting his shaft and thrumming through his bloodstream.

Blissful heaven.

Restrained hell.

When her fingers teased his balls, he knew he was in trouble. He was close. Too damn close. Too damn soon.

"Get your ass up here," he growled, and cursed inwardly when he opened his eyes to peer down at her. When he'd first seen her in his bunk, she'd been the epitome of beauty. Now she was the goddess of sexuality with her lips ruby red, her cheeks flushed, and her hair partially covering her phenomenal breasts.

She released his cock with a pop and licked her lips. "Why?"

"Because I said."

She quirked a brow but began crawling up his body.

"No." He shook his head. "Just your ass. I want my mouth between those thighs."

Her lips parted, her shock evident. Then she was complying, maneuvering ninety degrees to straddle him backward so her pretty pussy was in his face. He didn't wait for her to get comfortable. He clutched her thighs and yanked her cunt down to his mouth, sinking his tongue deep.

She cried out and relaxed into him, letting him taste his fill as her lips sank back over his cock.

The volume of the movie increased, the *boom, boom, boom* of an action scene so loud it vibrated the walls. He didn't care. He gave no fucks about his friends overhearing. He gave no fucks about being caught. The only fucks he gave were about Leah and making her come before he lost control.

The taste of her was playing havoc with his senses. The scent of soap and the musk of her arousal making him mindless. He sucked on her clit, sucked as hard as she was sucking his cock and then some. Her taste was all through his mouth, her juices coating his tongue. He couldn't get enough. Never could. Never would.

He wove one of his arms further around her thigh, his thumb reaching for the clit piercing he both loved and despised. He flicked the jewelry, let his touch grind over it, again and again until she was bucking his face, his beard likely leaving a rash against her delicate skin.

Her palms pressed against his legs, spreading them wide as the sound of her suction battled over the garbled television.

"Ryan..." She was panting against his shaft. "Don't. Stop."

"Wait..." He tried to pull from her, otherwise he'd lose himself in her mouth, but she wouldn't allow it. She took him deep, her tongue working frantically along his length, her fingers walking over his sack to the sensitive area before his ass. So close. So close.

She whimpered and her entire body went taut with release—arms, legs, lips. The grip of her mouth was so tight as she mewled that he couldn't stop himself from following after her. His orgasm surged. Pulse after pulse coating the back of her throat. So much pleasure he couldn't think straight. Couldn't breathe through the taste of her.

He continued lapping her pussy, flicking her clit, repaying the gift of ecstasy. They descended together, the strokes of his tongue growing languid as she lessened the friction on his cock and relaxed on top of him.

Yet, he still wanted more. He continued to taste her. Slower. Gentle. Deliberate. He learned her folds, inside and out, lapping top to bottom. She wiggled and he held her thighs tight, her pussy still over his face.

"Ryan..." She groaned with another wiggle. "Let me go."

Never. Not now. Not ever. But he released his hold, ignoring the hollow ache in his chest as her evaporating heat left him cold. She climbed over him, turning awkwardly so they were face to face before collapsing into her previous position against the wall.

He hadn't done that before. Hadn't lost himself in a woman's mouth. Julie never wanted to do it and he never asked her to. It wasn't a big deal. He knew his opinion of Leah shouldn't change because of what just happened. Nope. Not at all. But it had. He was more enamored, more hypnotized, more in need of...more.

He kicked off the boxer briefs hovering at his knees and pulled her into his chest. "Come here." He gripped her hips, dragged her on top of him, then over to the other side of the mattress closest to the curtain. "I don't want to suffocate you in the corner."

"Thank you." Her eyes were dreamy, equal parts sex-drugged and sleep deprivation.

"You tired?"

"I am now." She smiled and nuzzled into his chest like an exhausted kitten. "Tired and content."

He pulled her close, resting his chin against the top of her head as he closed his eyes. "I love seeing you like this."

"Naked? I'm not surprised."

"No, seeing you relaxed." He chuckled. "And with your guard down."

She nodded. "It's nice to be able to feel that way with someone. Being vulnerable has its advantages."

"You're not vulnerable with me." He kissed her forehead. "I've told you I'd never hurt you."

"I know."

There was something hidden in her reply. An underlying fragility he didn't want to pinpoint. Her confidence in him would take time, and he wasn't going to push her. He had her love. He had her affection and her lust, too. Even though he hated hiding what they shared from the rest of the world, being the only one to know how she felt was enough for now.

"Hey, Mace?" he called over the drone of the television. "Can you quit the noise?"

The volume decreased along with the vibrations of the walls. "You two done?"

"For now." He had plans for later. Many plans.

There was a grumble, then the television cut completely.

Leah remained against him, her fingernail tracing intricate lines over his chest as the others prepared for bed. Toilets flushed, doors slammed, curtains were slung back and forth. Then the lights were off. The hum of the engine the only sound apart from the whisper of her breath.

"Good night." She lifted her chin and grazed tempting lips against his.

"Night, gorgeous."

She rolled over, her body spooning into his, chest to back, ass to crotch, thigh to thigh. He could feel her everywhere, against his skin, even under it.

His love for her was pulsing through his chest, affecting every breath. He leaned his forehead against her shoulder trying to deny how destroyed he would be if he ever lost her. There was no way back from here. No peace without her. No hope if she wasn't in his arms.

There was only her. Only them.

And he was going to make sure it stayed that way.

Eighteen

LEAH WAS THE FIRST AWAKE IN THE MORNING. RYAN WAS BREATHING HEAVY beside her, his arm wrapped around her back, her face nestled against his chest. He had her cocooned in his embrace, kept safe and warm from the reality on the other side of the curtain.

They hadn't slept much. Not between the silent lovemaking and whispered conversations as they flittered in and out of consciousness. She was finally done with fighting. This was her life now. With him. All they had to do was make it work.

All in good time.

She inched forward, holding her breath in an effort not to wake him.

"Where are you going?" he mumbled against her shoulder.

She smiled, loving every aspect of waking up beside him—his heat, his security, his graveled tone. "Coffee."

He clutched tighter, making her chuckle.

"I'll only be gone for ten minutes. I promise."

"Not a minute longer." His voice was rough from sleep, dark and devilish.

She eased his hand from her waist, kissed his knuckles, and slipped under the screen. After a quick trip to the storage cupboard to retrieve her clothes and cell, she changed and freshened up in the bathroom. She'd been in there for five minutes max. but the sweet sound of Ryan's slumber greeted her when she returned to the aisle.

She inched the curtain across and stared at him. Her man. Her love. There was no looking back now. No need or desire. There was only determination to move forward. To secure her boss's approval, kick Julie from their lives, and slink away from the Slicker publicity.

The first hurdle was her boss, and without a plan in place, it would come down to good ol' fashioned pleading. All she could bank on was her feminine wiles and a track history of bringing successful men to heel. She wouldn't be able to admit they were already together. Those details would only work harshly against her. But if she acted as though she was seeking approval before making a move, maybe her boss would take pity on her.

She released the bunk cover and exited the curtained sleeping area to drink in the sight of a barely waking Kansas City.

An orange glow crept along buildings, turning night into day. Darkness into sunshine. She gave Pat a finger-wave through the rearview mirror as she approached and he flicked out his earphones with a smile.

"Mornin'."

"Morning." She sank onto the corner of the booth seat, placed her cell on the table, and hunched toward him to take in the view.

"How long until we're at the stadium?"

"Twenty minutes if the traffic is good. But we'll be in the secure parking area if you want to catch a few more hours sleep."

"I'm good." The confinement of the bunk wasn't conducive for slumber. Neither was the erection that had nuzzled against her ass on and off all night. "Want a coffee?"

"Nah. I stopped a few hours ago and bought some gas station sludge. It'll keep me going for a while."

"Poor thing. Let me know if you need anything. I'm going to get some work done while there's peace and quiet."

"No problem." He nudged his earphones back in place and focused on the traffic as she made her way to the compact kitchen to switch on the drip machine. While she waited for liquid goodness, she checked social media, scanning the usual blogs and headlines to make sure the Reckless world was stable. Apart from an increase in questions regarding Mason's sexuality, everything was quiet on the band-front. Slicker were still a major topic of discussion, with Ryan's involvement highlighting most tweets and posts.

Once her coffee was ready, she slid into the booth and started brainstorming. Ryan was doing well to keep his relationship in the spotlight, but there needed to be more. More hype, more publicity, more sales. She no longer wanted to sit on the sidelines and watch him manipulate the media. She needed to take charge. To grab the promo stunt by the horns sooner rather than later to get the rabid Grander monkey off their back.

Ideas came to her in quick succession and she ended up having to scavenge through cupboards for a notebook because her typing fingers couldn't keep up. Page after page of garbled notes were scribbled. All they needed was a chart topper. One measly chart which would've been a cinch for Reckless and would end up being a miracle for the lesser-known Slicker.

She was preparing to make a second coffee when the bus slowed and turned into the stadium entrance.

"It looks like security are already here and waiting." Pat pulled the bus to a stop and cut the ignition. "I'm going to stretch my legs and have a smoke. You good?"

"Yep."

"I'll close the door once I'm out, so y'all can have some privacy and catch some more sleep." He descended the stairs, the doors closing seconds later.

Someone groaned from the bunks, followed by the rustle of sheets, then silence. The guys wouldn't wake for hours, giving her more time to concoct one of the many necessary plans. And with the planning came excitement. She was pumped to speak to her boss. Figuring out a way to gain her wildest dreams was making her giddy... Or maybe that was the caffeine.

Either way, she was optimistic for a future with Ryan. The pleasure in her chest couldn't be denied. If she could make this work, she'd have everything she'd ever wanted—the career, the future, the love.

But...

If...

How...

When...

She shook away the confronting questions and took another gulp of coffee. Her cell began to move, the vibrations signaling an incoming call. *Bruce.* She wondered if her thoughts had been loud enough to wake her boss.

"Hey," she whispered. "You've hit the grindstone early."

"Not by choice."

"And why is that?"

"I just got off the phone from some no-name blogger who warned me of a podcast she uploaded last night. Apparently, it's starting to gain traction and local radio stations are airing snippets in their gossip news—"

"Hold up. What blogger? What snippets? I've already scanned social media this morning and nothing triggered my radar."

Another ring tone sounded from the bunks, followed by the clearing of a throat and Ryan's gravelly voice.

"I can't remember the name but I've got the details in an email along with a link to the podcast. She wants you to contact her about an opportunity to respond to the claims."

When the third ringtone sounded she stood, her stomach flipping at the sudden influx of communication. One call at this hour was understandable. Two was a coincidence. But three signaled trouble.

Big trouble.

"What claims?"

"I haven't listened to the interview yet. I wanted to contact you first, but she said there's some controversial stuff in there about Reckless."

"Who did the blogger interview?" Felicity better not have opened her damn mouth. Or Hannah. Fuck, if it was Scott she'd kill him.

"It's the disgruntled wife of your guitarist. Apparently, she's flinging accusations at her husband, the band, and you."

Fuck.

"Can you forward me the information?"

"I did, two seconds before I connected the call. And if this blogger is to be trusted, the information would've been shared minutes ago, after the last news update."

Leah closed her eyes. Judging by the phone calls taking over the bus, the manipulator hadn't lied.

"After all these years in my employment, I hate having to ask you this, but..." He paused and she knew exactly what would come next, the disappointment, the questioning. "Have you crossed a line? Is there something I should be worried about?"

Images from last night flooded her. Ryan's cock in her mouth, his tongue on her breast, his fingers in her pussy. "I don't know why Julie would involve me, but she's been stalling with the divorce. It could be some sort of power play."

"Band drama is inevitable, Leah. We both know that. I do, however, get antsy when my managers hit headlines. It's not the look I want for my company."

"Give me half an hour to see what we're up against—"

"I will. But if this is trouble, you need to shut it down. You're supposed to blend into the shadows. And if you can't do that, maybe it's time to take a vacation. Recharge and let someone else take over for a bit."

"You don't even know what she's said."

"No, I only know you took your first emergency leave a few months back because of something Ryan did."

A kiss. *That kiss.*

"Bruce, I disclosed all the information about that situation with you. You know I wasn't to blame. You trusted my judgment and the promise it would never happen again." Only it had, and now her argument was killing any chance she had to renegotiate her contract. "I took a break when I needed it back then. You need to continue to trust that I know what I'm doing." Even when she didn't trust herself.

"I trust you. I just don't like hearing about more drama from your camp. It's not like you to drop one ball, let alone two."

"I haven't dropped anything," she grated. "Let see what the mess is and I'll call you back."

She waited for his muttered agreement before she disconnected the call and rushed to her bag to retrieve her earphones. Ryan was still talking. Mason, too. Both conversations heated and angry.

As she returned to the booth, she navigated to her emails, found the link, and turned up the volume.

"Welcome listeners. Tonight we have Julie Bennett joining us from the

comfort of her Manhattan apartment. Good evening, Julie."

Leah scanned forward, bypassing the introductions as she slumped in her seat.

"—been married to Ryan for how long now?" the announcer asked.

"We started dating in school and married a few years after graduation. I was with him before Reckless was born and stayed with him throughout the trials and scandals."

"But Ryan's the charmer of the group, right? How many trials and scandals could there have been?"

Leah held her breath. Held it tight until her chest hammered with impending collapse.

"None that were publicized. But there were many behind the scenes. I was constantly fighting with him over his relationship with his band manager. That woman has been trying to sink her claws into Ryan for years."

The hostaged breath escaped, all of it, every last ounce to leave her completely hollow.

"You're talking about Leah Gorman?"

"Yes. She was a plague on our marriage and I suspect she'll continue to do the same for Ryan moving forward."

Leah cradled her head in her hand as the diatribe filtered into her ears. So much for begging Bruce for a change in her contract. So much for tying loose ends in an effort to gain peace with Ryan. So much for turning daydreams into reality. His ex had just placed months, if not years between Leah and a happy resolution with the man she loved.

"Leah is a narcissistic, power-hungry viper who will stop at nothing to get what she wants... I'm sure she tried to seduce my husband... She's a manipulator... She's the reason for our divorce..."

The words became garbled, each syllable intertwining with the next to increase the static in her head. She paused the podcast, removed the earphones and slid the cell away to wade through the mental carnage.

"You heard?" Ryan's voice carried from her side.

She nodded.

"Is it bad?"

She continued to nod as she stared at the table. In comparison, it didn't hold the weight of Blake's drug addiction scandal or Mason's leaked sex tape. It was a bitter attack. A defensive, soon-to-be ex-wife lashing out. But this time it was personal. The assault was aimed at Leah's career. Her future. Her happiness. And Julie had successfully struck gold.

"What did she say?" Ryan crouched beside her, his hands resting on her thigh.

The touch shot through her, the sensation painful in its pleasure. "The day you were handed the divorce papers, you said I was the cause of your failed marriage." She gave a derisive laugh. "I thought you were attacking me in an attempt to release your anger. But you weren't, were you? I *did* ruin your marriage. I'm the reason the two of you were never happy."

"She said that?"

"Yes, she did." Leah met his gaze, those wide eyes staring back at her. "On a popular podcast that is now being distributed to god knows how many radio stations."

"*Fucking hell.*"

"Don't ignore the question, Ryan." She turned to him and tried to read his expression. What was done, was done. There was still no looking back. But she needed to know if she'd been kidding herself about her superior level of professionalism. Had her feelings been obvious? Had she wordlessly convinced him to sabotage his marriage? "Am I really the reason Julie asked for a divorce?"

"Yes." His unreserved response stabbed through her stomach as the hand on her thigh tightened. "I fell out of love with her because I was in love with you. Because I wanted to be with you. Because I couldn't stop imagining how great we'd be together. So yes, you are the reason for the divorce, and I'm not going to feel guilty, because she fell out of love with me years before I gave up on the marriage."

"But we haven't been close since Australia. We've barely been friends."

He nodded. "And she knew that. She also knew being at odds with you had changed my mood more than any argument with her ever had."

A brief flicker of adoration sparked and was soon smothered by shame. There was no denying she'd crossed a line. A big, fat line her boss wouldn't approve of. But the threat to her career wasn't what hurt the most. It was the amassing destruction she'd caused.

Ryan's divorce was her fault. Even though she'd tried to hide her feelings, she'd cost him his marriage.

"Don't feel guilty, Leah." His eyes turned lethal. "I welcome the divorce. I don't want to be with her."

"You didn't always feel that way. I was there when the document was handed over. I witnessed the devastation on your face."

"You witnessed my shock at being blindsided. And my anger at being a failure. You didn't witness heartache over her leaving me. We stopped being in love a long time ago. We'd merely been going through the motions."

"Then why did you stay?" His jaw flexed, his nostrils flared, and the unmistakable loosening of his palm on her thigh told her he was contemplating a lie. "Tell me the truth."

"I will." He nodded. Cringed. "I wanted a family. I wanted to be a father. And she kept promising we'd make a start. It wasn't like I could be with you. And no other woman has ever tempted me. So I stuck around in the hopes a baby might revive the marriage."

"You would've stayed with her if it meant having children?"

His lips parted, the brutal words poised to devastate her when Mason pulled the curtain back from the bunk area and strode forward.

"I just got off the phone to Sid." His hair was tangled, his face creased from sleep. "She said we have another nightmare on our hands."

"Yeah." Ryan stood, forgetting their interrupted conversation. "How did she find out?"

"She heard something on the radio and wanted to give me a heads up."

"Who told you?" Leah stared at Ryan.

"My lawyer. That guy is making a mint because of Julie's bullshit."

Silence descended, the weight of indecision settling between them.

"You won't let this affect what you've got going on, will you?" Mason eyed her. "The two of you are still good, right?"

She sucked in a breath, held it, and became strengthened by her impending response. "Ye—"

"Julie's not going to bring us down." Ryan tugged her to her feet. "I won't let it happen."

His determination starved her shame and she went willingly into his arms. "It's going to make things harder, though. We'll need to lay low. I can't take any more trips on your bus. There'll be no more hiding in plain sight."

"Changing your routine will only make you look guilty." Mason rested a hand against the back of the booth seat. "I'm not saying you should shake the bus walls every night, because frankly, that shit was traumatizing, but if you keep your distance, there's going to be more questions to answer."

"I prefer questions to being caught red-handed and losing my job."

"Hey." Ryan got in her face, gripping her upper arms. "Nobody is losing their job. I promise you."

Why did she believe him? There was no justification. No reasoning. But yet she became reassured by his words. Strengthened.

"We'll pull through."

She stared into those eyes, drowning in their warmth. Her pessimistic thoughts wanted to rebel, it was her heart that clung to his promise.

"We've got this." He kissed her forehead. "Trust me."

She nodded and sank against him, breathing in his scent. "I need to call Bruce back."

"What are you going to say?"

"I'll tell him the truth—Julie has been hassling your lawyers for weeks, trying to get a rise out of you. It wasn't like we weren't expecting the drama. We just didn't know the shape it would come in."

"Or that you would be the target." Ryan gave a sad smile.

"Not only me. My boss's company will take a hit because of the mark against my reputation. Julie has also undermined what you're trying to do with Felicity. You'll need to release a formal statement about the claims and spin it so the fans think it's petty jealousy."

"I agree." He squeezed her hand. "But I need to speak to her first. I told my lawyer I'd go to New York with the rest of you tonight and get some answers."

No. She stepped back, her heart, mind, and soul refusing to get on board with the thought of him going anywhere near the toxic woman. "If you're seen, the tabloids will use it against your relationship with Felicity."

His shoulder hitched. "That's a risk I'll have to take. I can't have her going after you."

"No." She retreated another step. "We've spoken about this. You can't make decisions based on your feelings for me."

"He's not," Mason interrupted. "To anyone else, this is merely about his divorce."

"And Julie isn't going to leave me alone unless I see her in person." Ryan grazed a thumb along her jaw. "So that's what I'm going to do. We'll talk, I'll give her whatever she wants, and then I'll never see her again. End of story."

"She doesn't deserve a damn thing."

"Hear, hear," Mason muttered. "Have I told you how much I don't envy your woman situation? The hole you're digging is getting bigger by the day."

"I can handle it."

Leah wasn't so sure. Yes, his fortitude was admirable, but if it came with the price of ignorance, they were in trouble. "Don't be quick to brush off how monumental this is. There's a lot of fingers in this pie—Felicity, Hannah, my boss, Grander. Not to mention Blake and Gabi. One wrong move and we're all in trouble."

His lips curved, the acknowledgement gently reassuring as he cupped her cheeks in his palms. "I won't be quick to brush it off. But you need to remember my promise that nothing is going to stop me from making this work."

Nineteen

RYAN NESTLED INTO THE JET SOFA, HIS HEAD AGAINST THE ARM REST, HIS LEGS stretched over the far end, and tugged Leah's body tighter into his chest. She'd been lying in front of him since they fled the Kansas City runway, her quiet contemplation soothing his soul. The flight was smooth. Quiet. None of the usual post-concert adrenaline was present as his friends waited anxiously to arrive home to their loved ones. He, on the other hand, tried to mentally prepare for the showdown with Julie.

He'd already called her, and the two-minute conversation hadn't been what he expected. She was definitely up to something. Her bitchiness had been on hold, her answers almost apologetic when he'd grilled her about the stupidity of the podcast interview.

"Run away with me," he whispered, nuzzling into the silken strands of Leah's hair.

She glanced over her shoulder, her cheeks lifting, a tiny glimmer of a never before seen dimple. "Don't tempt me."

"I'm serious." At least he could be, depending on her answer. There was too much white noise surrounding them. If they disappeared, maybe the drama would, too. They could start over. Make a new life.

"And give up Reckless?" She lazily blinked up at him. "You're crazy."

"I'd do it for you."

Her smile faltered, the twinge in expression letting him know he'd be on his own if he walked away from his friends. "I'd never forgive you if you left the band. Music means the world to you."

"You mean more." It was the truth. He could give it up. He could walk away from Reckless and never look back because this feeling—with her in his arms, smiling up at him—was beyond anything he'd ever experienced. He wasn't merely happy, he was at home. This sensation wasn't neatly packaged into a box titled—Love. It was about devotion. About strength. This thing between them consisted of unfaltering faith and reciprocated vulnerability.

He wanted to spend the rest of his life with her more than he needed to be on stage. Music would always be there. You couldn't stop a torrent with a stone. All he'd have to do is find another outlet.

"And if you walked away," she whispered, "we'd never see each other. I'd be with Reckless and you'd be somewhere else. The distance you experienced with Julie would start to settle between us. We'd drift apart." She turned away and nestled further into his chest. "Working together is the best and the worst part of this situation."

"I know." He sighed and nuzzled his face into her hair. "Are you still going to meet with your boss?"

"No."

He closed his eyes and fought against frustration. "Because of Julie?"

"It's bad timing. My boss is now annoyed with me for casting a shadow over the company. Telling him how I feel about you, even if I did lie about us already being together, wouldn't turn out well. It's best to wait."

"How long?"

"However long it takes. At least until your divorce is final and the tour is over." She wiggled, turning her body around to face him, her beauty making it hard for him to form a protest. "I don't want to rush this. I think my initial plan to speak to him was a smidge optimistic to begin with. If I hold off, it will give me more time to find the leverage I need."

"And you're happy to wait?"

"I have to be." Her gaze raked his face, the gentle touch of her appraisal filling his chest with heavy beats. "Who knows? By then, it could be better to tell him the truth. If we can be together and not let it get between our working relationship, it might work in our favor." She gave a sassy smile.

"All you need to do is keep your protective nature in check."

"That won't be a problem if Mason shuts his pie hole."

She chuckled, the brilliant laughter peppering his lips.

"Did I hear my name?" the lead singer called from the other side of the cabin.

"No," they said in unison and shared goofy grins.

It was as if the tension had been paused. The drama on hold. They were smiling through the impending onslaught, both content to live in the moment.

"You know, even with all the crap going on, I'm still the happiest I've been in...ever." She wove an arm around his waist, her fingers gliding under his shirt. "How can I feel this energized when my world is upside down?"

He had no response. No words, at least. Only a kiss. He tasted her smile and fought for control when her nails dug into his skin. Every inch of him was alive for her. Especially his heart. Her hold was beyond anything he could've imagined. When she inched her mouth away he waited, thankful for the pause in proceedings so he could leash his dick.

"When are you meeting with Julie and your lawyers?"

"There's no lawyers. I'm going to the apartment."

She caught her expression a second too late, allowing him a glimpse of her disapproval.

"Don't worry. I can handle her."

"You're too sweet, Ryan." She lowered her gaze, focusing on his beard. "She'll manipulate you."

"Let her try. I'm already prepared." He leaned down, reclaiming those sweet lips with a quick peck. "She has no hold over me anymore."

She whimpered, their noses brushing. "Will you call me afterward?"

"As soon as I leave. I promise."

Her mouth tentatively glided back and forth, her teasing tongue adding to the delirious mix. "You've promised a lot."

"Mmm." He nipped at her, earning a gasp. "I'll promise you everything."

"And I'll take it. I want everything you have to give, Ryan. And everything I have is yours in return."

He nudged his knee between her legs, parting her pants-covered thighs.

"Everything?" he whispered. "How 'bout another pair of panties to add to my collection?"

She laughed. "Everything but those. At least while we're in the air."

He deepened the kiss and cupped the back of her head. Her moan slid down his throat, through his stomach, directly to his cock. Sharp nails dug into his flesh, scarring skin as she ground her pelvis against his thigh.

"Cut it out, you two."

He ignored Blake and kept her head in place, unwilling to let her go. On the jet it was easy. They could shut the door to the hostess area, flick the do-not-disturb light, and act like the world didn't exist. Professionalism would steal her away soon enough and he doubted he would get another chance to taste her until they rejoined the tour.

"We should critique them until they stop," Mitch suggested.

Ryan responded by lowering his hand from her hair, down her back to cup her ass. *Critique that, motherfuckers.*

"Cut them a break," Sean added. "Let them enjoy their slice of heaven."

"And what about our living hell?" came from Mason. "I caught an eyefull of Ryan's dick last night."

"I thought you liked dick?" Sean had a death wish. "At least the poll on Twitter says you do."

Leah pulled back, her bright eyes staring up at him. "If they're trying to stop me from wanting to kiss you, they're failing. I could stay here forever."

He grinned and the resounding silence meant Mason must've responded to Sean with a middle finger gesture. "Then that's what we'll do."

This time her smile faltered, the happiness fracturing. She closed her eyes and nestled into his chest. "I'm going to catch some Zs before we land. Can I use you as a pillow?"

He rested his chin against the top of her head and pulled her close, resigning himself to the limited time they had before arrival. "I wouldn't have it any other way."

Twenty

HIS APARTMENT KEY SLID INTO THE LOCK. WHY? HE'D TESTED THE FIT AS A joke, a little confirmation to Julie's bitchiness, and he'd been proven wrong. He'd assumed updating the security would've been a high priority on his wife's divorce schedule. Apparently not. He turned the handle, pushed inside, and returned to the contempt of a failed marriage all with a simple step over the threshold.

"Julie?" He kicked off his shoes and padded onto the plush carpet. "It's me."

"I'm in the kitchen."

He continued past his retired guitars still on display in the hall, their glossy shine letting him know she'd polished them during his absence. Her care didn't make sense. And the Betty Crocker scent of caramel and chocolate floating through the air made him nervous. His wife didn't cook. At least, not for him.

"You didn't change the locks." He walked through the kitchen doorway and acknowledged his body's lack of response to the sight of her. There was no anger, no disappointment, no attraction. The mountain of emotions he'd once harbored over this woman was now a void.

She turned to him, her loose dress dancing over her thighs. Her hair was different, colored to a dark brown with light highlights, the length now resting an inch above her shoulders. "I couldn't bring myself to sever the final link between us."

He withheld a scoff. "After your bitter online interview, I expected you to have burned or buried all the stuff I left behind."

She reached for a cloth and began cleaning the flour from the counter. "It was the only way I could get your attention. You've blocked every attempt I've made to get in contact with you, and I knew, once I got the band involved, they'd send you home to deal with me."

"This isn't my home anymore, Julie. If you want more from the divorce settlement, you need to take it to my lawyer."

"That's not what I want."

"Then what is it? Why am I here?"

She lowered her gaze and reached for the tray of freshly baked cookies. "Want one?"

"No." God, no. He wanted a signature and an amicable farewell. Not a damn cookie. "Tell me why I'm here." He stepped further into the room and took the divorce settlement from the back pocket of his jeans.

"I needed to see you." She cleared her throat. "I wanted to tell you I made a mistake."

"Which one?" The barb escaped without thought. "Marrying me? Or waiting too long to call it quits?"

"My mistake was letting you go."

"Excuse me?" Her revelation didn't faze him. It couldn't. Not when he was lost to someone else.

"I made a mistake when I asked for a divorce."

"No." He shook his head and shot his attention to the kitchen window, unable to face her. He wasn't going to do this. Not now. Not when she'd already dragged him through weeks of hell. *Years* of heartache. "I'm not in the mood for games." He placed the stapled pages on the counter and slid them toward her. "If you read over this, you'll find it's a fair settlement."

"You're not listening." She slid the pages back. "I no longer want a divorce."

"Don't do this." He tried to keep his cool, tried to remain civil and in control even though his subconscious was demanding he leave the fray.

"I was hormonal," she pleaded. "I wasn't thinking."

"Yeah, you were. You were thinking about how miserable we were. You were thinking about how you resented my career and hated me being away from home all the time. You were thinking that we'd gone too far to come back, and you were right."

"No." Remorse filled her eyes. "We haven't gone too far. I just had to realize how wrong I was. I needed space to clear my head."

"And while you took your time to figure it out, I moved on."

"I don't believe you." She shook her head. "That woman isn't your type."

No, Felicity wasn't, but Leah sure was. Leah was everything. She was the light in the darkness. The stability in a building tsunami.

"I want you to come home, Ryan."

He cringed.

"Not right now," she blurted. "I realize you're on tour. But once that's over..."

"Stop saying 'home' when you know full-well I haven't been welcome here for a damn long time." He couldn't remember when she'd officially kicked him out of their bedroom. He'd been relegated to the couch or the spare bedroom, only getting a temporary return pass when she wanted a physical fix. Once the sex was over he always got shoved back to the doghouse.

She wasn't entirely to blame. He'd willingly taken her shit. He'd gone along with it because he harbored the guilt of all their problems.

"Trust me. We'll be happier once the divorce is final." He took a one last visual sweep of the place they'd bought when happiness had still been a part of their lives. He relived the few fading memories of love and hoped they didn't disappear entirely. Then he turned on his heel and headed for the hall.

"Ryan." His name was a plea. "Please stop."

He paused, her agonizing tone making him glance over his shoulder. The slightest shift in her position made his heart seize. The light streaming through the window hit her at a different angle. The tiniest change in perception turning his world upside down. She stood tall, her hand sliding over her abdomen, the placement pulling her loose dress tight over a rounded belly. The air left his lungs in a heave and he thought his stomach would follow suit.

"I'm pregnant."

His blood infused with adrenaline, the heavy pulse of awe keeping him immobile. In an instant his life changed. Clarity skewed, perspective morphed, responsibility became a heavy weight, and fear and longing collided. In one revelation she crushed his dreams for a future with Leah and taunted him with the opportunity of a family.

"You're going to be a father."

Those words... That belly...

"How long?" He voiced the doubt bubbling to the forefront.

She lifted her chin, her hand possessive over her abdomen. "Five months."

A knife stabbed deep into his chest, piercing skin and sinew. They'd slept together in that time. Once or twice, depending on the validity of his shadowy memories. Both emotionless sexual experiences he didn't want to associate with the conception of a child.

"I've been trying to tell you for weeks, but you wouldn't answer my calls. I didn't want you to find out from anyone else, but the bump is getting too big to hide." She stared at the hand on her stomach, a maternal smile curving her lips. "We're going to have a baby."

The knife plunged deeper, through arteries and organs.

He'd endured loveless years in the hope of hearing those words. He'd gone to sleep not alone, but lonely for nights on end. He'd thought about baby names, and if he'd be a good parent, and if his child would grow to resent his career like his wife did.

Becoming a father had been his dream, and now it resembled a nightmare.

"I..." He swallowed, hard, the moisture barely coating the gravel in his throat. "I need to..." What? What did he need? Time? Clarity? A bigger set of balls to call bullshit on her manipulative announcement?

"Don't you want to feel her kick?"

"Her?" Images of little girls and pigtails blinded him. The echo of feminine giggles and a sweet voice calling him daddy filled his ears. He couldn't breathe, couldn't stop his limbs from shaking.

She stepped forward, offering the bow of her belly.

"Don't." He held up a hand, unwilling to connect with his child while he was in a state of shock.

"Isn't this what you wanted?"

"It is... It *was*." He shook his head to fight the lack of concentration. "I..."

"Is this about that other woman?" She took another step. "You don't love her, Ryan. I know you don't."

No, he didn't love Felicity. But he did love Leah. With all his heart, spare the newly forming extra beat now sounding for a child he'd never met.

"I want you to come back to me so we can be a family." She was poisoning him. Each word killing the plans he'd had for the future. "I want this to work."

"I... I can't..." He couldn't think. Couldn't even walk straight. He stumbled from the kitchen and into the hall, passing his guitars before snatching his shoes from the floor.

"*Ryan.*"

He scrambled for the front door and slammed it shut behind him. He had to get out of here, away from the memories devoid of happiness and the wife who would never love him again.

And the only person he wanted to flee toward was the woman he would destroy with the news.

L EAH CHECKED HER PHONE. AGAIN. RYAN HAD BEEN SCHEDULED TO MEET with Julie hours ago. *Three* hours, to be exact. He hadn't called. Hadn't messaged. Clearly, it wasn't a sign of mass devastation but her stomach sure felt like it.

Her pessimism had taken control, spitting in the face of optimism's raised white flag. Any minute now she was going to succumb and call him. For the moment, she was on the edge of restraint, making laundry her mission, shoving non-delicates into the dryer as if they were traitors. She assumed this was how Julie felt for all those months Ryan spent on tour. The jealousy was rich, cloying, coating every inch of her skin.

The tentative knock at the door was barely heard over the rambling in her brain. She had to pause, cock her head, and wait for a louder, more adamant knock before she convinced herself there was a visitor.

"I'm coming." She closed the dryer, wiped her damp hands on her pants, and made for the entrance hall. Only five men knew she was home from tour. Four of which should be balls deep in their women by now. That only left one. One man she hoped wouldn't be stupid enough to come to her apartment in broad daylight.

She yanked open the door and cursed his carelessness. "Ryan, what are you doing here?"

"Needed to speak to you." His eyes didn't meet hers, those emotional depths remaining downcast, morphing her frustration into fear.

"You were supposed to call." She pulled the door wider and beckoned him inside. "If anyone sees you…"

He trudged his feet forward and accidentally nudged her shoulder as he passed. Then an unmistakable scent hit her. The strong hint of alcohol and misery.

"Christ, have you been drinking?" She scrutinized him—the crumpled shirt, the slumped shoulders, the tangled hair slicked back from his face as if he'd worked his fingers non-stop through the lengths.

"Ryan?" She followed after him and gripped the waistband of his jeans, bringing him to a stop. "What did she say?"

He laughed, the sound brutal, if not maniacal. She'd lost him again. Julie had taken away the man she loved and replaced him with someone overcome with destruction.

"Either tell me what's going on or I'm calling Mason."

His glassy gaze met hers, increasing her panic. "That's not a very nice threat."

It wasn't a threat toward him, it was a defense for her. His look was terrifying, informing her this situation was something she couldn't handle on her own. "I don't know which hat to put on. Is this a professional issue? Is it personal? Talk to me." She bridged the space between them and pleaded with her eyes. "Please, Ryan. You're scaring me."

His face crumpled, the lines etching his brow digging deeper the longer he stared at her. *Oh, God.* She couldn't take this. She didn't know how to help him.

He fell to his knees before her, his shoulders slumping, his hair framing his cheeks. "I'm drowning, Leah." His head fell back and he peered up at her, his eyes stark, his face bleak. He reached for her, latching on to the material of her blouse, and tugged her down to the floor. "I can't breathe." He began to hyperventilate. Big breaths. Rasped, labored exhalations.

"I need to call Mason." She made to run for her cell and he stopped her with an arm around her waist, dragging her down to the floor.

"Stay with me."

"Then tell me what to do." She pressed her palms against his chest, placing space between them. "Talk or I'm getting straight on the phone."

His face crumpled, the man she knew nowhere to be seen. "She's pregnant."

Time stopped.

Her throat closed.

The world condensed to three things–Ryan, his ex, and a child. There was no Leah. No love. With two words he'd shoved her from his life whether he wanted to or not.

"No." The denial slipped free, giving pain a chance to sink in its place.

He simply stared at her, those shiny eyes all the confirmation she needed to give in to sorrow. "Five months. That's why she's been trying to call me." He sat back on his haunches, his arms limp at his sides.

"Five months," she repeated.

"It could be mine, Leah."

The clarification washed over her, an invisible landslide destroying everything in its wake.

"The baby could be fucking mine and I don't know what to do. I don't know how to make this right. She wants me to move back in with her. She wants us to be a family. She wants all these things I can't give her and can't turn away from either."

Each announcement wrapped barbed wire around her heart, making each torturous beat harder to bear. "And what do you want?" she whispered. "Where do you fit in to all of this?"

"I don't know." His sorrow begged at her, demanding the answers he couldn't find. "I wanted this with you. Not her. I want this to be our baby. Our family. Our future. I don't care that we've only been together for weeks. In my heart, I've always been with you. I can't go back."

"Hey." She ran her hands through his hair, making him focus. "You're in shock. You need to give this time to sink in."

"I can't do this without you. I'm drowning, my lungs are burning, but I can handle the suffocation if I'm with you." He began to ramble, the words tumbling in quick succession. "Leah, help me. Tell me how I fix this."

"Shh." She clutched his shoulders and dragged him forward, squeezing him against her chest. "We'll figure it out." She didn't know how. She didn't have a clue. There were only platitudes and useless words to fight the anguish. This was what he'd always dreamed of, with the one woman neither one of them wanted to be tied to.

Heaven and hell.

Dreams and nightmares.

Opposites forced together to create anarchy.

"I want you." He pulled back and cupped her cheeks. "I want a family with you. I want babies. *With you*."

"Ryan, *please*." She was in too deep, drowning right beside him with no one to save her.

"I need you." He kissed her, his alcohol and fear colliding with her pain and resignation. "I just need you."

His lips melted everything inside, leaving her in a worthless pile of nothingness. His tongue entered her mouth, increasing the insanity. Anguish turned into desire with every swipe of his mouth. Numbness built into warmth with the press of his body against hers.

She couldn't deny him. There was no power to push him away. She craved him, too. Yearned for the passion to temporarily hide the truth. She gripped his shirt, tugged it over his head, only to have him smash his lips back over hers, the kiss possessive.

They didn't stop, didn't break for air. Together, they stood, mouths connected, chest to chest. She touched him everywhere, unable to get enough of him, wanting to claim everything as her own before someone else could. When he pulled back, she fought not to crumple under the adoration in his eyes as he stripped her. First her blouse, button by button, then her pants, her underwear, each item removed with delicate finesse. The more skin he exposed, the more vulnerable she became to his touch. She was bare.

Physically.

Emotionally.

"I need to feel you." She began removing his jeans with mimicked worship, making sure to memorize every last inch of his skin as her palms trekked over his ass, his thighs. He was hard for her, his devastation no match for his passion even though his eyes remained bleak.

He swept her off her feet, his strong arms swinging her into an embrace as he brought them down to the couch. Weathered hands guided her to straddle his lap and she wiggled against his cock as their mouths reconnected. Her body wasn't ready. Arousal hadn't kicked in, only the demand for connection, but she sank onto his length, lessening the emotional agony with a bite of physical pain.

This felt like goodbye. Each press of lips a farewell, every stroke of his fingers leading to an inevitable end. She kissed her love into him, rocking their bodies together as tears pricked her eyes. Even with his cock inside her, he seemed miles away, the distance between them already growing.

She rocked harder, trying to bridge the gap. She kissed with more determination, hoping to remain tethered.

Nothing worked.

He did the same. Harsh strokes of tongue. Brutal jerks of his hips. The pleasure didn't increase. Only the suffering. His mouth found her neck, her collarbone, her chest. She leaned her head back, giving free rein to the moisture now seeping from her eyes.

She couldn't derive gratification from this moment. Her heart wouldn't allow it. But she let him take what he needed, rocking her hips along with his increased tempo.

"I can't lose you," he rasped, his fingers digging into the flesh of her ass.

Too late. She was already lost. "I'll always love you, Ryan."

Her words seemed to shove him toward climax, his movements becoming unfettered. Chaotic. He pounded into her, thrust after thrust of persecution and comfort. Black and white. Right and wrong. He came undone in her arms, his shout of release guttural, almost animalistic in her ears. Tight hands clung to her. Harsh breaths called to her. Jerks turned into undulations, the gentle rock of his hips signaling an end that was more than physical.

"I'm sorry." He kept his head bowed, his chest rising and falling as he cradled her against him. "I'm ruining everything."

She shook her head, keeping them close so he didn't see her tears. "You haven't done anything wrong."

"Then why does it feel the exact opposite?"

"Because sometimes life isn't fair, and good people are punished." She wiped her cheek on her shoulder, removing the moisture.

He pulled back and met her gaze. "Oh, God, Leah." He cupped her cheeks, his thumbs wiping away her tears in gentle strokes. "What have I done?"

"Nothing." The word stuck in her throat. He hadn't done a thing... Yet he'd done everything, too—lifted her up, placed her on a pedestal, admired her without reservation. Then Julie kicked the platform out from beneath her. "This isn't your fault."

She comforted him the best she could, listening to his cathartic whispers as a stabbing pain built in her brain. When his words tapered, she excused herself and fled for the bathroom, grabbing her cell along the way. She needed to find calm in the chaotic storm. She needed to decrease the pressure pushing down on her head. The long-forgotten sense of a panic attack was building with each hyperventilated breath, her loss of control imminent.

She locked the door, cleaned herself up, and gripped the counter as she hung her head and stared at the tiled floor.

He was having a baby.

Julie would remain in his life.

She gulped in air and pressed a palm over the throbbing in her skull.

Their relationship was over.

He had to build a future without her.

"Stop it." She held her breath and stood tall. "You're stronger than this." She waited until the need for air became a physical burn, then sucked in a long, deep breath. "No more."

She closed her eyes and pictured nothingness. No Ryan. No Reckless. No panic. She forced the calm she needed. "Focus."

Dissect and assess. Evaluate and strategize.

"One thought at a time," she whispered.

OK. Here goes.

When the news of the pregnancy came out, his reputation would be hammered—inevitable. He'd be accused of fleeing his fatherhood role to snatch a new piece of ass in the form of Felicity Knight—inevitable. Her own reputation would be tarnished due to the recent blog interview. Speculation would be rife. Accusations would be harsh.

All inevitable.

But there were things she could control.

Felicity and Slicker were a chart topper away from being a distant memory.

The rumors of her own involvement with Ryan would dissolve without evidence to back up the claims. The last thing he needed was more fuel to the wildfire.

No. She sucked in a deep breath and choked on it as a sob escape. The last thing he needed was their relationship getting in the way of him making the right decision about what he wanted for his future. And the last thing she needed was another threat to her career when she'd already begun to lose the man of her dreams.

Being a parent meant everything to him. Having a family was his aspiration. As much as she wanted to cling to him right now, she needed to step back and give him the space he needed to come to a conclusion with a clear mind.

"It'll work out." It had to. Right?

She slid her cell off the counter and scrolled through her contact list. The number of people she could rely on was short. Miniscule. If you took out the three men who would despise her for interrupting the little time they had with their partners, it only left one person she was willing to ask for help.

She tapped Mitch's name before she could regret it and sent him an urgent message. There was no time to wait for a response. Her plan wouldn't change if he left her hanging.

She washed her face, brushed her hair, and added a light dash of mascara. While Ryan was quiet on the other side of her apartment, she tiptoed from the bathroom and grabbed a change of clothes. She was in business mode now, and a work dress would give her the strength she needed to smother all the feels and bolster her professionalism.

When she walked back into the living room, Ryan was passed out on the couch, legs and arms splayed in all their naked glory. Quietly, she picked up his clothes, willing to give him extra moments to sleep off the effects of the alcohol. She had his belongings in a folded pile on the armrest when he sniffed and raised his head to give the room a once over.

"Shit." He swiped a lazy hand over his beard. "How long was I out?"

"Not long."

He looked her up and down, the narrowing of his eyes taking in her change in appearance. "What's going on?"

She handed him his clothes as he sat up. "You need to get dressed."

He frowned as he pulled the T-shirt over his head, his gaze still holding her. "You opposed to having me naked?" He yanked on his underwear and stood to do the same with his jeans.

"No." She gave him a disheartened smile. "But it's illegal to go out in public like that."

"I don't want to go out in public."

She squared her shoulders, poised to speak.

"You're kicking me out?" he whispered.

"I'm giving you space in the hopes it will help you make the best decision for your future."

He frowned. "You think I want to go back to her?"

"No. But you want this baby. And you've already told me you would've remained married to Julie for the sake of a child."

"That was before."

Before us. Before love. "You owe yourself the time to determine what you want."

"I want you."

"I know. And in the heat of the moment, while you're still in shock, I believe you. But when the alcohol wears off and you're able to think clearly, and long-term, your outlook might be different."

"I don't need clarity."

"Well, maybe I do." She swallowed, knowing he wouldn't give in while this argument remained focused on him. "Bringing a child into our relationship changes everything. If we stayed together, I'd be a step-mom. A parent. I'd have to deal with Julie for as long as we were together." She tapped her fist to her chest. "Those are huge changes for me."

He balked, the shock quickly settling to comprehension. "I understand."

No, he didn't. He didn't understand how she had to change her tactics and make this a selfish request just to get him to listen. This was all about him. His child. His life. Her reluctance didn't matter.

"I'll get going, th—"

There was a knock on the door. The cavalry.

"Who's here?"

He backed away and she struggled not to go after him.

"Mitch. He'll help you get to a hotel." She strode for the door and pulled it open to welcome Mitch and Alana. There was no comfort from their appearance. Only the guilt of betrayal. "Come in."

"You OK?" Alana gently gripped Leah's wrist while Mitch strode ahead.

"I'm fine. I just need help getting Ryan out of here. If he walks out alone, it'll cause headlines we don't need."

"Are you sure that's all it is?"

Leah nodded and turned to see Ryan at the end of the hall, Mitch at his back.

"Did you tell them?" he asked, his face shadowed.

"No. I haven't said a word."

"And we're not going to ask." Mitch clapped Ryan on the shoulder. "Whatever has gone down is between the two of you. I'm only here to make sure you get to a hotel safely."

"Or you can stay with us," Alana offered. "We don't mind."

"For the record," Ryan started forward, "I don't want to go anywhere." He stopped in front of Leah, his hand skimming her waist.

He leaned into her and she welcomed the brief swipe of his lips. Nothing would ever beat the taste of him. Alcohol riddled or not.

"I'll see you tomorrow," he murmured against her mouth.

"OK." She squeezed her eyes shut, not strong enough to withstand his stare.

There was a brush of his fingers, another swipe of lips, then he was gone and all that was left in his place was defeat.

RYAN CLIMBED THE JET STAIRS AND PIVOTED SIDEWAYS TO ALLOW FOR HIS heavy duffle to fit through the door.

"Sorry I'm late."

The hostess smiled and grabbed for his bag. "No problem. Take a seat and we'll get going."

He hunched over and worked his way into the main cabin, closing the security partition behind him and flicking on the Do-Not-Disturb light. Everyone else was onboard. Mitch and Alana were in the back in the recliners, looking at him in uninformed pity, while Mason, Sean, and Blake sat on the sofa opposite Leah, staring at the tablet she held up in display.

"Nice of you to join us." Mason leaned back, one arm spreading across the top of the head rest. "We were about to leave your ass behind."

He ignored the taunt as the jet engines rumbled to life. "I lost track of time." Truth. He'd spent the night detoxing, trying to clear his head in an effort to think straight. He hadn't been able to sleep, hadn't been able to do much of anything other than type messages to Leah and then delete them again. He must've passed out somewhere around mid-morning because he woke with an hour to spare before their flight was scheduled to leave.

"You look like shit." Sean scrutinized him. "Did you and the boss have a late one?"

"No. I crashed in a hotel."

Blake narrowed his stare. "Didn't want to risk getting caught?"

"Yeah. Something like that."

Leah kept her focus on the tablet, refusing to meet his gaze. It wasn't hard to see why. Puffiness surrounded her eyes, the pink skin barely covered by make-up.

"What are we looking at?" He dropped down on the sofa beside her and fought not to greet her with a kiss.

"I was explaining the plan to try and get Slicker on a chart. Time is running short and we can't afford to let this slide any longer." She swiveled the tablet in his direction, showing the document filled with bullet-points. "The only way we can achieve our goal is to focus all our efforts on one major promotion."

Right. He should've expected this response. While he'd spent the night searching for answers, she'd focused on distraction.

"I've suggested the second performance in San Antonio. The show is almost sold out and the stadium holds around nineteen thousand. It's a good size crowd to get our point across. It also gives me a week to organize promo material and advertising."

She shot him a two second glance, the sight of those bloodshot eyes enough to suffocate him. "Will seven days be too long for you?"

It wasn't a question of time constraints with Felicity. Her concern surrounded Julie and how many days his wife would allow before announcing his impending fatherhood.

"I'll make it work." He hadn't spoken to the child incubator since she'd shared the baby news. But he would. Soon enough.

"Any longer than that and we're cutting our chances to organize something else if our first attempt isn't successful. Any shorter and we won't have time to build the hype before the show."

"Just so you know," Mason interrupted, "I don't plan on doing this twice. I'll pull whatever strings necessary to ensure we get the job done right the first time."

"Leave the strings to me. I don't need you causing more headaches."

Ryan kept his focus on her, hating every second she didn't return the affection. "Seven days is fine."

She nodded and swiped to a new page on her tablet.

"Can we hold up for a sec?" Blake glanced between them. "Three nights ago I fell asleep to the soundtrack of you two getting your fuck on in the bunk beside mine. The following night you were all over each other on that very sofa." He pointed to where Ryan sat. "Now you can't even look at each other. What gives?"

Leah remained silent, her gaze downcast.

"Things are complicated at the moment," he admitted. "We've got stuff we need to discuss."

"There's nothing to discuss," she murmured. "We need to focus on the tour."

Silence descended as he stared at her profile, the growing noise from the engines increasing as the jet inched forward.

"What'd you do?" Mason grated, leaving no doubt Ryan was the target of his question.

"He didn't do anything." Leah tapped the tablet screen. "Can we please concentrate on the task at hand? I'll want you guys to sign a heap of promotional material, and we'll get local media involved. I'm sure Grander will help, too."

The jet increased its speed, the accompanying sound mimicking the roar in his chest. His friends stared at him in question, some in accusation, while the bird propelled into the air. The velocity had him holding on to the arm rest, his fingers digging deep as words failed him.

He *had* done something wrong. He'd done *everything* wrong. And he couldn't figure out how to fix it. The thought of getting back to the complicated existence of their secret relationship seemed like a fairytale in comparison to the current shit-storm.

"Lee?" Blake inched forward. "We'll have to pause the business talk because I need to know what's going on with you."

Leah raised her chin. "It's nothing that won't blow over." She held Blake's gaze, her throat working over a heavy swallow as the jet began to level out. "I crossed a line. I made mistakes. And I'm hoping you'll let me fix them without making a big deal about it."

"Leah..." He didn't know what to say. This burden was supposed to be on his shoulders. So why could he see more crushing weight on hers?

"We're family." Alana pushed from her recliner and came to crouch at Leah's side, Mitch following after. "Let us help."

Leah's jaw worked, her forehead creasing in a show of self-control. He couldn't handle it. Her pain was his pain, the agony clutching at his ribs and tearing bones apart. His Wonder Woman was breaking, and the worst part was knowing this was her restrained. Whatever she'd put herself through last night would've been far worse.

"Julie's pregnant." He tore his attention from her and met Mason's judgment. "I found out yesterday."

Silence hit like an atom bomb as matching expressions of horror beamed back at him. There was no happiness. No congratulations. The upcoming birth seemed more like an announcement of death.

"Fuck. Me." Mason balked.

"Yeah... That about sums it up."

Leah crossed her arms over her chest and stared in a daze. He couldn't stand the indifference. She needed to scream at him. To react. The hollow detachment was pure torture to his guilt.

"I want to say congratulations, man," Sean started, "but that shit won't leave my mouth without me cringing."

He shrugged. "I hadn't expected high-fives."

"Please tell me you're not thinking about going back to her." Blake rested his elbows on his knees. "She's toxic. With or without a kid."

"But a baby needs a father," Mitch argued. "He can't leave her high and dry."

"Christ," Leah hissed. "Cut him a break, he only found out yesterday."

He returned his focus to her, loving how she stood up for him. Loving her more than life itself. "Truth is, I'm still struggling to come to terms with it."

Personally, he was confident he could make a rash decision and handle the consequences. But Leah needed time, and through all the mess and destruction, his main focus remained on her.

"You're stupid if you think that kid is yours." Mason didn't hide the disgust in his tone. "She could've spread her legs for half the US population while you've been separated."

"Mason..." Alana warned. "I think we need to be supportive."

"We've been supportive of Julie's crap for years." Sean slunk back in his seat. "I think I've reached my limit."

"God, you're an asshole." Leah shoved to her feet and squeezed by Mitch. "I can't stomach the garbage all of you are spewing. With the myriad of defiled women lying in your wake, you'd think the four of you would be less judgmental about an unplanned pregnancy."

She strode through the cabin, her footsteps shaky, and shut herself into the bathroom with a slam of the door.

Then the silence returned. This time thicker. Heavier. Nobody looked at him. He was visually shunned and made to feel like a leper, and rightly so. His friends had put up with Julie's bullshit for years, keeping the majority of their thoughts to themselves even when his wife hadn't.

"I'm sorry, Ryan." Alana broke the tension. "I wish I knew what to say."

"Yeah, me, too." Mitch leaned forward and landed a soft punch to Ryan's shoulder. "I gather Leah didn't take the news well."

"How could she?" He stared at the bathroom door, wishing he was comforting her instead of explaining himself. "All I want to do is tell her it's going to be OK, but I can't bring myself to lie to her."

"Oh, Ryan." Alana took Leah's seat on the sofa beside him. "It'll work out."

"You might just need a break," Mason offered. "Forget about her while you pull your shit together. It's not like she's going anywhere."

"Forget?" He gave a bark of laughter. "I wish. She's all I can think about, but now I've got a kid, and no matter what happens, it's going to affect her."

"Fuck, man." Mitch shook his head. "I wouldn't know what to do."

Alana's hand rested on his thigh with a reassuring squeeze. "Like Leah said, you only found out yesterday. There's no rush to make a decision."

"Yeah, no rush." He sighed. "Apart from knowing I'm holding her happiness hostage."

•••

Leah sat on the lowered toilet seat, staring at the unfavorable reflection in the bathroom mirror. She looked like death. No exaggeration. There was major luggage under her eyes, her skin felt dirty, and even her hair lacked the usual bounce. And no amount of foundation or mascara could diminish the carnage.

It hadn't been an easy feat to scrape her heart off the living room floor. The process required numerous boxes of tissues and a scathing mental chastisement before she reclaimed her resolve and pieced together the broken parts of her soul.

Like always, distraction helped. It soothed and consoled, shoving away the spiral of demise hovering over her shoulder like a shadow.

She spent hours working out a plan to get the Slicker-Grander issue out of the way. She even gave the duo a nickname—Slander—but the title seemed a lot funnier at two in the morning when she was delirious and recovering from her emotional breaking point.

A gentle tap sounded, followed by Alana's soft voice from the other side of the door. "Can I come in?"

"Yeah." Leah reached out and flicked the lock.

Alana pushed inside, an apologetic grimace on her face. She leaned against the clear wall of the shower and cleared her throat. "Is there anything I can do?"

"No. Nothing can be done. And losing my shit at the guys doesn't help."

"They deserved it. Ryan needs their support, not their judgment."

"True." Leah stared down at her hands in her lap and wondered why she hadn't grown smarter with age. The last few weeks had been spent in the mind of a love-struck teenager. A careless, love-struck fool.

"You should've told me yesterday. I could've stayed with you."

"I couldn't broadcast his private life." She continued speaking to her hands. "And besides, it's not like we had a three-year relationship. We were together for a few days. I'll get over it."

Eventually.

"You're not going to fight for him?"

"No." In this she was adamant. "It's too risky. It always was. We were stupid to think this would work out differently. If Julie hadn't been the detonator, my job would've been."

"But the two of you are great together."

"And so are fries dipped in ice cream but that shit isn't healthy. We've gotta move on."

Alana remained quiet, the silence voicing innumerable questions Leah didn't want to answer. This wasn't going to blow over in a day, or a week. Her feelings for Ryan were always going to hover, no matter what he decided. There was no easy out. No quick fix. Just pain and torture she needed to ignore for the sake of her career and the band.

"For once, I don't know how to react," she admitted. "My entire world has turned upside down. I always thought I was independent. That I was this kick-ass manager who was strong and sure and capable. I was invincible until Ryan kissed me. Then, all of a sudden, I put everything at risk with my stupid feelings—my career, my income, my friends, my future." She sniffed, then tensed her jaw, refusing to let pity take hold. "Nobody understands that I wouldn't merely lose my job if my breach of contract was common knowledge. I would've lost everything."

"Here, take this." Alana reached into her pocket and pulled out a perfectly pressed handkerchief.

"Thank you." She dabbed at her nose.

"I'm still listening. Please keep going."

Leah sighed, hating the shame accompanying what she was about to say. "I don't have friends outside of the band, Al. Or family. There's no high school buddies. Nobody I can rely on for an uninformed opinion. I pushed everyone away in an effort to invest all my attention into building Reckless. I don't even have a god damn hobby."

She clutched the handkerchief in her fingers to curb her frustration. "Reckless defines me. Without them, I'm nothing. Yet, my happiness with the band and my love for Ryan are two completely separate things. They're mutually exclusive. I can't have both. It's one or the other. And Julie's pregnancy made the choice a simple one."

Alana shook her head. "I refuse to believe this is the end for the two of you. Not when you love each other."

"I want him," she admitted. "I want him so bad it makes my entire body feel bruised. But I can no longer risk myself, or the family I've built. I won't risk losing *me*."

"What if you could buy out the clause in your contract. Or renegotiate?"

"There's no way my boss would agree, not when Julie implicated me in that online interview. It'll be even worse once the pregnancy is announced and thrown in the blender along with his fake relationship with Felicity. There's too much scandal."

"But what if?" Alana straightened. "You never know what's going to happen next in the music world. Any number of things could change your situation. Your boss could sell the company. He could retire and someone new might be more amiable to your needs—"

"That's a little far-fetched."

"I don't care. You can't lose everything you've ever wanted with him because of this."

Leah stood and looked Alana in the eye. "What I want is for Ryan to do what's best for Ryan. He spent years doing what was best for Julie. Then he became caught up in this Slicker scandal because it was best for the band. And now he's contemplating what path to take for his future and I know full-well his own interests aren't at the top of that list."

She sighed, long and low and cathartic. "He's thinking about me when he needs to be thinking about the right choices for him. And none of this can be determined overnight. It can't even be determined in a week or a month. He can't anticipate how his life will change once his palm rests against Julie's belly and the baby kicks for the first time. He can't predict the pride and reconnection he'll feel when he holds his child and knows Julie created that gift."

She gave Alana a sad smile, not caring if she understood, because her mind was made up.

"I don't want to be a ball and chain during any of that process. I already ruined his marriage. I won't risk getting involved and destroying his chance at a family, too."

"You didn't—"

"Don't try to argue." Leah held up a hand, already anticipating the response. "He already admitted I was the reason his marriage ended. So there is no way I'm going to take this baby away from him, too. With me out of the picture, maybe they can make it work."

She could sense another protest and was losing the strength to fight.

"Look, I'm not sure what the future holds. Who knows, something crazy might happen and Ryan and I might find our way back to each other. But for now, I need to sever all ties and concentrate on my job. It's the best thing for both of us." She straightened her shoulders, preparing to face her musicians.

"Please tell me if there's anything I can do to help."

"No, I'm good. I promise." Leah yanked open the door, her step forward blocked by Ryan's strong frame. Remorse gleamed in his eyes, freezing her in place. How long had he been standing there? What had he heard?

"I'll give you two some privacy." Alana squeezed past and made for the Reckless men trying to discreetly eavesdrop with their mouths shut and heads quirked toward the impending conversation.

"Ryan?"

He blinked away the deer-in-headlights expression and stepped into the space the opened door provided, giving them a modicum of privacy. "How are you holding up?" He clutched either side of the frame, his gentle voice in contrast to his now predatory stance.

"I'm taking it as it comes."

"You've settled back into Wonder Woman mode?"

"I'm far from Wonder Woman." Unless the superhero had started dropping balls left, right, and center.

"Not to me."

She snorted. "Well...thank you. You should know that Felicity is behind you all the way, too. I called her last night to give her a heads up on the possibility of drama unfolding from the Julie camp. I didn't give her specifics. I only made her aware she may need to pull out the no-comment card and flash it around if a storm arrives."

"Shit." He frowned. "I didn't even think to call her."

"Nobody expects you to think straight right now. This is why you need space to clear your head." She gave a sad smile. "I also called my boss, and although he didn't say it aloud, I know he's disappointed in me. I should've had the situation with Grander settled already. Instead, I got caught up in my feelings for you and justified every reason why Bruce has the no-relationship clause in my contract."

"But you were happy. *I* made you happy."

"And you still will. But from now on it has to be as friends."

He flinched. "No."

He reached for her, strong fingers scorching the burning heat of her cheek. He couldn't do that. He couldn't touch. Couldn't soothe. Not anymore.

"You wanted space yesterday and I reluctantly gave it to you. But I'm not going to go back to being friends. I don't want to be with her."

She nodded. "I know. But would you feel the same if I hadn't torn the two of you apart?" He opened his mouth and she continued before he could protest. "I always thought I hid my feelings. Now I realize that was a lie. I sabotaged your marriage. I made it obvious I loved you. I didn't have to say the words. You could see it. Everyone could. And my lack of professionalism cost you dearly."

"In all honesty, sweetheart, that's bullshit."

"Is it? You were madly in love with her when you first married. I remember, because I tried to deny I was jealous. And at the first sign of trouble, I jumped at the opportunity to be your confidante. I never should've crossed that line, because deep down, I knew what I was starting." She grabbed his hand from her cheek and squeezed his fingers. "The truth is, if I hadn't ruined what the two of you had, right now you'd be celebrating the news of your child. You'd be so happy, Ryan. And through the envy, I would've been happy for you, too."

"I disagree. The two of us were inevitable—"

"Because of my feminine wiles and subliminal messages. How could you resist?" She chuckled through her desire to crumple. "And now you need to put all that in perspective. We have to go our separate ways so you can concentrate on the pregnancy and I can focus on Slicker to ensure the tour doesn't get extended."

She dropped his hand and the jovial expression to drive home her message. There was no negotiating, even though his searching gaze made her want to falter.

He nodded, slow at first, then more convincing. "I'll do what you want, Leah. I'll think about it. I'll make the decision that's best for me, and when it brings me straight back to you, will you accept that? Will you support me having a child with someone else?"

She sucked in a breath, held tight until it turned toxic. He still didn't understand. Those gentle eyes and loving heart weren't allowing her message to sink in. "Ryan, my support is inconsequential. We both know this will never work. Julie is only one force trying to tear us apart. My contract is the other. It's best if you let me go and concentrate on being the father you've always wanted to be."

"You're placing me back in the friend zone permanently?" He inched closer, his hand returning to her cheek.

"I'm sorry."

"Don't be, because it's not going to happen." His fingers brushed her skin, trailing over her jaw, her neck. Even his gaze lingered like a physical caress, his affection hitting her on every level. "Fighting the need to kiss you is killing me."

She closed her eyes at the rapid sense of forming tears. She wanted his kiss. Wanted to rip it from him without apology or remorse.

"I love you, Leah."

She whimpered—like a fool, like a weak, pathetic kitten.

"I can hate myself for it later, but right now all I want to do is place my lips against yours."

She sucked in his breath and descended into the darkness of inevitability as his mouth touched hers. She was at his mercy, untethered, floating aimlessly. There was so much love in their connection, so much necessity in the softness of his mouth, his lips, his tongue.

All of it redundant.

"Ryan…" She pushed at his chest, demanding space.

I love you. I should've agreed to run away with you. And even crazier than that, I wish like hell I was the one carrying your child instead of a woman we both despise, but…

"Please don't make this any harder than it needs to be."

San Antonio, TX

"RYAN?" Felicity nudged him in the ribs, dragging his attention out of the staring match with the carpet and back to the journalist sitting before them. "Sorry. What was the question?"

"There's no more questions." The woman offered her hand to shake. "I can see the final weeks of the tour are taking their toll. I'll let you both get back to work."

Ryan clasped her hand and they stood together. "We appreciate you taking the time to chat with us."

"It was my pleasure." She released her grip and pocketed her notepad as her cameraman began packing up equipment. "We'll broadcast the segment on the news tonight. We wish you all the best with the show."

He remained quiet, zoning out of the present and back into his thoughts while Felicity pushed to her feet beside him. At Leah's request, he'd joined Flick in interview after interview to promote tomorrow night's epic performance. The two of them were the face of the event. Slicker and Reckless joining forces to create unstoppable magnificence.

They'd promoted the outdoor activities available to people who didn't have tickets to the concert. They'd boasted the thousands of promo items up for grabs and how the show would be live streamed to people outside the stadium for one night only.

He'd done everything Leah had asked, including keeping his distance for the last six days. Their interaction had been kept to a minimum and strictly band related. He hadn't voiced his concerns about her wellbeing. He hadn't confirmed if Alana's comments were true—that Leah had been a mass of anxiety and nausea since New York.

He kept his promise. Even though it destroyed him.

"I guess this is it." Felicity turned into him as the news crew left the room, pulling the door shut behind them. Her face was solemn. Big eyes and a furrowed brow. "Tomorrow this crazy charade will be over."

"Yep." And a new one would begin.

He tugged her into his arms and sank his chin against the top of her head. "Are you and Hannah excited?"

She shook her head. "I know I didn't hide my resentment when we first started this crazy scheme, but I'm going to hate pretending we're enemies even more."

"Me, too." Their fake relationship would end as soon as Julie announced her pregnancy, and then Felicity would play the role of scorned lover until the gossip died down. All he had to do was sit back and watch the carnage. "Hopefully, it will all work as planned and you'll gain more followers from all the shared sympathy."

"Popularity is the last thing on my mind. I'm more concerned about ruining your reputation."

"Don't be." He'd already kissed his good name goodbye and finger-waved that fucker farewell. "As long as the two of us are still friends behind closed doors, I'll be happy."

She hugged him tighter. "We'll always be friends."

Friends. The word stuck in his head, reminding him of the one friendship he'd always valued above all others. There was no way he could last months, putting space between himself and Leah. Not even weeks. He'd already endured six days of hell where he'd had to watch her suffer from a distance. He couldn't take much more.

"I've lost you again." Felicity leaned back and met his gaze. "What are you thinking about?"

"I think I'm done waiting."

"For what?"

"For her."

A knowing grin curved her lips. "About time."

"It's only been six days."

"And you made up your mind on day one."

"True." He inclined his head. "But Leah needed time, too—"

"To strengthen her resolve about never getting back together."

He stiffened, the tiniest sliver of fear brushing the surface. "No. She wanted me to have a clear head."

"Ryan..." She looked at him as if he'd missed something. As if he were a child who hadn't caught on to an easy concept.

"What?"

"No woman ever wants a man to take his time making a decision about a relationship. You either want it or you don't. At least, that's the way I see it." She shrugged. "From my point of view, she was banking on your kindness to give her space to move on."

He shook his head. "No." Leah wouldn't play him. Yeah, she'd openly said they were back to being friends, but he hadn't believed it. He couldn't believe it. Not when they were in love.

There was a knock at the door. "Ry?" Blake's tattooed fingers gripped the wood before his head came into view. "Come on, we've got three million posters left to sign before tomorrow night."

"Give me a minute." He raked his hands through his hair. Was he back to square one? Would he have to repeat history all over again, convincing Leah they could make this work, all because he'd done the right thing in giving her space?

Fuck.

Blake pushed the door wider and stepped inside. "What's going on?"

"I think Leah's been playing chess, while I've been playing checkers."

"Is that supposed to make sense?" Blake gave him a blank stare.

"Probably not." He pulled tighter on his hair. *Think, think, think.* Space was one thing. Termination was another.

"Did you hear me? We've got sixty-three billion posters to sign, and if they don't get done today, Leah's going to shove the colored markers in a place I won't appreciate."

"*Give him a second*," Felicity grated.

Blake raised a brow. "Bossy. Just the way my boy likes 'em. You sure you two haven't hooked up?"

"He's got a dick." She rolled her eyes. "So, no, he's not my type."

"Lesbian?" Blake glanced to his left, pinning Ryan with a wicked grin. "Did you cause that, buddy?"

"Are you referring to lesbianitis?" Felicity cocked a hip. "Because, yeah, it's totally catchy."

"Don't get your ovaries in a twist. I was merely referring to Ryan's special skill set. One kiss from him sent Leah fleeing to the other side of the country. So..." He shrugged. "You never know."

"*I* know," she growled.

"And I totally respect and admire your decision." Blake raised his hands in surrender. "In fact, I'd love to introduce you to my wife and maybe encourage you to sprinkle some of your girl-on-girl tendencies her way."

Felicity gaped and turned her wide-eyed stare to Ryan. "Is he serious?"

"Unfortunately."

"How do I make it stop?"

Blake chuckled. "I'm kidding. Lighten up."

Movement in the doorway drew Ryan's attention. Inch by inch, Sean silently backed into the room, his focus still on the hall.

"Out." Blake pointed to the door. "This is my hiding spot."

"Nope," Sean whispered and shut the door gently. "I'm not going anywhere." He leaned against the glossy wood and repeatedly flexed his right hand. "If I have to sign one more poster, I'm not sure I'll regain feeling in my fingers."

A bang cracked through the room and Sean went barreling forward as the door flung wide, Mason and Mitch scuffling in after.

"I think we lost her." Mason panted, slamming the door shut.

Felicity looked from Sean to Mason to Mitch. "You're all running from Leah?"

Mitch nodded. "Don't look at me like that. Satan's got nothing on that woman when she's running behind schedule."

"Ohh...kay..." Felicity frowned as she crept closer to Ryan's side. "I think that's my cue to leave." She kept her gaze on the rest of the band as she placed a quick peck on his cheek. "If I don't speak to you before you figure out what you're doing with the lady in question, good luck."

"Thanks." He gave her his best I-can-handle-this smile and watched her leave the room.

"Did we walk in on something?" Mason picked up a wooden chair and jimmied it under the door handle.

"They were *not* having sex. I can assure you of that." Blake winked at Ryan and tapped the side of his nose with his index finger.

How was he supposed to react? How? His friends were fucking morons.

"I'm not even going to ask." Mason tested the door handle and nodded at a job well done. "I don't think demon woman will get through that."

"Then I think we have a problem." Ryan pinched the bridge of his nose. "Because the woman you're trying to keep out, is the one I need to go after."

They all glared at him.

"You're not exposing our hiding place. Whatever it is can wait." Mitch sank into a chair and kicked a leg over the arm rest. "Leah's not in her right mind, anyway. It's like PMS, hysteria, and bipolar all rolled into a package of heels, tits, and flawless make-up."

It didn't matter. If Felicity was right, he didn't want to give Leah another second thinking he was letting her walk away. He had to bridge the gap. At least temporarily. Until he worked out a plan that made everything fall into place. "I've seen her at her worst. It won't bother me."

He made for the door and Sean stepped in front of him.

"You've seen her at her worst, but have you witnessed her Jekyll and Hyde impersonation? Because since this morning, she's got that shit down pat."

"And I'm not pointing fingers," Mason added. "But I think we're all pretty clear on who should be taking the full brunt of this ass reaming."

Ryan turned to face everyone, arms wide. "Then let me out. I'll take it."

"Or will you make it worse, my little grasshopper?" Mason tented his fingers in front of his chest and tapped them together. "Why do you need to see her so urgently?"

Admitting he may have made an error in judgment wasn't on the top of his to-do list. They would slay him. Verbally, at least. Then again, they may confirm he hadn't made a mistake after all. "I think I fucked up."

"Clearly," Mitch drawled. "You have a fake girlfriend, impregnated the wrong woman, and ditched the one you were supposed to keep. What's your point?"

"I didn't ditch Leah. She was the one who told me to take time to think about what I wanted."

Blake stepped forward. "I thought you were the one who asked for space."

"No." He shook his head. "The baby hasn't changed the way I feel about her. I'm not going back to married life."

"Does Julie know that?" Mitch asked.

"Not yet."

"How about Leah?"

"I told her the day I found out about the baby. And then again on the jet. But she still wanted me to take more time."

Sean groaned. "No wonder she's in an epically bitchy mood. You've left her hanging."

Ryan's heartrate increased. "I gave her what she wanted—time. Space. How can I be in the wrong?"

"For starters, don't listen to a woman when she says she's 'fine,' or that 'nothing is wrong,' or if she ever utters the words 'I'm not mad'—"

"Or 'I'm almost ready,'" Mitch added. "That shit is *never* true."

"And never, ever believe her if she tells you to take time to think about your relationship." Mason clucked his tongue and shook his head. "What she's really saying is 'do you love me enough to make an on the spot decision about our future?'"

"Umm…" Ryan wasn't sure if he should be shocked at their insight or petrified that he'd clearly made the wrong move. Either way, he was fucked if these four were now the experts and he was the novice. "Thanks… I guess it's more important than ever to go find her."

"Touch that chair and I'll be forced to hurt you." Sean cracked his knuckles, not an ounce of humor in his features.

"But you just said—"

"We said you fucked up," Mason muttered. "We didn't say we were letting you expose our cavern of protection."

Sean inched closer to the door. "She's in Lord-of-the-Flies mode and we all refuse to be Piggy."

"But what we can do," Blake drawled, "is help you find those balls of yours so you can tell her how it's going to be."

Fucking morons. He couldn't understand how they weren't laughing through the pitiful misogyny. It didn't matter, though, because he already knew they weren't going to let him out. Not without a fight.

"Fine." He slumped onto the nearest chair, resigned to wait it out. "In all your infinite wisdom, please tell me exactly how I'm going to get Leah back."

Twenty-Four

LEAH'S FEET WERE KILLING HER. SHE HADN'T WALKED THIS MUCH IN YEARS, but the back and forth from the dressing room to the parking lot was well worth the blisters. The stadium had been surrounded by fans hours before Slicker took the stage. Now, with ticket holders inside, the people outside were still amassing to see the live performance feed.

Scott had already emailed her with a report to show Slicker's sales had increased over the last hour. Their social media followers had, too. Volunteers were handing out promotional items to those who downloaded on the spot, and although there would be hell to pay for the stack of Reckless posters left unsigned, she was sure her men would work the crowd into a frenzy once they walked on stage and blew their chart target out of the water.

Everything was working seamlessly.

So why did it feel like the world was ending?

Ryan had done what she wanted. He'd given her space. But all the distance achieved was heartache. Her anxiety was out of control. Her mood mimicked a heartrate monitor. Up, down, up, down. She couldn't cement the professionalism she'd always clung to. It was elusive, hiding behind a sea of tears and a blanket of nausea.

Tomorrow would be worse.

Even if they successfully removed the Slicker burden, Ryan's fake relationship with Felicity would be replaced with an announcement of an unborn child from his real wife. A charade would be interchanged with something more tangible and destructive.

"Leah?" a voice called through her ear-piece.

She paused in the middle of the hall and pressed a finger to the device to respond. "Yeah?"

"I've got a stack of people trying to get backstage. Did you organize some sort of pre-show event I don't know about?"

"No." She continued down the hall. "It's the same as usual. The last thing we need is more people back here."

"Some are adamant."

"I don't care. If they don't have a pass, they don't get backstage."

"Roger that."

She stopped outside the Reckless dressing room and tapped her knuckles against the wood before letting herself in. They were immersed in laughter as she entered, all their faces alight, the flashes of teeth, dimples and smirks unwavering as they turned their attention to her.

"Evenin', Cruella." Mason stood beside the refreshment table, a bottle of water in his hand.

The rest of them were lounging in different positions. Mitch was seated on a backward wooden chair. Sean was laying on the sofa. Blake had a hip cocked against the armrest. And Ryan... He was in the far corner of the room, leaning against the dressing table counter.

She didn't meet his gaze. Couldn't. Not tonight.

"Are you all ready?" They stared at her and smiled from an unknown high she hoped wasn't drug related. "Why do you all look overly excited?"

"'Cause it's an exciting kind of night," Mitch drawled.

Sean sat up and pulled a pair of drumsticks from his back pocket to twirl in his fingers. "You look nervous."

Good. Exuding nervousness was better than the heartbreak she was trying to hide. "Once tonight is over, I'll be fine."

"Thank fuck for that," Blake muttered.

Mitch snorted.

She made a mental note to retaliate in the near future. "Do you all remember the drill for tonight?"

"Yep." Mason took a gulp from a water bottle and nodded. "Do whatever it takes to encourage downloads. Exchange sales for posters. Offer to sing more songs. Sell off sexual favors."

"I think you can hold off on the sex." Sean continued to twirl his sticks. "We don't want people demanding their money back."

"For once, can we please take this seriously?" She sighed. "We've got a lot riding on the success of tonight's show."

"Don't fret." Mason smirked. "I've got a few tricks up my sleeve to ensure Slicker's spot on a chart."

"A few tricks?" His involvement in the business side of things was never good. The arrogance he expelled always burned bridges she had to mend. More work. More unease. "What have you done?"

"A magician never reveals his secrets."

"For fuck's sake, Mason." She was living on exacerbated hormones, little sleep, and a lack of sustenance because stress continued to make her nauseated. And he thought taunting her was a good idea? "If you don't quit increasing my anxiety, *this* magician is going to pull your lungs out of your ass, and I'm more than happy to reveal how I plan to do it."

Mitch snickered.

Sean chuckled.

Ryan cleared his throat.

"Point taken." Mason took two steps and slumped into a seat, a grin fighting to break free from the corner of his lips.

Why were they all sporting jovial moods? Usually they were in the zone before a show. Focused and stoic. They had to be up to something. Or on something.

A shout of "five minutes" came from the hall and the men began to move. Sean stood. Mason made for the bathroom. Mitch and Blake headed for the refreshment table and grabbed bottles of water. The only one who didn't budge was Ryan. He remained in her periphery. A solid rock in a flowing stream.

"Can I talk to you?"

She pretended he wasn't addressing her.

"Leah," he murmured, his voice barely heard over the flushing toilet from the bathroom.

She played with her ear-piece and ignored her panic as Blake and Mitch walked into the hall.

"Leah," he repeated, this time louder.

Reluctantly, she met his gaze and held her breath through the pain of it. Every time their eyes met her entire body reacted—heart, mind—even her soul.

"Can you come over here for a minute?"

She remained in place, unwilling to move. "What's up?"

His lips quirked. "Come here." There was a demand in his voice now, the subtlest insistence she couldn't deny.

She sighed, trying to simulate frustration when her throat was closing from yearning, and strode toward him. "Is something wrong?"

From the corner of her eye, she watched Sean leave the room. Then Mason was heading for the door, about to leave them in dangerous solitude.

"Good luck, Ry."

Good luck? She shot a frantic glance to Mason as he reached for the door handle. All he did was laugh before escaping. *Shit.* They were definitely up to something.

She paused a few feet from Ryan's position against the counter and met her reflection in the mirror behind him. She looked calm. Almost in control. Until he lunged for her, one arm weaving around her waist to pull her into his position against the counter.

She froze, every muscle tight.

"Ryan." She poised to push away from him, her palms on his muscled chest, her heart gagging her throat.

"I need to tell you something."

"Can you tell me while we're not touching?" She tried to laugh off the situation and failed when it came out as a whimper.

"No. I need your full focus."

"Well, you've certainly got it."

That grin continued to beam back at her, a tiny glimmer of wickedness shining around the rough appeal of his short beard. "I wanted to tell you I'm calling Julie after the show."

"OK..." She swallowed.

"I'm letting her know there's no chance I'm moving back in with her."

"OK..." She swallowed again.

"What I'm not going to tell her, is that from now on, I'll be with you." Those eyes gleamed at her, honest and true. Their depths filled with unwarranted confidence.

"Ryan..." Her ear-piece crackled and one of the security guards spoke her name. She pressed the talk-back button and tilted her face from Ryan's. "What is it?"

"I'm still having problems with a woman demanding to get backstage. I'm not sure if I should have her removed from the premises."

"I'll be there in a minute." She yanked the ear-piece out and let it hang over her shoulder. "I need to go."

"Wait." Ryan wiped a stray strand of hair from her cheek, his fingertips inspiring tingles all the way down her neck. "I love you, Leah. There's no point wasting more of our time trying to find excuses. We need to make this work, no matter what it takes." He edged closer, their noses a mere inch apart, their breath mingling. "We snuck around before. We can do it again."

There was a loud knock on the door followed by a hollered, "Two-minute call."

She stiffened and tried to pull away, her attempt failing due to the strong arm wrapped around her. "We'll discuss this later." In weeks. After the tour ended.

His fingers caressed her cheek, her chin, her neck. "There's nothing to discuss. I only wanted to prepare you." His tempting lips turned somber, no humor, no comfort. Only sincerity. "After the show you'll be on my bus. In my bed. In my arms. The rest will sort itself out." He bridged the distance between them, his beard scraping her jaw as he whispered in her ear. "You and me. Forever."

She closed her eyes and whimpered at the press of his mouth below her ear. "But my job..."

"We'll sort it out." He placed another scorching kiss to her skin.

"The baby..."

"We'll sort it out." His lips brushed her throat.

"No." She shook her head but couldn't tear herself away. "I can't think when we're together. I can't do my job."

"We'll…" He nipped her skin. "Work…" He bit. "It…" He sucked. "Out."

She felt the sensations all the way through her chest. From the peaks of her nipples, then lower, to the newly forming pulse in her clit.

There was another shout from outside, this one garbled.

"You better go."

He nodded, his arm still around her.

"Tell me you love me."

She didn't want to. The admission would be a sign of surrender, when she wasn't done fighting.

"Tell me," he whispered. "Because I can already see it in your eyes."

"Ryan, it's better if we wait until the end of the tour."

He grinned, unfazed by the rejection. The beauty of his expression stole her breath. This man was sweet and loving and protective. He was happiness personified. The temptation she may soon be willing to risk absolutely everything for.

"We can talk la—" Her words vanished as the door flew open.

She shoved from his chest, her gaze flying to the mirror and the reflection of the woman now standing in the doorway, a security guard rushing in behind her.

"I'm sorry, Leah." The guard ignored the compromising position before him. "I didn't want to risk manhandling a pregnant woman."

"It's OK," she lied, because clearly, everything was horribly wrong. She stepped away from Ryan and focused on Julie, the familiar face now a mix of shock, pain, and anger that transformed her features like a kaleidoscope. "We can take it from here."

The guard slinked away as Julie crossed her arms over her chest, pulling the loose top tight over the small mound of her belly. "Why am I not surprised?"

"You shouldn't be here." Ryan strode forward, approaching his wife. "You said you'd lay low until the announcement."

"I did lay low. Now I'm here so we can share the news together. Obviously, I didn't realize I'd be interrupting something. At least not with her." Julie wrinkled her nose. "I guess my years of jealousy were justified."

A dull throb formed in Leah's brain. Another anxiety attack waiting on the periphery. This was the end. Her position as band manager was seized by the hangman's noose. Eviscerated with the opening of a door. There'd be no more Ryan. No more Reckless. No more life filled with achievements.

She'd fucked up.

She'd failed.

Again.

She turned her back to Ryan and Julie, their conversation drowned from the hysteria taking over her mind. Bile bubbled up her throat. She closed her eyes. Swayed.

"Leah, are you OK?" Ryan grabbed her arms and lowered to eye level.

"Yeah. Of course." She blinked up at him, pretending, like always, and then turned to take in the empty room. "Where's Julie?"

"She ran. I have to go after her." He scrutinized her. So much dreary desolation in one handsome face. "I'll make sure she doesn't say anything."

She nodded through the doubt. Julie would take pleasure in sharing what she'd walked in on. Without hesitation. "Go. I'll stall the perfor-mance."

He smashed his lips to hers, quick and hard, but still there was no relief. Only anger at herself for causing this mess. When he pulled away she waited, watching him leave before she dragged her feet from the room.

"I'm sorry, Leah." The security guard was waiting in the hall, his brows drawn tight. "I didn't want to physically restrain her, and I wasn't even sure she was telling the truth about being Ryan's wife. I've never seen her at a concert before."

"Forget about it. You did the right thing." She'd been the one in the wrong. At each and every turn since Ryan first kissed her in Richmond.

"I'm not going to say anything," he added. "I mean...about what I walked in on."

"Thanks." She slunk away, hiding her wince from view. His silence wouldn't matter. Julie's enthusiasm would be enough to convince Leah's boss of the breach in contract. Especially when Ryan's wife had already set the ball rolling last week with the online interview.

The fooling around was over. It had to be.

She was too damn tired. Too drained.

The years of fighting her love for him, then battling to keep their shared feelings a secret had taken their toll. The collateral damage was piling up. She had to bow out. Now. While there was still one preemptive strike available to help salvage everything she'd worked for.

She palmed her phone from her pants pocket and scrolled through her directory. Bruce's name resembled a white flag. She was giving up. Giving in. She pressed the screen, the resulting rings sinking into her chest like lead.

"What can I do for you, Leah?"

She stopped in front of the door leading to side-stage, the crowd chanting for Reckless on the other side as she closed her eyes. "I have a feeling more drama is about to unfold from Julie."

He paused, the contemplation filled with disappointment. "Did you cause the drama?"

"No." She squeezed her eyes shut at the depth of how low she'd sunk. "She snuck backstage and misconstrued something she walked in on. She's pregnant and emotional. She doesn't—"

"Leah…"

She hung her head.

"This has happened one too many times," he murmured.

"It's all a misunderstanding," she lied. It kept happening because she was in love. The vicious cycle kept spinning because her professionalism was being smothered by uncontrollable emotions over someone she wasn't supposed to have.

"Then, if you plan to keep your job, you know what you need to do."

"Yes." She nodded and turned the door handle. "I know."

•••

Ryan ran down the hall, closing in on Julie. "*Wait.*"

She stopped, pivoted, and slumped against the wall to stare back at him. Her eyes were glazed, her hand pressed tight against her baby bump as if it needed protection from him.

"You can't mention a word of this."

She scoffed. "I most certainly can."

"But you're not going to. We can't get back together, Julie. It's not going to happen. I want to be with her. But that doesn't mean I'll support you and the baby any less. I've already spoken to my lawyers. They've arranged a payment schedule to help cover medical expenses in the coming months, and once the baby is born and paternity is established, I'll have bank accounts set up for you and our child."

She stared at him, her eyes narrowing.

"That's the best I can offer. I'm going to be a part of this baby's life, and I'm also not going to give up on what I have with Leah."

"What makes you think you can make it work with her? Once she loses her job, the two of you will have the same relationship we had. You'll be separated most months of the year. You'll grow distant. You'll never make it work."

"She's not going to lose her job."

She gave a derisive laugh. "One phone call from me and she will."

"She's not your enemy, Julie. If you want someone to blame, I'm your man. Leah has only ever tried to keep us together." *God.* How hadn't he seen that? He raked his fingers through his hair. "I told her she was the cause of our divorce, but I was wrong. She tried to save our marriage. *I* was the one who ruined everything. *I* was the one who quit trying because I couldn't stop loving her. This is all on me."

"It doesn't have to be. You can still fix it. I can give you the family that she never will."

"If she doesn't want kids, I'll deal with it."

Julie stared into the distance and drew a deep breath. "It has nothing to do with her wanting kids. You'll never be able to give them to her. This is your only chance."

He waited for her to elaborate, to establish any sort of meaning to the puzzle. If she wanted to manipulate him, she could take her best shot, he was more than willing to be her target. He just wouldn't be her victim.

"I tried to give you children for years. It never happened. It was one unsuccessful attempt after another."

It never happened.

It. *Never*. Happened.

He dropped his hands to his sides, unable to hide the effect of her verbal sucker-punch. "The baby isn't mine."

"It could be." She raised her chin and met his eyes. "The father didn't want to settle down. He doesn't want a family. But you do. This is all you've ever wanted. And it's the only opportunity you'll get."

He had no words, not even a scoff. Torment clogged his throat. Grief cemented his lungs.

"Ryan, I know you're hurt, but you need to listen to what I'm going to say." She pushed from the wall and came to stand before him. "We tried to make a family, year after year. I never once became pregnant." She glanced down between them and ran a hand over her belly. "Obviously, the lack of success hadn't been because of me."

"*Fuck.*" His shout reverberated off the walls, startling her. *Fuck. Fuck. Fuck.*

He ran a hand over his face, trying to wipe away the disgust. He'd gone from hating the nights in the tour bus, to loving the thought of them because he could hide away with Leah. He went from thinking the world was against him, to not caring as long as he had the woman he loved in his arms. He'd gone from despair to hope due to Leah's love, and he'd cast it all aside for this woman. For loyalty. For responsibility.

"We can still make this work," she murmured. "Nobody else needs to know. You could have everything…"

One by one his dreams of having children burned to ash. He wouldn't learn to braid hair, or teach guitar. He wouldn't cradle his own child. Couldn't give a father-daughter speech about the merciless charm of boys.

"Yeah." He began to nod. "I want everything."

Her eyes brightened, her hope spurring the words clogging his throat.

"I want the apartment." He straightened. "I want the car." He leaned close. "I want the bank balance." He smirked, the expression filled with a threat he hoped she understood. "I want every damn thing I gave you that you didn't deserve."

Her face went pale. "Ryan—"

"As soon as tonight's show is over, I'll be on the phone to my lawyer. He'll be informed of your infidelity and told there's no length I won't go to in an attempt to drag your name to hell and back… Unless you sign the next settlement that's drawn up, and never contact me again."

"*Please.*" She tried to implore him with the bat of feminine lashes. At one point in their relationship it would've worked. "Do you realize you're giving up your dream?"

Giving it up, letting it go, and never looking back.

"I do." He turned and strode for the side-stage door. "And funnily enough, I'll still be happier than I ever was with you."

This was all because of his need to do right by people. He hadn't pressed her for paternity. He'd blindly trusted someone he no longer cared for at the cost of someone he adored. No more. He was going to take a leaf out of Mason's book. *No.* He was going to rip out every fucking page. If the lead singer of Reckless Beat could be an unscrupulous asshole in the name of getting what he wanted, Ryan was going to do the same.

His veins thrummed with the need to make shit happen.

He was done pandering—to Grander, to Leah's boss, to life in general.

He shoved the door leading to the wings, and let the rush of chanting voices wash away the carnage. One by one he passed the crew, security, and approached his non-blood family.

This was where he belonged, with Leah by his side and his friends at his back. He strode for her shadowed form, shoving past Mason and Blake to grab her around the waist and steal a gasp from her mouth.

She pushed at him. "Stop."

He didn't. He took her fear and killed it with a kiss, molding his mouth against hers, parting her lips with a harsh swipe of tongue.

She shoved at him. "What the hell do you think you're doing?"

"I'm saying fuck-you to the world." He stared down at her without remorse. "Once I get off that stage things are going to change. I don't care about Felicity or Julie or Grander. I won't even give a shit about your god damn boss. I'm done, Leah. After this show, it's all about us."

"No." Her gaze darted around at the witnesses standing in the shadows.

His friends glanced back and forth between them, and followed him as he walked backward onto the darkened stage, the technicians encroaching with guitars. As he stared at her, he mimicked a smirk he'd seen Mason pull too many times to remember. "Fight it all you like." He kissed his fingertips and blew the love her way. "In a few hours, you're mine."

L EAH STOOD SIDE-STAGE, TAKING IN THE CROWD PARTICIPATION. SHE'D successfully batted away hysteria for the last two hours, scurrying away to different hiding places during their short set breaks.

"How many of you have downloaded Slicker's album?" Mason's shout resounded through the stadium, soon smothered by a wave of screams. "And how many of you fuckers haven't?"

"Maybe we should take off our shirts to encourage more sales?" Blake crooned into the microphone.

"I don't know about them—" Ryan leaned into Blake's side, "—but I'd one-click to ensure you kept yours on."

Mason glanced to the wings and met her gaze as he continued to chat up the crowd. She gave him a thumbs up, the simple gesture letting him know they'd reached their target, even if it was in an obscure way.

Scott had updated her with half-hourly sales reports, and the number of downloads was impressive but not enough to hit the mark. At least she hadn't thought so, until she checked the retail sites and found Slicker featured under a bestselling header. They'd succeeded. They'd won. And the relief was merely a drop in an ocean of turmoil.

She didn't know what had happened between Ryan and Julie. She wasn't sure if she wanted to know. All she could think about was the ticking time bomb and how Ryan's kiss in front of the crew had made the avalanche of destruction all the harder to bear.

Mason gave a jerk of his head and led Reckless into another song. She was beyond proud of her men. They were an unstoppable team—emotionally and successfully. Each of them had stolen a piece of her heart in a different way. Sean was the brick wall, the man who hid his soft heart behind a gruff exterior. Blake was the fighter, the strength who could endure hell and teach her the sun would always rise tomorrow. Mitch was the stoic soldier, holding his head high no matter what challenge came their way. And Mason was like a brother. She hated him at times and couldn't help loving him in the same breath. Even though nobody else noticed, he was the glue keeping the band together. He just did it in the most abrasive way possible to keep his asshole reputation intact.

Then there was Ryan, the love and heart of Reckless. He was everything she wasn't—sweet, kind, selfless. Too much perfection. He didn't even have to speak, his unwavering compassion shone bright in his eyes. She'd never met a more generous man, and being with him, no matter how short the duration, would forever be a memory she would cherish.

But it was time to clean the mess she'd made.

She took in the sight of them on stage for one last time and tried to smile as her gaze skipped from one brilliant man to the next. Then she pivoted on her toes and made her way to the backstage hall, the weight of judgmental stares following her into the dressing room.

The next fifteen minutes were spent alone, strengthening her resilience and bolstering her resolve. When they barreled through the door, hyped with enthusiasm and covered in sweat, she stood from her seated position on the sofa and grinned like her world wasn't ending.

"Congratulations." She walked to the refreshments table and handed them all a bottle of water.

"How'd we do?" Mitch's cheeks were flushed, the adrenaline making his breathing heavy.

"Slicker reached bestseller status on Amazon MP3 downloads *and* iTunes. Not only that, they also reached number one on their chart."

"Number one?" Blake balked. "Bullshit."

"Crazy, huh?" Her chuckle was half-hearted. "I think the rest of the world will have the same reaction when they see Slicker in the Classical genre."

"Their shit isn't classical by any stretch." Mitch snorted.

"No, it definitely isn't." She turned her attention to Mason's smirk, knowing he was the culprit. "What did you do?"

"I told you I had a few tricks up my sleeve. One of those was a man on the inside who agreed to tweak Slicker's metadata."

Mitch grinned. "Scott is going to be pissed."

"Like I give a shit." Mason drove an arm around Ryan's neck and ruffled his hair. "You're off the hook, motherfucker."

Ryan responded with a shove of his elbow and a free-spirited grin. His elation was clear while she was steadfast in hiding her misery.

"Is it time to celebrate across the board?" Sean asked. "With the delay in getting your ass on stage, we assumed the two of you were sorting your shit out and doing some genital reconnaissance."

"Soon." Ryan met her gaze, his confidence taunting her need to argue. "We hit a slight detour when Julie showed up." He shoved from Mason's hold and walked toward her. "But we're even more on track now than we were before."

She shook her head and wandered behind the sofa, placing the furniture between them. "No. Not this time. All we've done is make a bigger mess."

"That's where you're wrong." He strolled after her. Unfazed. Unhurried. "Felicity and I can quit this charade tomorrow, and Julie and I will never see each other again."

"What about the kid?" Sean asked.

"It isn't mine."

Ryan spoke without emotion, as if he hadn't dropped a fifty-pound bombshell. She tried to read him, to determine if the fortitude in his eyes was born from his need for her, or the necessity to remain distracted from the new changes to his future.

"The divorce is going ahead without fault, and it'll be just the two of us. You and me."

His tone held a promise she wanted to grasp. Instead, she remained true to herself and her career, and stopped at the far end of the sofa, her shoe covered toes brushing the suitcase hidden from sight.

"Nothing is going to stop this now," he continued. "We can hide if you want. Or we can ditch the theatrics and demand what we've always wanted."

"You can demand all you want, Ryan, but all it will do is drive us apart when I lose my job." She leaned over and gripped the trolley handle of her luggage, extending it to the full height. "And we can't hide, either. Even if I could trust Julie to remain quiet, you made the option impossible with your side-stage kiss."

He stopped approaching, his gaze lowering to the handle in her fist.

"What's with the suitcase?" Blake pinned her with the question but it was the stiffening of Ryan's posture that put her on edge.

"You're running again?" Mason snarled.

"No. Not running." She shook her head. "This time I'm following orders. Bruce has demanded I take a temporary vacation. Otherwise, he'll make it a permanent one."

"You told him," Ryan murmured.

She raised her chin, deflecting the disappointment in his tone. "I had to get on the front foot and inform him more drama might be coming our way from Julie."

"Then take it back. Tell him you were mistaken." He started approaching again, making her heart stutter with harsh beats. "Julie won't talk. I promise you that."

He kept promising. This time she didn't believe him. She wouldn't let herself. "I can't. We all know I haven't had the band's best interests in mind. So I need a break. Dylan will meet you in Houston to take over my role for the rest of the tour."

"Like hell he will." Mason scowled. "Put your bag back on the bus. You're not ditching us."

She took his judgmental arrogance head on, not caring that it increased her defeat. She hadn't anticipated the lead singer would act any differently. He couldn't say, "Stay, I need you here." Or, "Come on, Leah, we'll stick by you, no matter what." It wasn't his style. But she heard the sentiment through his anger nonetheless.

"This is temporary." She cut her gaze to Ryan, hoping he'd be kinder. What looked back at her was more punishing. He wasn't angry or resentful, his eyes were filled with forgiveness and painful understanding.

He slowly nodded, his response subdued. "Do what you have to do. And I'll do the same."

The underlying threat slid down her back like molasses, the delicate authority ringing in her ears. She ignored it. She ignored everything—Blake's heartbroken smile, Sean's disapproving frown, Mitch's wide, concerned eyes. "I'll still be available to talk if you need me. Please call whenever..."

Her words drifted as Ryan turned his back to her, wordlessly gaining the attention of his friends.

"It's time to get Plan A underway." He gripped the back of the sofa and scrutinized his audience. "Are you guys still on board?"

Blake nodded. "Let's do it."

"I'm all for it," Sean added.

"You know I'm in," came from Mason.

"Mitch?" Ryan focused on the lead guitarist. "What about you?"

"Come on." Mitch glared. "Do you really need to ask? I'll do whatever it takes because I know you guys would do the same for me."

"A simple yes would've sufficed," Blake muttered. "This isn't the Davies' show."

"What are you talking about?" Her voice was meek, barely audible over the sense of impending doom. They were all immersed in a conversation she didn't understand, and wasn't sure she wanted to. "What's plan A?"

They ignored her, all five of them muttering among themselves, one over the top of the other, the noise coalescing—*What was the plan again? Do you need us to do anything else? Are we doing this in the bus or a hotel?*

"I'll go with Ryan." Mason spoke the loudest. "The three of you will have to deal with Leah."

Have to deal with her? Was he striving for a blunt-force trauma to the balls?

"Ahem." She cleared her throat, and still they ignored her. Time for the big guns. She circled her thumb and pointer finger, placed them over the curl of her tongue and whistled loud enough to make them flinch. "*Explain.*"

Mitch, Blake, and Sean still had the respect to act apologetic. Mason, on the other hand, was smirking in defiance. But, as always, her interest came back to Ryan. Once she left, this could be the last time she was around him for months. There'd be no wavy, chin-length hair to fantasize about running through her fingers. There'd be no kissable lips to dream of, or hugs to strengthen her.

He was grinning now, his mouth curved in a delicious show of excitement that scared the hell out of her. She frowned at him, not knowing why or how he could be happy at a time like this, and released the grip on her suitcase as he approached.

"What aren't you telling me?" she whispered. She could smell him, the mingled scent of sweat and aftershave. The deep breaths tattooed her lungs, warming the icy chill inside her as he ran one hand around her waist and pulled them together.

"Do you trust me?"

"Do I need to?"

He winced, the slightest fracture to his confidence. "I have a plan to solve our problems."

"If it were that easy, I would've thought of it myself."

His wince didn't waiver. It still hung between them, increasing her heartbeat as the rest of the band listened on in silence. "It's not easy. And it might not work. But I have faith it will. I wouldn't risk everything if I wasn't ninety-percent sure."

"Everything? You mean *my* career, *my* life, and *my* future." He wasn't risking those things. His risk had nothing to do with him and everything to do with her.

He leaned in close, his breath brushing her ear. "You are my everything. You are all that matters and all I want. So yes, I'm risking everything, because nothing else is as important to me as you."

She closed her eyes and battled to keep her head high. "Tell me the plan."

"I can't."

She snapped her eyes open and met his gaze. "You want me to risk everything without even knowing what you're doing?"

"I want you to trust me... And Mason, Sean, Mitch, and Blake. We all came up with the idea yesterday."

She read those soulful eyes, trying to measure the risk. The only thing she could see was hope mixed with pleading.

"Are you going to do something stupid?"

"Probably. Will you forgive me if I do?"

She stared over his shoulder, at the men who were her family. At Mitch who had devastation written all over his face. At Blake who was guarded and resolute. At Sean who was smiling through his concern. And finally Mason, his superior brow taunting her like the tormenting brother he'd always been.

"I trust you, but—"

"That's good enough for me." Mason jerked his head at Sean. "Grab her suitcase. Take her to a hotel and do what we discussed."

"Ahh." She reached for the trolley handle and gripped tight. "Hotel? No." The guys should be boarding the tour bus for Houston, and she'd already arranged for the jet to fly her out of here. "If I'm not in the air in two hours, I'll lose my job before your plan is underway."

"Our plan is already underway." Ryan placed a sweet kiss on her forehead. A sweet, destroying kiss that had her toes curling in innumerable directions. Damn that mouth. Damn his appeal. "Just give me some time."

He backtracked, leaving her mouth agape and her heart threatening to throw a tantrum while Sean wrestled the suitcase handle from her grip.

"We'll accompany you outside, m'lady." Mitch came to her free side and placed a hand at the low of her back. "But you might have to arrange a car. I'd have no idea who to call."

She scowled at him, the little confidence she'd had slingshotting from the room with their lack of foresight. "Do any of you know what you're doing?"

"I'm sure one of us does." Sean squeezed past her, suitcase in tow.

"Come on." Blake tried to shoo her forward. "Let's get going."

She couldn't. Her feet refused to move. They were going to do something senseless. Reckless, as their world-famous name suggested. "Ryan..." she implored.

"I'll see you soon." There was no kiss goodbye. No sweet farewell. He strode for the door, pausing inside the frame. "Remember, I love you."

Jesus Christ. She parted her lips, poised to protest his departure, but Blake wrapped a hand around her mouth, silencing her call. He held her hostage as she wriggled, the fight soon leaving her body while the sound of Ryan and Mason's footsteps disappeared down the hall.

"Relax," Blake whispered in her ear and slowly slid his hand from her face. "Let him do what he needs to do."

"And if my career gets shot down in flames?"

He gave a sad smile. "Then we all go down with you."

After grabbing their overnight bags from the tour bus, Mitch, Sean, and Blake dragged her to a nearby hotel and booked the penthouse suite. Since then, she'd sat on a corner of the plush sofa, arms crossed, glaring at the muted television playing a movie none of them were paying attention to.

Blake was on the floor doing sit ups. Sean was staring straight ahead, eyes unblinking in a daze. And Mitch was on his phone, probably messaging Alana, who should be on the crew bus to Houston.

"I'm going to have to leave in ten minutes."

"Sure thing." Blake didn't pause in his exercise count. "As long as we hear from Ryan by then."

"And if we don't?" The so-called plan had already taken an hour.

"Then you stay." Sean mumbled, practically asleep with his eyes open.

"That doesn't work for me." She pushed to her feet. "The jet would already be waiting at the airport." She'd already delayed the flight as long as possible and the sixty minutes of clock-stalking hadn't been fun. Yes, she wanted this to work. She'd silently prayed Ryan's plan fell into a neat little package of happily-ever-after, but time was running out.

"Not going to happen." Sean still hadn't blinked.

"It *has* to happen. Bruce expects to meet me first thing in the morning and I'm supposed to message him when I touch down."

"Sweetie…" Blake sat up straight, his shoulders slumped as he panted. "We'll let you walk out of here once Ryan gets back, but until then, calm your tits and get used to it."

"Nope." She cocked a hip. "I'm leaving."

Sean finally blinked to consciousness and met her gaze. "We'll see."

"Yeah." She gave him a sinister smile. She wasn't scared of his bulk or the buzz cut hiding his teddy bear center. "We *will* see."

She sauntered for her suitcase at the start of the open plan kitchen, grabbed the trolley handle, and then made her way to the front door. Muttered curses followed, and then the padded footsteps of a rushed stride.

"Get your ass back to the sofa." Sean's voice was tired, the on-stage adrenaline long gone, now leaving him in a defeated withdrawal.

No way. She continued walking and spoke over her shoulder. "I know dealing with a different manager is going to be painful, but it's only temporary." She reached the door handle and twisted. Her chest expanded with the relief of freedom and then constricted with the reminder of her lonely future. "I'll be in contact all the time."

Sean's palm hit the door, slamming it shut in her face.

"Get. Your ass. On the. Sofa." Each word was enunciated in a terrifying growl.

"Sean—" Her reply was cut off by a scream. *Her* scream as he lifted her off the ground and threw her over his shoulder like a sack of wheat.

"I'm too tired for this shit." He swung around and carried her back into the living room, ignoring the hard-core wiggle she increased in an effort to break free.

"Down. *Now!*"

He did as instructed, unceremoniously dumping her on the sofa, her arms and legs flailing. Blake and Mitch didn't fluctuate from their positions. They didn't even pay her attention as she began to hyperventilate in livid anger. "You don't want to do this."

"Yeah." Blake returned to his steady rhythm of sit-ups. "We do."

"I'll run."

"With a suitcase and those heels?" Sean raised a brow and dropped down beside her. "Just sit tight until tomorrow."

"*Tomorrow*? You can't be serious. I thought this was only going to take an hour. Two, tops. What could Ryan be doing—"

"They took the jet and went back to New York." Mitch slid his cell onto the coffee table and met her gaze. "It's going to take time."

"New York?" *No.* She shook her head. *No.* "What are they...? Why are they...?" *Christ.* She needed answers. Nothing good could come from them going home. She reached into her jacket pocket and pulled out her cell.

"Don't even think about it." Sean snatched the device from her grip, leaned to the side, and slid it beneath him.

"Oh, no, you didn't." She gaped, her focus on the place where his thighs met the sofa cushions. *Fuck.* "You just ate my phone with your ass."

Blake threw his head back and laughed. A long, loud, and over-tired sound she wished she could mimic. No luck. She was furious.

"Payback will be unimaginable." She stood again, this time smoothing out her clothes and raising her chin to curb her frustration. Her brows descended into a scathing glare before she stalked across the room, heading for the bathroom, Sean's chuckle a taunting companion.

"You can only pay me back if you stick around."

Twenty-Six

RYAN WAS THANKFUL HE'D HAD THE FORESIGHT TO GET THE JET TO SAN Antonio. The strategy had been far simpler yesterday—get Slicker on a chart, convince Leah they were going to make this work, ditch the tour bus to Houston, and spend the night in a hotel suite. Just the two of them. No clothes. No sleep.

Instead, the jet was touching down in New York, the illuminated night sky greeting him through the tiny window.

"Stop worrying. I've had to listen to your brain tick the whole way here." Mason raised his head from a sleeping position on the opposite sofa. "Nothing is going to go wrong. In fact, I dare someone to take us on."

"Don't be a jinx." Ryan had failed in trying to claim the don't-give-a-shit attitude Mason had perfected. Evidently, not everyone could enjoy being an asshole. "If something goes wrong…"

"Nothing will go wrong. We'll be in and out of here like a teen getting his first lay."

The jet pulled to a stop, the flight attendant opening the door to the main cabin seconds later. "I've arranged for the car you requested. It's already waiting on the tarmac."

"Thanks." Ryan stood, not needing to grab any luggage because he'd left San Antonio with nothing but his cell, wallet, and the clothes on his back.

The drive into Manhattan was smooth, the early morning hours quiet while most of the city slept, the desolation in contrast to the frantic buzz inside his chest.

"Are we in the right place?" Mason asked from the front seat of the car.

"Yeah." The tree-lined street was dead to the world. The houses devoid of inside lights. "Look for number thirty-six."

The driver slowed, taking in the numbers until they reached their destination. When the vehicle stopped, so did Ryan's heart. Outside the window was a three-story townhouse, the narrow building dark and confronting.

"We'll be back soon." Mason spoke to the driver and climbed from the car.

Ryan wasn't as quick to rush to the fray. He'd been in a panic to get here, but now the plan loomed in front of him, he questioned what he was doing. Leah could end up hating him. She may never speak to him again. The prospect had him second-guessing everything. Even the depth of his breaths.

"Hurry the fuck up," Mason called from the street.

Shit. Ryan unclicked his belt, opened the door, and slid into the night air. "Keep your voice down."

"Why?" Mason snorted. "I'm pretty sure I established a bad reputation with this guy years ago."

"You may have." Ryan started for the house. "But I'm hoping to make a good impression."

"At three in the morning? Good luck with that."

They climbed the four steps and stopped at the front door. Mason didn't give him a chance to compose himself before a loud rap of knuckles pounded against the wood. *Fuck.* His heartrate increased. He began to fidget.

"Come on," Mason grated, staring up at the windows. "Wake up." He knocked again, this time pounding with the side of his hand.

A light brightened a third-story window. Seconds later, another illuminated on the second floor, followed by ground level. Footsteps approached. A shadow crossed the door. The lock clicked. Then they were staring at a balding man, his squinted eyes harsh with scrutiny. "What the hell do you think you're doing?"

Not a good start. Not a fucking good start at all. "Hi, sir…" Ryan ignored Mason's raised brow that mocked his greeting. "I'm a member of Reckless—"

"I know who the hell you are, Ryan. We've met before. What I don't know is why you're banging on my door in the early hours of the morning."

"I wanted to speak to you about Leah."

"Damn it." Bruce ran a hand over his wrinkled face. "You're involved with her, aren't you?"

He straightened, preparing to fight. For her. "I want to be." Deflection was key. *Don't lie. Just divert.* "I've had feelings for Leah for a long time. And I've known, because of her job and my wife, that I couldn't do anything about it. But I'm here today to ask you for permission—"

"No." Bruce shook his head. "Don't ask. Don't even go there."

"Hear him out." Mason leaned against the side of the building, relaxed, oblivious to what was at stake, or simply not caring.

"And delay crawling back into bed? Why? I already know the answer, and it won't change. All this conversation will do is send Leah into the unemployment line."

"Please." Ryan stepped forward. "I'm begging you. Take the clause out of her contract."

There was a beat of contemplation as aged eyes narrowed. "You love her that much?"

"Yeah, I do." Hope sparked to life in his chest.

"And how about your wife? Did you feel the same way about her, too?"

Shit. Optimism took a nose-dive, freefalling without a parachute. "I was young and ignorant when I married Julie. I didn't know what love was."

"But you vowed your life to her. Now you're claiming Leah is all you want."

Ryan darted a pleading gaze to Mason. He was flailing, throwing punches that didn't connect while Bruce had begun slamming this conversation out of the arena. "I appreciate what you're trying to say. You think I'll change my mind in the future. And I get that. I understand why you feel the way you do."

"No." The older man shook his head. "You don't understand. Otherwise you wouldn't be here. Do you think you're the first person to ask for the contract to be changed? Out of all the celebrities my company represents, do you think you and Leah are the only ones to get swept up in the glitz and glamour and think it's love?"

"We're not swept up in anything. I've been in love with her for years. And she feels the—"

"I suggest you quit talking before you admit something I can't ignore."

Mason pushed from the wall. "You'll ignore whatever necessary to keep us as a client."

"That's where you're wrong." Bruce scowled at the lead singer. "Your worth is only as valuable as the reputation it gives my company. If your manager can't control her feelings, it reflects badly on everyone under my employment and all the artists they represent."

"Then put a price on it," Mason demanded.

"I could buy her out of the clause." Ryan stood firm, unwilling to give up, no matter the cost.

"And when things end and I'm stuck with a bad reputation and a band who is no longer willing to work with their manager? What then?"

"It won't happen. Leah and I are good together. We'll continue to make it work."

"Continue?" Bruce sighed. "You'll *continue* to make it work?"

Ryan didn't give a shit about his admission. "Look, I'm not asking on a whim. I wouldn't be here unless my future happiness was dependent on your answer. Leah's, too. I've never seen her date during her entire time as the Reckless manager. She's never needed or wanted to. But she needs this. She needs me and I feel the same way about her."

"Just put a fucking price on it," Mason snapped.

"Even I know Leah wouldn't appreciate a price on a relationship." Bruce scoffed. "But you want a number, so I'll give you one. How does two million dollars sound?"

Ryan fought to withhold a wince.

"Don't even think about it." Mason grabbed Ryan's shirt. "Let's get out of here. He's not going to negotiate."

"I could get the money together." Ryan couldn't move. He couldn't quit staring at the man who held his happiness hostage.

"I'm not going to let you do that." Mason stepped in front of him. "Leah would kill you. *I'd* fucking kill you. You're not wasting two mil on a chance with her. It's not worth it."

"It's not wasting two million on a chance. It'd be two million for an opportunity."

"He's fucking with you, Ry. And besides, your track record with women isn't a glowing recommendation to throw money at. You've got a wife who's pregnant with another man, and Blake tells me you turned your other conquest to the dark side."

"Not funny." Ryan glowered. "I have no other option."

"Yeah, you do." Mason tugged again. "You just don't want to take it."

True. Plan B was worse than the risks with Plan A. The revulsion at his action would be doubled. More people would be involved, diluting the affects but stretching them further. "I don't think..."

"Thinking's never been your strong suit." Mason dragged him down the cement steps and onto the sidewalk. "Now we do it my way."

•••

Leah sucked in a deep breath, filled her lungs, and then let loose with an off-pitch rendition of Adele's latest release.

"*Fuck.*" Mitch jerked upright from his dozing position on the sofa, while Blake and Sean cringed.

She'd never been more proud of her lack of vocal talent.

"Enough." Sean shoved to his feet and stamped his grumpy ass into the kitchen, stopping in front of her seated position on the counter. "If I'd known payback would come in the form of singing, I would've drugged you hours ago."

"Oh, sweetie," she cooed. "Retribution hasn't even started."

Since her first failed attempt at escape, she'd tried to leave two more times. The first was in commando mode and involved a rather embarrassing crawl along numerous feet of hallway carpet before the click of a cell's recording device encouraged her to stand. The second was when all three men had been dozing in varying positions around the living room. Mitch had sprung to his feet with the opening of the door and proceeded to run straight ahead, tripping over Blake on the floor. He hadn't braced for impact. At least not with his hands. His face took the brunt of the fall, the resulting blood rushing from his nose enough to kick her conscience into overdrive.

"Why don't you get a few hours' rest?" Sean leaned against the opposite counter, his shoulders slumped, his head drooping. *Please.* Daylight is going to break any minute now."

"If your career was on the line, would you be able to rest?"

He raised his chin and met her gaze with determination. "If I were you, I'd have faith in the men who love and adore you."

She glanced down at her swaying feet, cursing the effects lack of sleep had on her emotions. "Do you forget how well I know you all?" She shot him a look through her lashes before lowering her focus again. "My position is already perilous, and then Ryan made it worse by kissing me in front of the crew. If Bruce finds out..."

"He already has."

Her gaze shot up.

"Sean," Blake warned, the bass guitarist striding into the kitchen. "Let's keep this quiet until Ryan gets back."

"No." She pushed from the counter. "I deserve to know what's going on with my own career."

"We've got your back. That's all you need to know." Mitch came up beside Blake, wiping a rough hand over his face. "This won't end until we're all happy with the outcome."

"We're all happy?" Incredulity dripped from her lips. "Since when did you claim dictatorship over my life? This is *my* career. *My* choice. Not yours."

They had the sense to look remorseful. The three of them now struggling to maintain eye contact. This wasn't a game anymore. It wasn't fun or comical. It was her future they played with. Her decisions they stole.

"Do you understand what you've done?" She pinned Blake with a stare. "You're going to be a dad soon. You may have a daughter."

He stiffened.

"When she's a grown woman—fit and capable to make her own decisions—would you find it acceptable to have the people she works with make choices about her future on her behalf?"

"It's not like that," he grated.

"Then what is it like?"

His jaw ticked, the beat of contemplation narrowing his gaze. "Do you remember when we were back in Australia and you found out the infidelity rumors about Julie?"

Ice water washed through her, along veins, through nerves.

"It's like that," he continued. "You made the choice not to tell Ryan, even though he deserved to know, merely because you thought it was the best thing for him."

"It was best for the band," she clarified.

Sean inclined his head. "It was a professional decision." He approached, grabbing her upper arms and staring down at her. "And so was ours. We can't continue the tour without you. Not even for a day. It's not something any of us are willing to do. So you can either look at it as if we're trying to protect you—which we are. Or you can see it as the best career move we'll make, because both apply."

"We'll make this right, Leah." Mitch gave a sad smile.

She sucked in a deep breath and demanded the anger to dissipate as Sean pulled her into his chest.

"I assume you've been in contact with Ryan." She reluctantly slid her arms around his waist, taking comfort in whatever way she could.

"We've messaged back and forth."

"Then tell me—" she retreated and met his eyes, "—what did Bruce say when he found out?"

His eyes softened, the lack of excitement filling her with dread.

"In short, he wasn't happy and refused to negotiate."

Translation—her contract remained in place and now her boss had the evidence to send her packing.

"Don't give up on us." Mitch came to her side, wrapped a hand around her neck and kissed her cheek. "You've fought for us from day one. It's our turn to fight for you."

"**D**ON'T START REGRETTING IT NOW," MASON MUTTERED FROM THE OTHER side of the cab. "The damage is already done."

"I'm not." Ryan stared out the window, watching the hotel come into view. He'd been trying to imagine the different ways Leah could respond to the news, and nothing he came up with was favorable. Not to begin with, anyway. She'd either be upset or livid, and the reaction would take hours, if not days, to simmer. "It's going to take some time for her to forgive us."

"We already knew that before we started. But at least you can be with her now. If I would've been in the same situation with Sid, I wouldn't think twice about what we've done."

"That's because you're an asshole." The cab pulled to a stop and Ryan handed the driver a stack of bills, giving the guy a healthy tip because he hadn't acknowledged the celebrities in his back seat.

"True." Mason opened his door and slid from the car.

They regrouped in the lobby, ignoring the curious stares of people who were awake at this ungodly hour.

"So, how are you going to tell her?"

Ryan threw his arms wide, fucking clueless. "I'm still hoping inspiration hits before I get upstairs."

"Want my advice?"

"No."

Mason laughed. "Well, you're going to get it anyway. I suggest making sure she's on the other side of a locked door. Or tied to a secure structure."

"Thanks for stating the blindingly obvious." A loud whistle split the lobby and Ryan glanced toward the sound, finding Sean waving them toward the elevators. "Good timing."

Mason started forward.

"Wait a second." Ryan placed a hand on his friend's shoulder. "Before we get upstairs, I wanted to thank you."

"For what?"

"Supporting me even though my decision is going to fuck with the band."

Mason shrugged. "We'll bounce back. We always do. And besides, it's not only you I'm supporting. It's Leah. Reckless never would've made it this far without her."

"Have you ever told her that?"

"And ruin the dynamic we've got going on?" Mason started for the elevators. "Nah. We're right where we need to be. If she knew how much I adored her it'd get weird. And I don't like weird. I prefer the bitter animosity we share."

"Right..." It made no sense. But then again, nothing they'd done tonight had.

"Who's sharing bitter animosity?" Sean asked, holding open the elevator doors.

"Leah." Ryan stepped inside the confined space, Mason following close behind. "How is she?"

"I convinced her to pass out about an hour ago and I'm not looking forward to seeing what happens when she wakes up." He pressed the button to the top floor. "I suggest greeting her with a mouth and groin guard."

"He doesn't want suggestions," Mason announced. "Lover boy thinks he knows best."

Sean chuckled. "Then we should have the paramedics on standby."

Ryan ignored the banter as they ascended. He appreciated the distraction technique; really, he did. But he needed to focus. He still hadn't figured out how to break the news. Inspiration hadn't even hit once they quietly made their way into the penthouse, Blake and Mitch greeting them in the living room.

"Hey," Blake murmured. "How'd you do?"

"Not as good as we'd hoped." Mason made for the kitchen and grabbed a bottle of soda from the fridge. "We had to settle for Plan B."

"So that means…" Mitch let the sentence hang.

"Yeah." Mason nodded. "It means more fun times ahead."

The resulting silence hit Ryan with a truckload of guilt. This was all on him. He'd been selfish. He'd put himself first. And no matter how much it made his chest ache, he couldn't regret it.

"What was Plan B?" Leah's voice murmured from the other end of the room.

He swung around, finding her leaning on one shoulder against the hallway wall, her suit crushed, her hair loose and framing her face. Those beautiful eyes blinked in lazy strokes, the blush of sleep darkening her cheeks. "Give me a second."

She crossed her arms over her chest and turned on her toes, walking out of view.

"Do you plan on telling her alone?" Mitch asked.

"Yeah." He deserved the brunt of her anger. Nobody else. She was independent. Resourceful. Accomplished. It wouldn't be easy for her to accept what he'd done. He could barely accept it himself.

"Want me to go in first and remove any loose items she might want to throw?"

Ryan met Mason's gaze, hearing the humor but also seeing the concern staring back at him. "I can handle it."

Mason nodded. "Do right by her."

"I will."

• • •

Leah sat at the foot of the bed, listening to the mutterings of an ominous conversation in the living room. There was no excitement. No whispers of celebration.

242

She heard his footsteps approach, could see his frame through her periphery as he entered the room and closed the door behind him.

"Leah…" His voice was so soft. So sweet.

She raised her head and met his gaze.

"You know I love you, right?"

Her stomach dropped. "That's not how you start this conversation, Ryan."

"And the guys…" He continued, "They love you, too."

Her pulse spiked. Breathing became hard. She wanted to shake this beautiful man. To shake and shake and shake until he divulged the disaster he'd created. "Please, don't drag this out."

His expression faded. There was no warmth, no heat, no sense of hope to cling to.

"I had a meeting with your boss."

She closed her eyes and hung her head. "I know."

"I'm sorry, but I had to." He came to stand before her and crouched at her feet. "I thought I could convince him to change your contract."

"But you couldn't. Could you?"

He shook his head. "No."

A ragged breath escaped her lips. "How much does he know?"

"Everything. We tried—"

"And when you failed, he fired me."

Ryan winced. It was all the confirmation she needed. "I'm sorry, but please hear me—"

"You had no right." She pushed to her feet and slid from reach.

"Let me explain." He grabbed her waist, swinging her around, making her compliant with his hard stare. "You need to know how I fixed this." He backed her into the wall, his weight crushing, his possession maddening. "I found a way for us to be together."

She denied him with a jut of her chin. "Bruce never would've agreed."

"You're right. He didn't. But he said I could buy out the clause for two million dollars."

"Oh my god." Her mouth gaped as she struggled in his hold. "You didn't…"

"No. I didn't. But I would've. Two million. Three million. Ten." He got in her face, his nose almost brushing hers. "I don't give a fuck. I would've done it if Mason hadn't insisted on taking another option first."

His harsh tone. His cursing. His hold. It all diminished her anger. Attraction was making her pliable. Infatuation was making her weak. She couldn't allow his appeal to take over her head. Not when it had already consumed her heart and parts further south.

"It's love, *not* stupidity." He ground his hips into her, as if he knew the route to acquiescence was through her vagina.

"From my limited experience," she snarled, "they seem to be the same thing."

"Are you going to let me finish, or do you insist on growling at everything I say?"

Honestly? She wasn't sure. She wanted to know the damage. Knowledge was power and all that. But knowing also meant pain. It meant harsh reality and punishing truths.

"Go on," she whispered, slumping against the wall. "I won't interrupt you again."

He quirked a brow. "I find that hard to believe."

She kept her mouth shut, belying him.

His responding chuckle was short and breathy, flittering away as quick as it settled. "Plan B involved Scott."

Fear of the unknown morphed into terror and she shook her head to fight it away. "No."

"You promised." He settled further against her, his fingers raking down her arms, stopping at her wrists. He gripped her gently and raised her hands to the wall, demanding surrender in a tender and Ryan-esque way.

"As I said," he murmured, his lips brushing her cheek, "Plan B had a different strategy. With most of your boss's clients with Grander, it gives Scott a lot of power. And we asked him to do us a favor." His mouth painted a distracting trail as he spoke, from her cheek to her neck, up to her ear. Each new breath tempting her to fall victim.

"Don't stop." She wasn't sure what she was referring to, the affection or the admission. Either way, she needed more.

"We asked him to play hardball and tell your boss all the upcoming releases from his Grander client list would be placed on hold if he didn't comply."

"*What?*" She yanked her wrists from his grip. "Are you serious?"

"Do I look like I'm kidding?"

No. Unfortunately, he appeared entirely sincere. Each stroke of her gaze back and forth between his eyes didn't clear the idiocy.

"So it wasn't just my life you decided to mess with? It was innumerable artists who are meant to be your allies." She scoffed. "No wonder Mason suggested this avenue. It reeks of his taint."

"We were willing to do whatever necessary."

"Then undo it."

"Can't." His fingers stroked her cheek, his gaze lazily raking her face. "It's already done. I was in Scott's home office when the early-morning call was made."

"And why would he make that call, Ryan?" She implored him with her eyes, hoping for a different answer to delete the horrific one already running through her mind. "What did you give him in return?"

He didn't react, didn't give her any inclination of remorse.

"Let me guess, you offered him something he couldn't refuse."

"We did what needed to be done." He gripped her chin with his thumb and spoke against her lips. "And we would've done more if necessary."

She wanted to hate every word coming out of his mouth. She wanted to detest them with the same ferocity as her frown. But how could she? How could she despise her men making a deal with the devil in an attempt to save her?

She closed her eyes and let her head fall back against the wall. "After all we've been through with this tour, you still signed another contract." She couldn't believe it. They'd worked too hard to escape Grander's clutches to give up right before the finishing line. "How many albums?"

"One."

She opened her eyes, still not seeing the remorse that must be hidden somewhere.

"A greatest hits collection," he continued. "We only need to provide three new tracks."

"And you agreed?" Her eyes began to burn. "Even though it means going back to Grander and extending the hold they have on Reckless? Those songs will be wasted."

"We see it as a good investment."

"We?" she murmured.

He inclined his head. "All the guys, plus Sidney, Alana, Melody, and Gabi. Everyone knew what was at stake."

Her vision blurred. "Wait." She pressed a palm against his chest. "I'm confused. You said I was fired. How does this fix our problems when I'm still legally obligated to comply with a non-compete?"

"There's no non-compete. Bruce agreed to a mutual dissolution to the contract. He doesn't want his company tarnished, and deep down, I think he was content our manipulation gave him a way to do right by you."

"I'm a free agent?" She wanted to be happy. The tingling sensation was already igniting behind her ribs, held captive by the reasons her freedom had been achieved. The cost was too high. They'd gone too far.

"We did good, didn't we?"

She leaned forward, brushed her lips against his and then pulled back. "It's another album. Those three songs could've gone toward establishing your own label. I would've fled the tour earlier if I knew that's what you were going to do."

"I know." He nodded. "That's why I didn't tell you." His smile returned, the glimmer of happiness touching every dark part inside her chest. "We know you've given up a lot because of your dedication to the band. You put your social and family life on hold for us. You made Reckless your world, and we love you for that. It's only fair we return the favor."

She would've forsaken more if there was anything left to give. Existence didn't seem worthwhile without those five men. One in particular.

"Forgive me?" He leaned his head against hers, his presence every-where.

"You're crazy, do you know that?" Insane. Unhinged. *Reckless*. But she loved him. She loved every single thing about him.

"Yes. But do you forgive me?"

She gave a defeated laugh. "Give me more than five seconds."

He smirked, the kick of his lips enough to initiate a rapid pulse in her clit. He trailed his forehead along hers, then his beard was scraping her cheek, his mouth finding the heavenly spot below her ear. "What can I do to speed up the process?"

"You got me fired." She placed her hands on his shoulders, needing to be grounded. "Redemption will take time."

"I bet I can make you forgive me in less than fifteen minutes."

She chuckled. "And how do you plan on doing that?"

He gripped the hem of her blouse and tugged. "Take this off and I'll show you."

"I'm not getting naked, Ryan."

"Are you sure?" His fingers moved to the center of her blouse, the deft digits flicking undone one button. Two.

"Forgive me yet?"

She shook her head. "No." She stared him down, her scrutiny almost a glare as he continued popping buttons until the front of her blouse gaped.

"That's a shame." He pushed the material from her shoulders.

Her nipples tightened beneath her bra as his attention lowered to her body. He admired her with fascination. With undiluted desire. Everywhere his gaze led, she could feel it—her cleavage, her shoulders, her throat.

Strong arms wove around her, unhooking her bra. He picked at the thin straps, encouraging them down her arms, to fall to the floor. "How about now?"

"Nope." She bit her lip over the frantic flutter of her heart.

He narrowed his stare and lowered the zipper to her pants, slow, gentle. Then in a rush, he shocked her by shoving them down her thighs, along with her panties.

"How about now?" he growled.

If she wasn't becoming mind-numbingly aroused, she would've chuckled at his growing intensity. Instead, she raised her brows in a taunt and shook her head. He stepped back, giving her a slow appraisal, the heat in his eyes making her burn. He pulled off his shirt, ruffling his long hair. Then his belt buckle was clanging, his jeans being thrust to the floor, exposing the length of his erection. An always-impressive length.

"I'm still unforgiven?"

She didn't answer. Didn't respond. Not apart from the frantic breaths between them.

He lunged for her, thrusting his body against hers, shoving her back against the wall, the result a resounding thud through the room. He grasped her wrists, raised them, holding them on either side of her head.

His hips ground into hers, his cock teasing the piercing in her clit. She whimpered, the sound derived from pure torture. She wanted him. All of him. He continued to lazily thrust, hard cock sliding over wet pussy. Not penetrating, only teasing.

"Forgive me."

"No."

He leaned to the side, his palm trailing over her waist, to her ass and lower to her thigh. He encouraged her to lift her leg and she wrapped it around him, her hands still on his shoulders. Fingers tickled her ass and then found her heat. Delicately, he parted her folds, sliding back and forth, each stroke finalized with a tap to the jewelry in her clit.

She closed her eyes, her core jolting, her lungs burning. His breath brushed her cheek, then his beard, the rough scrape a precursor to the gentle brush of his lips over her carotid. She ran a hand between them, reaching for his cock, but he tilted his hips.

"Not until you forgive me."

His fingers moved faster, the slide, slide, slide, deepening. Penetrating. Finally, she had something to clamp down on and the sensation of fulfillment made her moan.

"Forgive me, Leah," he whispered, almost making her acquiesce with his sweet tone.

"No."

His free hand slammed against the wall, hitting hard. She'd thought it was a game. A prelude to make up sex. But he was serious. He didn't realize he wasn't to blame.

"Ryan—"

His fingers plunged deep, weakening her knees. She rested into him, needing his strength.

"Want me to continue?" he growled.

She nodded, her head bobbing in time with the clenching of her pussy. "Yes."

"So you forgive me?"

"God damn you," she yelled. "*Yes.*"

He inched back, taking his dreamy cock with him. She mewled. Then he was shoving between her thighs, lifting her knees and driving his cock home, his shaft sliding deep into her core.

She cried out, her fingertips digging into him.

He thrust hard, over and over, his chest lashing her nipples, his mouth finding her own. He held her leg in place, inching it higher, allowing him to sink deeper. He murmured to her as he gyrated, words of love, strength and commitment—*I couldn't bear to lose you. You're all I have. All I want. I'll make it up to you. I'll do whatever I can to make you happy.*

She closed her eyes, enjoying how his harsh thrusts turned into languid, torturous strokes. "I'm happy, Ryan."

Each movement of his hips came with a masculine groan, the strong shove into lust now mixing with hope and optimism. She could finally enjoy him. Without reservation or restriction.

"You're such a wonderful man," she whispered. "Some parts more than others."

She met the next gyration of his hips with one of her own, the pleasure exploding with the slam against her clit.

"I'm glad you think so." He buried his face in her neck and sucked hard on her flesh. "Because you've got me for the rest of your life."

"I hope so."

She continued meeting his pace, increasing the friction one thrust at a time. His breathing grew heavier, his throaty growl becoming deeper as her pussy contracted tighter. He lifted her, encouraging both legs around his waist as he pistoned, each undulation hammering her ass against the wall.

"I love you."

She moaned at his admission and clung to his shoulders. Everything was heightened—her pleasure, her love, her optimism. Her abdomen began to tingle, the peppered sensation turning into a heavy throb of her core.

"Ryan..." She wanted to repeat his sentiment, but she was too late, her words cut short by her unpredictable orgasm. "*Fuck.*"

He growled, guttural and deep, his climax colliding with hers. His mouth found hers, his lips stealing breath and kisses at the same time. She drowned in the affection, burned from his passion.

Then everything quietened as the pleasure faded and the world slowed.

He leaned her against the wall and stared back at her with soft eyes and luscious lips. "Minx," he whispered.

"Manipulator," she countered.

He froze, every defined muscle taut in the passing beats of silence. "Are you really angry at me?"

"No." She shook her head and gave a genuine smile. "I couldn't be more overwhelmed with gratitude, even though it'll take time for the guilt to wear off." The price may have been high but her relief was even higher. Finally, she would get to be with him. All day. Every day. No hidden feelings. No sneaking from public view. "I love you for what you did for me."

His lips tweaked, his grin speaking of pride. He leaned one elbow against the wall and beamed down at her, his chest rising and falling with heavy breaths. "We're free—"

The door hinges squeaked and she swore as she pulled Ryan closer, hiding her nudity the best she could. Mason's face came into view through the crack of the opening door, his expression turning horrified before he slammed the door shut.

"*Fuck you*, assholes," Mason called down the hall, the echo of laughter coming from the living room. "I fucking told you those weren't fighting screams... Now, if you'll excuse me, I'll be in the bathroom, shoving my fingers down the back of my throat."

Twenty-Eight

THREE WEEKS LATER
Richmond, VA

RYAN TAPPED HIS FOOT TO THE BEAT AND SUCKED IN THE ELECTRIC ATMOS-phere of the last show of the tour. The hometown fans were hysterical, screaming their lungs out without a care for the music they were drowning out.

Even the thrown underwear was piling up at an unprecedented rate. There were bras and panties flying everywhere. Each time a new item sailed forward, he'd glance side-stage at Leah to see those pretty eyes roll. She pretended to be disgusted, but he knew she loved the attention the band received.

It was all her doing, after all. She'd built them, carving out their careers to make them a worldwide success.

"Thanks for the warm welcome, Richmond." A large pair of red panties landed at Mason's feet and he picked them up with the toe of his boot. "Thanks, again," he drawled, this time with less enthusiasm.

Ryan turned his usual appraisal to Leah and this time found her focused on the cell in her hand, her brow furrowing before she strode from view.

That woman had him so far under the thumb he doubted he'd ever regain his sanity. Every second away from her made him feel lost. She was the perfection who guided him and Felicity through the potential nightmare of Julie's pregnancy announcement.

Leah had written Flick's public statement that told the world her fun with Ryan was over and she planned to stick by him with friendship as he struggled to come to terms with his ex-wife's infidelity. The result was a wave of sympathy from fans. He was no longer the black sheep. His favorable reputation had slid back into place... At least temporarily.

He wasn't sure what the world would have to say once the news of him and Leah broke. But for now, their relationship remained private. They were happy to enjoy one another in peace while they flew under the paparazzi radar—hiding in the tour bus and sneaking into hotel rooms in the middle of the night.

The quiet wouldn't last long. They knew that. They also knew they were strong enough to withstand whatever the vultures threw at them once their personal lives were made public.

At the intro to their next song, a large pair of black knickers flew forward, missing the stage. He glanced for Leah again, this time finding her back in her usual spot, her frown still evident as she made a T signal with her hands, calling for a timeout.

He nodded and came to Mason's side and gave him the message via a jerk of his head in Leah's direction. The lead singer didn't skip a beat. He belted out the final verse of the song and then addressed the crowd.

"We're going to have to take a short intermission. Don't you fuckers go anywhere. We'll be back soon."

The five of them jogged from the stage, handing off their instruments to the approaching technicians.

"What is it?"

She didn't look at him; instead she focused on Blake. "Gabi's mom called. You need to get home."

Blake's face turned bleak. "What happened?"

"Gabi has gone into labor a little early." Leah beamed. "You're about to become a father."

"She's having the baby?" Blake stepped forward, grabbing Leah's waist. "She's having the baby!" He lifted her off the ground, swinging her around before dumping her back on her feet.

"The jet is already preparing for your arrival, and a car is on its way to the staff entrance of the parking lot."

"God, you're brilliant." Blake kissed her forehead, his eyes wide with shock. "I guess I better get out of here."

"Yeah." She chuckled. "You better. I told her I'd get you to the airport straight away."

"What about my luggage?"

"I'll handle everything. Just get yourself back home and send our love to Gabi."

He nodded, accepting fist bumps, arms punches, and other masculine shows of affection from the band and crew. "I'll see you all back home."

Ryan pulled her close as Blake ran for the stage exit. "He's right, you know."

"Hmm?" She cocked a brow, leaning into his hug.

"You're brilliant."

"I'm glad you finally noticed." Her smile was wide, her glossy red lips hypnotic as they brushed against his, without pause, without reservation. Just the way he liked it.

His cock stirred and he broke their connection to ensure he didn't have to walk back on stage with a tent in his pants. "How are you feeling?"

"Better."

"Liar." She'd stressed herself into an ulcer. Even after Julie had signed the divorce settlement and the media had quit hassling him and Felicity, she still hadn't relaxed. She wasn't herself and he couldn't wait to get them back to New York for some much needed recuperation time. "You need to see a doctor."

"I'll do it once we're home."

Home. Her apartment. The place they would soon live in together. The concept always added an extra beat in his chest.

Mason came up beside them, a bottle of water in his hand. "When the two of you are finished sucking face, do you mind adding to the conversation about our missing bass guitarist?"

"We could play with a man down." Mitch wiped the sweat from his face with his shirt. "It's only for one show."

Leah nodded. "You could. Or you could give Hannah the opportunity.

She knows the set."

"Since when?" Mason took a gulp of water.

"I had a discussion with her weeks ago about the possibility of this happening. Blake's replacement was always going to be at least a few hours away, and it wasn't like the baby had a strict schedule for arrival."

"Have you called her?" Sean asked.

"I have, but she's aware you might not approve."

"I vote for whatever brings us closer to the after party."

"Me, too." Ryan squeezed her tighter, demanding her attention. "And the hotel suite after."

Mason made gagging noises. "How long until she's ready?"

"Not long. Go and explain what's happening. Hopefully by then she'll be here."

"And what about Sidney? Did her flight arrive on time?"

"Yes. She's with Melody, organizing the caterers for the after party. Which reminds me—" She placed a kiss on Ryan's lips and stepped back. "—I have to double check the alcohol order. We can't be short on booze."

Reluctantly, he let her go, her warmth slipping from his fingers, her scent slowly leaving his lungs. "Be waiting for me after the show."

She gave him a wicked grin, one filled with promise even through the tired bags under her eyes. "You're so demanding."

"And you love it."

Her cheeks blushed, giving him all the confirmation he needed. Not that he needed any. He'd learned what she liked and there was very little she didn't, as long as they were together.

"I'll try my best." She gave him a finger wave and retreated with a seductive sway of her gorgeous hips.

"You're so fucked." Mason placed a condescending clap on his back. "There's no way you're ever getting that leash off your balls."

"Just like you with Sidney?" He met the lead singers gaze with a cocked brow.

"Yeah." Mason chuckled. "Just like me with Sid."

FIVE HOURS LATER

Leah laughed through a yawn. Everyone was drunk—the band, the crew, the security team, and Slicker. All of them mingling in the backyard of Mason's Richmond property as music poured through innumerable speakers.

Ryan stood behind her, his chest unyielding against her back, his arms wrapped around her waist. "Do you want me to ask Mason if we can crash in one of his rooms?"

"Not yet." There was no doubt his intent held a dubious amount of slumber, but she didn't feel like she was officially off duty yet. She wanted to make sure everyone ended the night in one piece. And there was still no word on Blake and Gabi.

She wouldn't be able to fall into a deep sleep until she knew they were all healthy and safe.

"Here you go." Mason stopped in front of her, Sidney at his side, and handed over a bottle of champagne. Not a glass. Not a flute. A damn bottle. "You can't abstain at an after party."

"Thanks." She took the offering and cradled it in her hands like a seasoned groupie.

"I hear congratulations are in order." Sidney spread her arms wide, engulfing Leah and Ryan in a quick hug. "It's about time the two of you got together."

"Good things come to those who wait." Ryan raised his half-filled scotch glass in a toast. "I'm definitely a lucky man."

Leah remained silent, happy to let him claim this was luck when it wasn't. Ryan was a deserving man. He was owed happiness. She only hoped she was enough.

"That's what we all say at the start," Mason drawled.

Sidney frowned and turned to her fiancé. "And then things change?"

"Obviously." Mason stared her down without remorse. "I haven't seen you in two weeks, and yet I've been home for hours and still haven't got you naked."

"I thought the hundred or so people in your back yard would've postponed your surge in libido."

Mason shook his head and clucked his tongue. "Do you know me at all, woman?" He grabbed her waist and tugged her forward. "Come on. You need to help me find Mel and Sean. I think they might be taking liberties in one of my bedrooms."

Sidney dragged her feet, scraping the heels of her sparkly black pumps. "I don't want to help you with that."

"Too bad. I've seen enough graphic horror with these two. I don't think I can take much more on my own."

Leah chuckled as they strode away, and placed the champagne bottle on the table by her side.

"You're not going to drink?" Ryan whispered beside her ear.

"Not when I'd pass out after the first sip." She hugged the arms around her waist and grinned as she spotted Hannah and Felicity slink away from their male band members to slip into the darkness of the tree line at the back of the property. Those two were going to make headlines soon and Leah had a feeling it would only boost their already promising careers. "I haven't been sleeping well." Or eating. Or functioning, for that matter.

"I know." He held her tight. "I hope it gets better once we're home."

"Me, too." She turned in his arms and drank in the memories that came with the hint of scotch on his breath. "Why don't you go and mingle for a bit? I need to use the bathroom."

"OK. I'll come find you soon."

She sucked in a deep breath at the loss of his warmth and strolled for the glass doors leading into the open kitchen area. The end of the tour was always an emotional crossroad. After weeks under the feet of five brilliant men, she then had to go home to an empty apartment. But not this time.

Ryan's toothbrush would live beside hers. The scent of his aftershave would fill her home. His arms would hold her during the night. Every aspect of her future was an exciting prospect. Even the parts she hadn't anticipated.

After using the bathroom, she made her way through to the living room and glared at the man standing before the floor to ceiling windows.

"Why are you here?"

Scott turned toward her, a beer bottle in his hand. "I thought the invitation might have been a Reckless olive branch."

"I'm sure it's more a case of Mason keeping his friends close and enemies closer."

"I'm not your enemy, Leah." He pivoted back to the window and sipped from his beer. "Never have been."

"That's news to me."

"It was business. You can't blame us for trying to hold on to our most successful band."

"I can." She crossed her arms over her chest. "And I will."

He shrugged. "Well, that's all over now. Grander has come to terms with losing you guys. We're not going to fight it any longer."

"Good." She began striding for the door, only to stop when he began talking again.

"Ryan seems crazy about you." There was no hint of a threat, just an undeniable poke at her protective nature. "If you're unconvinced I'm not out to get you, at least believe me when I say I could've demanded anything when he came to my home asking for a favor. He was desperate. Yet, I let him off easily."

"Do you expect a thank you?"

"No. But a lesser dose of animosity would be nice."

"I bet Felicity and Hannah feel the same way."

He took another gulp from the bottle. "Gay artists don't sell."

"They do if you back them. You need to start a trend instead of following archaic opinions. Maybe then you won't have every artist hating the sight of you." She continued for the door, this time not stopping until she was in the back yard and at Ryan's side.

"What did Scott have to say?" he asked in greeting.

She wove her arms around his waist and smiled up at him. "Have you been watching me?"

"Like a hawk."

Her cell vibrated in her front pocket and she pulled it out to see an incoming video call.

"*Shit.* It's Blake." She shot Ryan a glance. "Where is everyone?"

"You looking for us?" Mason asked from behind her, his arm around Sidney.

"Yes." She turned in Ryan's embrace, finding Mitch and Alana approaching hand in hand as Mason waved over Sean and Melody.

"Hurry." Her Reckless family rushed to nestle close, all of them staring at the picture that came on screen. Blake had his arm outstretched, holding up his cell as he lounged beside Gabi on a hospital bed.

"Oh, my, god." Leah's free hand came to her mouth at the sight of the baby cradled in Gabi's arms, it's tiny body swaddled in a pink blanket.

"It's a girl." Blake kissed the side of his wife's head. "Sophie Marie Kennedy."

A chorus of congratulations were offered, some more drunkenly ecstatic than others while Leah blinked through a sheen of tears. "Are you both healthy and happy?"

"Terribly happy." Gabi smiled through obvious exhaustion. "I'm just glad Blake made it here in time. I wasn't sure if he would."

"We're all so proud of you both."

"And we can't wait to get home to see you all," Alana added.

"Thank you." Gabi leaned into Blake. "I'm looking forward to introducing Sophie to her gorgeous aunts and uncles."

"What happens from here?" Sidney asked. "How long will you stay in the hospital?"

"We're not sure." Blake touched a gentle finger to the baby's nose. "But my first job is to buy a shotgun and let all those little fuckers know my girl is off limits."

"Blake." Gabi swatted her husband with her free hand.

"I'm not joking." Blake remained unapologetic as he spoke to his wife. "The most beautiful girl in the world is going to have thousands of admirers, so I'm starting my stockpile of bullets early."

Sophie let out a squawk and Gabi turned to face the camera. "We better go. I've still gotta work out this breastfeeding thing."

Another chorus of well wishes came forth as Gabi blew kisses at the camera. Then they were gone, leaving euphoria in their wake.

"The first Reckless progeny has arrived." Sean shouted with an empty glass raised in his hand. "This calls for tequila shots."

Ryan groaned from behind her and everyone else dispersed, following the drummer with heavy intoxication in mind.

"You're quiet," she whispered to Ryan, already sensing his unease.

"Want to talk about it?"

"No. I'm happy for them."

"I know you are. But I also know you're upset."

His scotch glass rose, and she heard him drink heavily from behind her. She didn't react. She had a sense any sudden movement might spook him.

"There's something I haven't told you," he murmured. "Julie thinks I can't have kids. She said she'd tried for years with no success. Then bam, she starts fucking around with some other guy and instantly she's impregnated. It doesn't take a genius to figure out I'm the problem."

"You're not the problem, Ryan." She trailed her fingers over the hand at her stomach, knowing without doubt he was wrong.

"You don't know that."

She shrugged. "Call it intuition."

He sighed, his disbelief heavy between them. She hadn't wanted to have this conversation yet. The whole kids thing was scary. She'd planned on waiting until they were back in New York, with the stress of the tour behind them.

"Ryan, there's something I haven't told you, too."

"I'm listening."

She gripped his hand and turned to him. "I've already been to the doctor. I went when we were back in Memphis."

His lips parted, his eyes widened. But it was fear morphing his features, not intrigue.

"I didn't want to talk to you about it until we were home. With the tour and media issues... I just... I didn't want this to be mixed in with all that."

"Is it bad?"

"It's something that's going to affect me for the rest of my life." She was struggling to keep a straight face. "It'll affect both of us."

"Fuck. Is it can—"

She placed a finger over his lips. "Don't swear."

"Then tell me."

She leaned in and whispered the news softly in his ear.

He pulled back in an instant, his hands cupping her face, his gaze scrutinizing. "Shut the front door."

"Shh." She grinned. "It's too early to let anyone know."

"But…" His mouth worked around silent words. "Julie said…"

"I don't care what Julie said. She was wrong. And from the doctor's estimation, I probably fell pregnant the first time we were together."

"I told you that condom was old… But I still don't believe it."

She chuckled. "My constant tears and inability to cope hasn't been a blindingly obvious clue?"

The corner of his lips lifted, his love hitting her with the simplest expression. "I thought that was because of me."

"No." She placed her mouth to his. "It's the hormones."

He nodded and bit his lip, his eyes brimming with unshed tears. Oh, god, if he started tearing up she was destined to sob like a baby.

"Don't cry, Ryan." Her vision blurred. "I couldn't stand to see that right now. I'd break."

He placed his forehead against hers, continuing to hold her cheeks as he closed his eyes. "I love you, Leah. I love you so much."

"I love you, too."

"Then marry me," he whispered. "I'll give you a proper proposal soon. I'll send flowers and have a ring…" His palms trailed down her arms to eventually cradle her hands as he lowered to one knee. "Please, Leah. I adore you. You're everything to me. Will you do me the honor of being my wife?"

A gasp escaped her lips, the attention of an entire drunken after party turning to face them. "I'd love to marry you."

He beamed at her, making her stomach flip-flop and her heart clench the longer his undiluted happiness radiated back at her.

"You better get back up here before we cause too much of a scene." She yanked him to his feet.

"Too late." Mason approached, a bottle of tequila in his hand. "What the fuck just happened?"

"We're getting married," Ryan announced, pulling her in for a kiss that curled her toes and probably those of innumerable people in the vicinity.

She sank against him, tangling her fingers in his hair as she wordlessly reciprocated his love.

"Fucking hell." Mason sighed and raised his voice to shout, "We're going to need another bottle of tequila."

Epilogue

LEAH CONTINUED TO STARE AT THE MARRIAGE OFFICIANT AS HE RAMBLED ON about vows and commitment. Why had she needed so many words? Why couldn't it have been a case of "Do you take him? Do you take her? Congratulations, you're married. Now go and sit down."

Her lower back was pounding, her swollen cankles aching, her stomach tight and uncomfortable. She didn't care who proclaimed otherwise, the last month of pregnancy truly did suck a bag of dicks. She was always tired and horny. Why the hell was she so horny?

She just wanted her baby in her arms, the soft cries of life tickling her ears.

"Ryan Bennett, do you take Leah Gorman to be your wedded wife, to live together in marriage? Do you promise to love her, comfort her, honor and keep her for better or worse—"

The words kept going. On and on, each one adding to her unease.

"I do."

She closed her eyes at the sound of that voice. Ryan would get her through this. It was only a few more minutes before she could sit and relax. It wasn't like they had a guest list to entertain. They'd only invited eight people. Nine if you included Blake and Gabi's daughter.

"Leah?"

"Hmm?"

"You need to say, 'I do.'"

"Oh." She opened her eyes and grimaced. "I do." Her voice broke as searing pain descended on her lower back.

"Hey." Ryan grabbed her arm. "What happened?"

"Nothing, just a twinge." She squeezed his hand. "Keep going."

More words were spoken. A ring slid onto her finger and she fumbled to do the same for Ryan through narrowed vision.

"I now pronounce you husband and wife. You may kiss the bride."

Ryan leaned in, his lips stopping an inch away. "Leah?"

A rush of warmth gushed between her thighs, the sensation trickling down her legs. *Holy shit.* She peered at the floor, unable to see her feet over the mountain of stomach, and had to step back to observe the puddle of liquid pooled on the floorboards.

"Umm…"

There was a mutter behind her, then another and another.

She raised her gaze to the officiant, then to Ryan.

"Clean up, aisle five," Mason called from the front row.

Asshole. She was going to kill him. Not today. Maybe not tomorrow. But one day soon Mason would taste her revenge from the years of brotherly bullshit.

"I think we need to get you to the hospital." Ryan wrapped his arm around her, supporting her weight.

"Would you like me to call an ambulance?" the officiant asked.

Ryan stole her attention, his panicked eyes repeating the question.

"No." She straightened and placed a fortifying hand on her lower back. "We can make it on our own."

"Are you sure?" Ryan swallowed, his Adam's apple bobbing. "I don't think I'm going to be able to remember how to drive."

She began to smile, the humor fading as pain crept into her abdomen, subtle at first, then building higher and tighter in intensity. She reached for his shoulders and bent over to fight the building agony.

Everything dimmed. It was only her and the pain. Only agony and the need to fight through it. Then slowly, the destruction ebbed and she blinked back to reality to find all their friends by her side—Mason and Sidney, Sean and Melody, Mitch and Alana, and Blake, Gabi, and baby

Sophie.

"I've got you." Ryan held her forearms, his grip unyielding.

"Me, too." Alana rubbed Leah's back. "Let's get you out of here."

"I think something might be wrong," she whispered. The pain was too rich. She hadn't expected the potency. Surely, giving birth couldn't last for hours if this was the torture involved. "Am I going to make it through this?" She looked at Gabi, then to the little baby now wriggling in her father's arms.

"You're going to do great." Gabi's fake smile faded as she glanced to Ryan. "Those contractions are fast. We need to hurry."

•••

"One more push."

Leah wailed, unleashing every ounce of empathy in Ryan's body and tying it up in knots. He was completely helpless, useless, while this unfathomably brilliant woman brought life into the world right before his eyes. Well... Not *right before* his eyes. He had no intention of moving his line of sight anywhere past her abdomen.

He was learning from Blake's mistake—*Buddy, I beg you. Do* not *go down there. You'll never recover.* Ryan didn't need to be told twice.

"You're doing a great job." He held her hand, wishing the painful squeeze of her grip was doing something to alleviate her torture.

"I can't do it." She slumped forward, panting. "I can't."

"One more push, Leah." The doctor poked his head up from between her legs. "I can already see the baby's head."

Ryan couldn't fault the hospital's support. They'd pulled out all the stops, ensuring Leah had additional staff to assist through the delivery of their child. Not that it seemed to be helping. She was in too much pain. Her agony killing him.

"No," she cried.

"Don't give up." He moved into her line of vision, demanding the attention of her unfocused eyes. "You're almost there." He guided the hair back from her face, wishing she knew how gorgeous she was in this moment. In *every* moment.

"One more push," the doctor repeated. "You've got this."

Ryan nodded, trying not to be daunted by the man staring between his wife's legs. *His wife.* Holy shit. What a day.

She wailed, bearing down on his hand like a warrior.

There was a mass of movement in his periphery, the doctor doing things Ryan didn't want to witness. The midwife assisted while another hovered close. Within seconds, another wail sounded. This one smaller. Meek and so undeniably heart-wrenching.

Everything after that sound was smothered by his harsh breathing and the rapid flow of blood through his ears. He clung to Leah's hand as the doctor murmured praise about the birth, then the placenta, and finally the announcement they were parents to a beautiful baby boy.

He didn't have time to take it all in—he was now a husband, a parent, the father to a son—before surgical scissors were placed in his hand and he was hacking at an incredibly tough umbilical cord.

Everyone moved in a rush, while he swayed on his feet. The doctor checked Leah for injury, the midwife took his child to the far corner for observations. And he merely blinked in a daze, unable to compute what had just happened until someone called out, "Ryan, would you like to hand your son over to Leah?"

A lady came toward him with a swaddled blue bundle while another went to his wife, removing her legs from the clinical stirrups, placing a blanket over them, and helping her to sit.

"I don't know how." He reached out, his limbs shaking, his heart thunderous.

"It's a great time to learn."

The nurse smiled and placed the tiny human in his arms. His son stole his breath, depriving him of thought. That tiny nose. Those cute lips. The bright blue, unfocused eyes blinking up at him.

"How is he?" Leah asked, her voice hoarse.

"Beyond words." He came to her side, each step cautious. "I'm so proud of you." He placed their child into her waiting arms and leaned against the bed. He couldn't move. Didn't want to. The caustic fluorescent light from the ceiling didn't dull the heavenly image.

He'd never been happier. More whole. Entirely content. His throat was clogged. And his eyes, *fuck,* they were burning.

"I love you more than life."

She grinned, the curve of lips lessening her look of exhaustion. "I love you, too."

"How are you feeling?"

"Invincible. You?"

"Complete. I never thought my heart could make more room after you took it over."

"I know what you mean." She ran her finger over the baby's forehead, trailing an intricate pattern over the flawless skin. "What should we call him?"

"How about Mace?" a familiar voice asked from the door.

Ryan turned and grinned at Mason and Sidney. "Not going to happen."

"Really? I think it has a nice ring to it." Mason came forward and placed a kiss in Leah's hair. "For once, you look like you've done some work."

Leah released a breathy laugh and accepted a hug from Sidney. "Please get revenge for me later."

"I promise." Sidney smiled, her focus on the already sleeping baby. "He's so cute. Have you thought of a name yet?"

"We have." Leah met Ryan's gaze as she announced. "Tyler Mace Bennett."

He nodded. Tyler Bennett. The name already suited the little guy.

"Are you shitting me?" Mason glanced between them. "You're shitting me, aren't you?"

"Mason," Sidney growled. "Watch your language in front of the baby."

"Shit. Sorry." Mason's brows drew tight. "But... Are you serious?"

"Yes." Leah rolled her eyes at the lead singer. "We decided on a name weeks ago."

The rest of their family entered the room. Alana, Melody, and Gabi all taking turns to give Leah a hug of congratulations before showering the baby in compliments while Mitch, Blake, and Sean did the same to Ryan...without the girlie affection.

"Why is Mason crying?" Sean asked.

"I'm not crying." Mason rubbed the end of his nose with the back of his hand. "I've got allergies, asshole."

Ryan chuckled and returned to Leah's side. She had her gaze glued to their son. The two of them more than he could've ever hoped for. "You're amazing."

"*We're* amazing." Her lashes lifted, the glassy depths of her eyes hitting him with a promise of forever. "I couldn't have done it without you."

"I think Sophie and Tyler will be best friends," Alana announced. "They'll be so cute together."

"She's not coming anywhere near the blue-eyed cherub," Blake grated. "I have a no-boys policy until she moves away from home."

"Good luck with that." Sean pulled out his cell and took some happy snaps. "I'm willing to place a bet they become more than friends before her sweet sixteenth."

"That's not funny." Blake squeezed by the women to get to Leah's side. "He's adorable... But make sure you keep his grubby mitts away from my daughter."

She leaned in to the kiss he placed on her cheek. "I'll try my best."

"Blake," Gabi warned. "He's not even five minutes old."

"I don't care. I'm laying down the law. My little girl is going to be locked up in her tower until she's fifty-five."

Leah snorted and then winced, the sign of agony quickly masked by a grin.

"Are you in pain?" Ryan asked.

"It's not too bad."

"That's our cue to leave." Melody started shooing everyone from the room. "The newest Reckless family deserves their privacy."

Leah repositioned herself, sitting taller. "You don't have to go."

"Yeah, we do." Mason shot her a wink. "Little Mason junior needs his rest."

One by one they filed out of the room, blowing kisses, whispering farewells, until it was down to the three of them. His family, alone for the first time.

"It's no longer just the two of us," she whispered.

"I know." He sat his hip against the bed and leaned into her. "It's the end of one chapter and the start of something new."

"I'm scared and excited at the same time. Who would've thought, all those years ago when we first met, that one day we'd be here?"

"I did. I thought about it. Dreamed about it. And it feels surreal to finally have what I always wanted."

She released a breathy chuckle. "You're such a sweet talker."

"True." He grinned. "And I'm going to teach this guy everything I know."

"If that's the case, Sophie won't stand a chance, and you might want to start preparing for Blake's wrath."

"That's the whole point, gorgeous." He ran his fingers over the short wisps of hair on his son's head. "We get to spend the rest of our lives making Blake's a living hell."

Please CONSIDER LEAVING A REVIEW ON
YOUR BOOK RETAILER WEBSITE OR GOODREADS

Look FOR THESE TITLES
FROM EDEN SUMMERS

RECKLESS BEAT SERIES

Blind Attraction (Reckless Beat #1)
Passionate Addiction (Reckless Beat #2)
Reckless Weekend (Reckless Beat #2.5)
Undesired Lust (Reckless Beat #3)
Sultry Groove (Reckless Beat #4)
Reckless Rendezvous (Reckless Beat #4.5)
Undeniable Temptation (Reckless Beat #5)

VAULT OF SIN SERIES

A Shot of Sin (Vault of Sin #1)
Union of Sin (Vault of Sin #2)

STANDALONE TITLES

Concealed Desire
Sneaking a Peek
"Phantom Pleasure" Halloween Heat V
Inarticulate

About the Author

Eden Summers is a bestselling author of contemporary romance with a side of sizzle and sarcasm.

She lives in Australia with a young family who are well aware she's circling the drain of insanity.
Eden can't resist alpha dominance, dark features, and sarcasm in her fictional heroes and loves a strong heroine who knows when to bite her tongue but also serves retribution with a feminine smile on her face.

Visit Eden's website to sign up to her newsletter for the latest book news.

W: www.edensummers.com

E: eden@edensummers.com

F: www.facebook.com/authoredensummers

T: twitter.com/EdenSummers1